What criti
Jennifer

"Who Needs A Hero is a wo
made their share of mistakes
complete each other."
—*Sizzling Hot Book Reviews*

"Ms. Hart writes all genres with ease and I enjoy her books but my heart will always be with Neil and Maggie because I am a total sucker for the Happily Ever After."
—*The Reading Reviewer*

"A must read for all people who love a good mystery and a jolly good laugh...laugh out loud funny."
—*Cocktail Reviews*

"A wonderfully fun whodunit"
—*ParaNormal Romance.org*

"Laugh out loud funny, realistic characters, snappy true to life dialog, and a sufficiently difficult mystery; all the required elements for an excellent read."
—*Manic Readers*

"I would not hesitate to pick up another of Ms. Hart's works as she definitely made me with one book a lifelong fan."
—*Joyfully Reviewed.*

"Jennifer L. Hart gives readers a contemporary love story constructed by two achingly real main characters."
—*Coffee Time Romance*

BOOKS BY JENNIFER L. HART

Mackenzie & Mackenzie PI Mysteries:
Sleuthing for a Living

Southern Pasta Shop Mysteries:
Murder Al Dente
Christmas Al Dent (holiday short story)
Murder À La Flambé
Murder Al Fresco

Misadventures of the Laundry Hag Mysteries:
Skeletons in the Closet
Swept Under the Rug
All Washed Up

Damaged Goods Mysteries
Final Notice

Other Works
Who Needs a Hero?
River Rats
Stellar Timing
Daisy Dominatrix
Redeeming Characters

SLEUTHING FOR A LIVING

---

a Mackenzie & Mackenzie PI mystery

Jennifer L. Hart

SLEUTHING FOR A LIVING

Cover design by Estrella Designs

Published by Gemma Halliday Publishing

To my neighbor and friend, Ms. Joan.
Thanks for all the stories!

CHAPTER ONE

Pretexting—misrepresenting yourself to achieve a hidden end goal.
From the *Working Man's Guide to Sleuthing for a Living* by Albert Taylor, PI

There was someone lurking in our apartment. Visible through the slatted blinds covering the bay front window, the beam from the flashlight roved over the mound of boxes and bags Mac and I had abandoned in our search for sustenance.

"Judas Priest," I muttered.

"I thought you said this was a good neighborhood," my sixteen-year-old daughter hissed at me.

"Well, it's not Beacon Hill," I whispered back, not taking my eyes from the bouncing beam of light. "But it was free, courtesy of Uncle Al's passing. Register your complaints with him."

Mac shifted the plastic bag filled with Thai takeout between her hands and darted a look back to our brand new pad. "We only moved in four hours ago. I haven't even unboxed my PC, and someone's robbing us." She thought about it for a beat and added, "And who's desperate enough to want your vintage He-Man trash can anyway?"

I glowered at her. "That's a collector's item." My gaze slid back to the window. The flashlight inside had moved down the hall.

"Do you have your cell?" I asked Mac. It was a rhetorical question, since my daughter was wired 24/7. When she nodded, I passed her the car keys and pointed to our ancient Jetta. The vehicle was a total eyesore—it needed a bungee cord to keep the trunk lid shut, and I'd covered the myriad dents and dings and rust with hair bands' bumper stickers. I'd lovingly dubbed the vehicle Fillmore, since he burned through gas and oil the way I went through a box of cookies, but he was better than not having a car. "Lock yourself in the car and call the police."

Mac's big blue eyes got even bigger. She sounded more like my mother than my offspring when she mumbled, "Mackenzie Elizabeth Taylor, what are you going to do?"

"Hit him with the He-Man trashcan maybe. With luck it won't come to that." I dug in my purse, hunting for the container of pepper spray my mother had given me as a stocking stuffer last Christmas. "Go on."

Mac's chin went up in classic Taylor girl *let's take it to the mat* fashion. "Come with me."

I didn't play the mom card very often. I didn't need to since I had the most mature teenage daughter on the face of the planet, which at the moment was more a curse than a blessing. Unfortunately for her, I had an additional sixteen years of practice at being a stubborn pain in the ass to my credit. No way would I let some creep loot our new apartment within hours of our taking possession. My mother would never let me live it down. "Mac, go, or I swear I'll never let you drive Fillmore again. It'll be public transportation from now until you're old enough to pay for your own therapist."

The streetlight fell on her worried expression. "Just don't do anything stupid, okay?"

"Go," I insisted, making no promises. Sometimes "anything stupid" was all a mother could manage.

After Mac was as secure as possible, I depressed the latch and opened the door that led to the four apartments in Uncle Al's building—now my building—well, mine and my mother's. The huge turn-of-the-century villa had been renovated into four separate apartments. The residence above us was occupied by Mrs. Burkowitz, who'd introduced herself the second we'd arrived, insisting both Mac and I call her Nona. She was sweet but wouldn't have my back if things went sideways. The other second-floor apartment was currently vacant, and I hadn't met the downstairs tenant yet. I was on my own until the police showed up.

My heart pounded, and there was a distinct roaring in my ears as I moved into the foyer, pepper spray in hand. The door to the apartment stood ajar. I swallowed past the lump in my throat. Though she lacked appreciation for my classic '80s paraphernalia, Mac was right—there really wasn't much worth taking in our new place, at least not of our stuff. No family jewels or giant wads of cash lying around the Taylor abode. My mom had insisted we keep all of Uncle Al's furniture, since mine was what I could afford, aka off-the-truck specials. Mac's computer equipment was all older stuff she'd refurbished herself, and most of it was bulky as all get-out. Hell, Fillmore was my most expensive item, and how sad was that?

I had second and then third thoughts about going inside. What if there was a tweaker or crackhead in there, someone crazy and desperate enough to attack me instead of just running away? What if he had a gun? Suddenly, my little vial of pepper spray didn't seem like much protection.

The distinct sound of something crashing spurred me into action. We may not have had much, but I'd worked hard for all of it. I wasn't about to let some drugged-out creep trash the place on a whim. And java help him if that had been my coffeepot. Decided, I skulked through the darkened living room. Sticking to the shadows, I paused only long enough to let my eyes adjust.

The intruder was in what had been Uncle Al's office and was destined to be Mac's bedroom, once we got around to moving all the clutter out and buying her a bed. The room faced the left side of the house and his flashlight was now invisible from the street. Cautiously, I peeked around the corner to get a look at our burglar. Even in the dim light cast by my LED nightlight in the hall, I could tell the guy was immense. He had at least a foot on me and looked three times as broad. And at five-foot-nine with the Rubenesque stature to match, I was no waif. He was sliding drawers open to Uncle Al's desk, rummaging through the contents.

Uncle Al had been my father's estranged older brother who dabbled at private investigation. He and Dad had some sort of argument years ago, and Uncle Al had kept to himself ever since. I'd only seen him twice, and one of those times had been at his wake. I'd done a cursory look through the room earlier, just to make sure dear old Uncle Al hadn't left any skin magazines where Mac might find them. There had been an epic amount of flotsam but nothing valuable. What did the intruder hope to find?

The sheer size of the man gave me fourth thoughts—I considered diving into the cast-iron tub and hiding until he left. Then he turned in my direction, and I plastered my back against the wall, trapped. I had no clue what the range on my pepper spray was but figured ten feet was asking too much from the little vial. I waited until he was just on the other side of the doorway, keeping out of line of sight as I called out, "The cops are on their way."

The footsteps stopped. "Are you Mackenzie?"

How did he know my name? Well, he *had* just been rifling through our stuff, but most people usually thought Mackenzie was my last name, not my first. His voice rumbled, the deepest I'd ever heard. It sounded like distant thunder over craggy mountains.

Swallowing, I forced a note of steely badass-ness into my voice. "Get out. And leave whatever you took."

Too late, I realized he'd have to walk past me in order to exit the apartment, either back through the living room to the front door. Or into my bedroom and through the French doors leading out to the back garden. I made a face, wishing I'd thought this through better.

"It's not what you think." He stepped out into the hallway, holding the flashlight off to one side. It reflected off the cream-colored walls so the left side of his face was somewhat visible. I'd expected something scary to match his hulking goon build and was a little taken aback. Even with the crappy illumination, I could tell he had sharp bone structure and full, almost sensual lips. His nose was straight, but with an obvious bump, as if it had been broken a time or two. The small flaw added character and depth to his natural good looks. His long jet hair was tied back into a ponytail.

The fact that he was a hot burglar changed nothing. He was huge and menacing and in my space. My arm flew up, pepper spray aimed and ready to rock. "Stay back."

"I'm sorry. I didn't mean to scare you. Can we just go into the other room and get some light so I can show you—"

"Mom?" Mac called from the front door. My blood flash froze. Oh no, what was she doing in here?

The stranger reached into his coat. Even in the low light, I could make out a gun holster.

My daughter was in danger. I didn't wait to see what he was reaching for, just hit the depressor and shot a steady stream of the goop directly into my own face.

Oh it burned. Like the time I'd accidently stuck a mascara wand in my eye, only ten thousand times worse. And in both eyes. My nose dripped, and I coughed, trying to suck fresh air into my singed lungs. My back hit the wall, and with a curse I slid down. Something snagged the hem of my jeans, pulling and tugging with little force and making growling sounds. He'd brought a dog with him?

"Run," I wheezed at Mac. "Get back outside, now!"

"It's not what you think," she began. "He's—"

The miniscule pooch continued to yap. "Mac, go!"

"Mom, he's a cop."

"Huh?" I whipped my head around to face Mac, even though I couldn't see her. "What?"

"Here." He put something in my hand, helping me trace the shape with my thumb. A police shield.

I coughed again and rasped, "What the hell is he doing in here lurking around in the dark? And where did this dog come from?"

Mac cleared her throat. "When I called Mrs. B to tell her what was happening, she said that the power had gone out. She asked Detective Black to come get a fuse for the fuse box, since he had a key. And he also brought Snickers home."

"Detective Black?" I repeated stupidly, the badge still in my hand. "Snickers? Wait, did you say home? That creature *lives* here?"

"Gggrrr ruff." Snickers danced around my feet all ferocious-like. I turned my attention from the tiny dog to the big man, *the freaking cop* that I would have dosed with pepper spray if I'd been less of a spaz.

"Yeah, she was Uncle Al's dog. The detective took him in until we got here." Mac made a derisive sound. "Congrats, Mom. You just tried to assault a police officer and our new tenant all in one shot."

I choked and wheezed, "The key word there is *tried*."

* * *

Detective Black helped me up off the floor and over to the couch and instructed Mac to get him a wet washcloth for my eyes.

"I know that's hell," he murmured, pressing the damp fabric over my face. "Keep blinking, it'll help."

"Get spritzed often, do you?" I couldn't help the acerbity in my tone. If he had just knocked like a normal person instead of scaring me half to death, I wouldn't be in this situation. And part of me was doubly miffed at looking like such an idiot in front of him. He was right though, my vision was slowly clearing, the burning subsiding.

His hands were gentle as he pushed my hair back over my ears. "No, all police officers have to endure nonlethal force measures before we hit the streets. Tasers, stun guns, and pepper spray. The spray is the worst though. Stings like he…" He coughed, casting a sidelong glance at my daughter, and didn't finish his thought.

"Don't worry. I know all the bad words. Mom made flash cards when I was eight," Mac said.

"Ix-nay on the ashcards-flay in front of the officer-ay," I hissed.

The detective's gaze went from one of us to the other and he shook his head. "I'm off duty. And am fluent in Pig Latin. Besides, I don't think teaching your daughter curse words is illegal."

"I didn't want her to be behind the other kids in public school," I explained.

Mac went down to the basement to change the burned-out fuse, but the small dog, Snickers, still skulked and growled by my feet.

I blew my nose then asked, "What's her problem?"

Detective Black scooped up the glaring critter. "Just a lot of transition lately. She's never been keen on strangers."

"Well they don't make them stranger than me," I quipped.

It was a lame joke, but he smiled anyway as he scratched Snickers behind her ears. "Noted."

There was some serious chemistry in the room, more than just the remnants of pepper spray. The only thing that ruined it was the snarling mongrel between us. Damn it, no one said anything about a dog. Not that I had anything against dogs, but I liked them better when I could coo at them, give them a scratch, and then go on my merry way. Dogs had a way of being less cute when they messed on a girl's carpet or chewed up her favorite pair of designer knock-off boots.

Note to self—padlock the closet.

"So, Detective Black," I said, turning my attention away from the territorial little beast, "have you lived here long?"

"Call me Hunter. And about six months," he said and set Snickers back down. "Your uncle offered me the apartment after I arrested him for trespassing."

I blinked my still watering eyes. "Really?"

"You didn't know?" He raised a jet eyebrow. His eyes were so dark there was no distinction between pupil and iris.

I shrugged and looked away from those intense dark eyes. "My father and Uncle Al had a falling-out several years ago, so I didn't really know him all that well. I think that's why he left the building to me and my mom, to get one last shot on the chin at The Captain. My dad was career Navy."

"So you're a military brat?" he teased.

"Recovering military brat," I corrected with a smile. "He's been retired for ten years." I didn't mention that I'd moved out of my parents' house long before that.

The lights flicked back on, and I blinked like a baby bat up at my new neighbor.

"Let me get a look at your eyes." Hunter leaned in close, presumably to examine my face. He smelled woodsy, like campfires and fresh air and pine boughs. The clean scent cut through my stinging nostrils and raw throat, and it took all of my energy not to sigh as he examined my eyes.

"Pretty," he whispered, so low that I thought I was imagining it.

"Mom?" Mac had returned, and we sprang apart like a couple of guilty teenagers.

Hunter rose from the couch and backed toward the door. "Pretty much standard. Do you have any honey? It will help with raw throat."

"We subsist mostly on frozen dinners and takeout." Mac gestured to the bag of Thai congealing on the counter.

He headed for the door and murmured, "Let me check with Nona. She might have some."

Mac chucked her thumb at the still open door to the hall. "Did I interrupt something? Because you know you're supposed to hang a sock on the doorknob when you have a boy over."

"It's not like that." I struggled up off the couch. "Besides, I'd have to be an idiot to start macking on the tenants."

My daughter rolled her eyes. "Mom, like you could help yourself."

"What's that supposed to mean?"

Before she could answer there was a tentative knock on the door, and Nona Burkowitz shuffled in, carrying a jar of organic honey. She was a short, heavy-set woman in her late sixties with silver hair that she wore in a tight perm. Her housecoat was floral, her stockings pink, and her glasses thick as her Queens accent. "Hunter said you needed some honey, bubala."

"Yeah, it'll go awesome with my larb." I peaked in the bag. "You want to stay for dinner, Nona? There's plenty."

Nona wrinkled her beaklike nose. "I can't eat that spicy foreign stuff. It gives me gas. Besides, I had a nosh with my book club ladies earlier. Though I could do with a cup of tea."

"Do we have tea?" I asked Mac, who was in charge of the grocery shopping. I did too much impulse buying.

She opened one of the boxes that clogged up the counter. "Maybe from Grams?"

"Don't trouble yourself, dolly. I don't mean to be a nuisance." Nona parked herself on one of the barstools, making no move to leave. "So, Miss Mackenzie, what do you think of our good detective? He's single, you know."

When I'd first encountered Nona the week before, she'd proudly introduced herself as the neighborhood's *yenta*—what non-Yiddish speakers referred to as a matchmaking busybody. Even through the teary afterburn of pepper spray I saw the speculative gleam in her eye.

"Maybe he bats for the home team?" I suggested, just to be a smartass.

Nona looked confused. "You mean the Red Sox?"

Mac made an exasperated sound. "She means maybe he's gay. And he isn't. I caught him ogling Mom's cleavage earlier."

Nona crossed her arms over her ample bosom. "He's schtupped plenty of women, but none of them are repeaters, if you know what I mean."

"I do." Mac was fighting laughter, her cute little elven, goth-princess face tight from holding her jubilation in. "Mom's a hit-it-and-quit-it kinda girl too."

"Hey, I resemble that remark. Besides I'm swearing off men."

"What about you, dolly?" Nona turned her focus on Mac.

I bit my lip and studied the honey jar. Mac didn't date, and I liked it that way. According to her, boys her age were too immature. I trusted her judgment as it was a far cry better than my own. Of course, I didn't want her getting knocked up at sixteen the same way her mother had, either. It was my own personal tightrope, and I had crummy balance.

My daughter made a disgusted noise as she settled in front of her open laptop, a bowl full of peanut rice noodles perched on one knee and deadpanned, "I'm saving myself for Justin Bieber."

I made a dramatic grab for my chest. "You hurt Mommy when you say such things."

Mac swirled noodles around the tines of her fork. "And why is this all about you?"

"Did you hear that? It was my soul shriveling to blackened husk."

Mac shook her head. "Always so dramatic."

I waggled a finger at her. "Hey, I'm just as invested in your future mate as you are. After all, he'll be changing my bedpan when you're out taking the world by storm."

One pierced eyebrow went up. "If I haven't put you in the home already."

I faux gasped. "You'd do that to me, the woman who gave you life?"

She shrugged. "Hey, you can still reconsider the whole swearing off men shtick. Find yourself a wealthy husband. Preferably younger."

"Never. Besides, you called dibs on Bieber."

Nona looked a little lost by our banter, and Mac took pity on her. "I'm not really looking for a relationship right now, thanks."

Big freaking sigh of relief.

Nona took her glasses off and rubbed them on her apron. "Well, you know where I am if you change your mind. Now I better get upstairs. *Castle* is on in ten minutes. That Nathan Fillion sure can fill out a bullet proof vest."

I shook my head when the door shut behind her then turned to look at my offspring. "How come I get the feeling that she gave up too easily?"

Mac thought about it for a beat. "Because you're used to Grandma's bullying? Some people actually can accept the word *no*."

"You are wise beyond your years." I grinned at her, and she grunted. Maybe she hadn't wanted to encourage Nona, but just to be sure I asked, "Seriously though, what about Pete?"

She snorted. "Pete the Pervert? Come on."

"He's not a pervert. He's a sixteen-year-old boy. They're all like that." As I well knew.

"Mom," she said in her *get real* voice. "He put a camera in our bathroom."

Okay, that was sort of creepy, even if he said it had been just a test run of his new motion-activated camera thingy. Still, Pete and Mac had been friends since preschool, and he'd had a crush on her about as long. I was sure he had a good heart and was relatively harmless, and really, what more could a mother of a teenage girl ask for? "Look, I'm not saying you have to date Pete. Just hang out with him once in a while. It'd do you some good to break out of your cyber shell and fly from the nest."

Mac took her dish to the sink. "How about you worry a little less about my love life and a little more about your job hunt. How's that going, by the way?"

"Fine." I poked at the congealing mess of takeout, my appetite gone.

"By fine do you mean not at all?" She raised an eyebrow.

"No, by fine I mean fine. I have a few irons in the fire."

Mac sat down next to me. "Are we in trouble financially? Is that why we had to move in here?"

"No," I flat-out lied.

"Mom." She cast me a disbelieving look.

I pushed my plate away. "Mac, this isn't anything you need to worry about. I know I don't act like it very often, but I am your mother. Have you ever had to go without food or shelter or even the best in vintage computer parts?"

"No," she admitted.

I reached out and ran a hand down her arm. "I'll find a new job—promise. Look, it's been a bear of a day, and I don't think Detective Hottie is coming back tonight. I'm going to take a shower and hit the hay. Will you keep an eye on the breathing dust mop?"

Snickers picked her head up and growled at me.

"Sure." Mac lifted the dog and got a lick for her efforts.

I made it to the door before she called after me. "Mom, you'd tell me if we were in real trouble, right?"

"Of course I would." I gave her my best reassuring smile and shuffled down the hall. The bedroom door shut with a snick, and I leaned against it, barely resisting the urge to bang my head into it repeatedly.

How was it possible that I was both under- and overqualified for every decent job in Boston? I hadn't been BS-ing Mac when I said I'd been scouring LinkedIn and pounding the pavement ever since the boutique dress shop I'd worked for went under three months ago. I'd been working odd jobs since I'd left my parent's place at sixteen and wasn't qualified for much else. Sure I could pick up a few part-time shifts, but that would be without benefits or much of a regular income. Besides, most retailers liked hiring kids Mac's age instead of a sad sack thirty-two-year-old. They worked for less money.

I headed into the bathroom and turned on the shower. Tomorrow I would expand my search and find something that I was good at. Waitressing maybe. I liked food as long as I didn't have to cook it. And the tips would help us put gas in the ever-needy Fillmore.

I'd just finished stripping and happened to glance up in the mirror when something unusual caught my eye. I turned around and reached for the book someone had wedged between a couple of towels on the top shelf. The cover was a nice leather quality, and the thing looked valuable. I opened it to the first page and read the handwritten letters.

The first page had only two sentences. *Working Man's Guide to Sleuthing for a Living*. And beneath that, *By Albert Taylor, PI.*

What interesting reading material Uncle Al had kept in the bathroom. My eyes were still itchy, but I decided that the shower could wait. After shutting off the water I headed for the bedroom and settled in to read.

CHAPTER TWO

Chain of Custody—applies to the documentation, custody, control, and handling of evidence in order to preserve its integrity.
From the *Working Man's Guide to Sleuthing for a Living* by Albert Taylor, PI

The journal was a fascinating read. I stayed up until two in the morning, engrossed with Uncle Al's pearls of PI wisdom. By the time the coffee had finished brewing I had a plan of attack.

"I know what I want to be when I grow up," I announced, pouncing on my sleeping daughter. Snickers, who had had been laying across her feet, snarled at the disturbance.

"Great," Mac mumbled and buried her face deeper into the pillows.

"Nice doggie." I backed off. "Wanna go outside?" The dog, obviously familiar with New England weather, laid her head back down.

Snagging Mac's pillow so she had to pay attention to me, I announced. "I'm going to be a private investigator!"

One eyelid cracked open. "Mom, get real."

"I am being real. It's not that hard, at least according to Uncle Al."

Mac yawned and sat up on the couch. "Did he come to you in a dream or something?"

"No, I found one of his old journals." I held out the *Working Man's Guide.* "He says, and this is a direct quote, 'If you think you would be good at being a private investigator, then you probably will be.' And I know I will be freaking fabulous!"

Mac took the book without much enthusiasm. "Don't you need like a license or a certificate or something?"

I moved over to Ol' Trusty, the coffeepot I'd scored for a dollar at a garage sale the year Mac was five. "Eventually. But the journal says I could go to work for a law firm right away as an unlicensed PI. They would give me cases and stuff."

"Cases and stuff." My daughter shook her head. "So you need a lawyer to hire you?"

Someone rapped on the front door, and I moved to answer it. "Don't sound so skeptical. I can do this. And take that creature outside before she piddles on the rug."

I pulled the door open with the chain still attached and peeked out in the hall. Hunter Black stood there looking scrumptious and bearing a cardboard takeout tray full of coffee and a bag of doughnuts.

"Be still my heart," I breathed.

"What was that?" he asked. He wasn't much of a smiler, though the spark of amusement in his gaze indicated that he'd heard me perfectly well.

"Coffee is my drug of choice. You're enabling an addict."

"It's just my way of apologizing for the mishap last night. May I come in?"

I shut the door, slid the chain free, and then opened it all the way. "If I tell you that the apology is unnecessary, do I still get the coffee?"

"I wouldn't want to be held responsible for your withdrawal," he murmured and handed it over.

"Hiya, detective." Mac waved from the couch. She was adorably rumpled, and her short red-gold hair stuck out every which way. "When you didn't come back, Mom thought she'd run you off for good."

"Yeah, sorry I disappeared so suddenly, but when I get called, I have to go." Those amused eyes turned back to focus on me.

I was too busy making sweet *amour* to French-pressed delight to pay much attention to their exchange. "Oh holy hoochie mamma, Batman. Mac, you have got to try this."

"You drink coffee too?" Hunter raised an eyebrow at my offspring.

"Is the pope Catholic?" Mac reached for a cup. "And don't mind Mom. She gets a little excited over her first cup of coffee. And her second and her fifteenth."

"You weren't kidding about the addiction, were you?" The detective set the bag of doughnuts down on the kitchen counter and shucked his jacket.

"I never joke about coffee," I told him, "or shoe sales. Everything else is fair game though."

"Good to know." He did that amused crinkling thing with his eyes again. If he ever did actually smile, or even laugh, my heart might stop.

We stared at each other, letting the moment stretch out between us. He seemed to fit the space well, looking completely comfortable perched on a barstool.

Mac rolled her eyes. "I better get ready for school."

"Have fun with that," I called, not taking my gaze from Hunter's. Oh this was Bad with a capitol *B*.

"You have to get ready too," she reminded me. "You're driving me, remember?"

Rats, I hadn't. "First day, new school. Oh, but shoot, Fillmore's oil light came on last night when we were on our way back from the Thai place. I have to stop and get some more liquid gold for him."

"You could take Al's car," Hunter offered.

"His what now?" Mac and I said in unison.

A slow smile spread across his face and I was right, the effect was devastating "You don't know? The keys should be in his desk." He strode purposefully down the hall toward Uncle Al's office.

Mac put down her empty coffee cup. "Did you know about a car?"

I shook my head. "Mom never mentioned it."

She worried her bottom lip. "So, is it okay if we just take it?"

"Not like Al's got much use for it. Besides, it can't be worse than Fillmore."

Mac nodded, obviously torn over the idea of using a car we didn't have permission from a dead man to drive. Time to say something parental. What would my mother, Agnes Taylor, say in this situation?

"Go get ready," I said. "You're going to be late." There, that sounded about right.

"Don't look at it without me," she begged, her curiosity obviously building as Hunter returned with a set of keys.

"She seems like a good kid." Hunter's low voice startled me.

Eerie, I had just been thinking the same thing. "She really is. Exceptional even. Not sure where she gets it from."

He focused those intense dark eyes on me again. "I could make an educated guess."

I wasn't a blusher. No way no how, blushing was not my thing. But I found heat creeping up my neck and was having a hard time holding his gaze, as if the compliment weighed me down somehow. Warning claxons reverberated in my head. I really liked our new tenant, like stupid liked him. And I had a strict *don't date the ones you could fall for* policy. Last time I had, I'd ended up with two pink lines on a pregnancy test the same week as my Civil War midterm.

Lesson learned.

"So is Mac short for something?" Hunter asked.

"Yup, she's a Mackenzie too. Unfortunately, I hadn't decided on her name before she was born and no one told me how freaking painful childbirth would be or how exhausted I'd be afterword. In utero I called her Mini-Me. I blame it on my fascination with *Austin Powers*."

Hunter was doing that thing where he looked like he was about to smile but it hadn't broken free yet. I wanted to see that moment when emotion overrode his considerable restraint.

"So there I was, whacked out on Demerol and more tired than I'd ever been in my entire life, and someone shoves a stack of papers in front of me and tells me it's for my daughter's birth certificate. So I see a space for a name, right? And I fill in *Mackenzie Elizabeth Taylor* because even in my doped-up state, I knew how to spell that one. So she became Mackenzie Elizabeth Taylor 2.0, the new and improved edition."

Bingo, there went the smile. And it was well worth the effort. "And her father?"

"He's not in the picture." I slid off the barstool and started fussing with things in the kitchen.

"I didn't mean to pry."

"It's a natural question. He's just not father material." I prayed he'd leave it at that.

Mac returned exactly five minutes later, backpack strap over one shoulder. "All set."

I eyeballed the hallway. "Where's Snickers?"

"In the bathroom."

Visions of the cranky little mongrel leaping up to bite my jugular assailed me. "What if I have to pee while you're at school?"

"You have lawyers to coerce into hiring you. Use their bathrooms."

"This is just a ploy so I set up your room sooner." I sent her a knowing smirk.

"Would I do that to you? My own mother?"

"Um, let me think about that for a second…hell, yeah."

Her quicksilver smile flashed. "You know me so well."

We followed Hunter out the door and were bitch-slapped by the chill autumn wind. October had copped-a-squat over Boston, and my hair whipped into my face in a sharp stinging sensation. Times like this made me envy Mac's short 'do. Hunter circled in front of our apartment and strode to the small gravel drive and the rickety shed behind.

"The anticipation is killing me," I grumbled while checking out our neighbor's stellar glutes.

"Down girl," Mac grumbled. "I forbid you to get naked with the good detective."

I scowled at her. "Who said anything about getting naked?"

Mac rolled her eyes. "Seriously? I'm choking on your pheromones over here. And it would make for dicey living conditions if he started giving us parking tickets because you nailed and bailed, so just say no."

"Remind me again who the parent is in this little duo? Because for a second I was sure it was me."

Mac actually snorted at that. "Says the woman who cried into her margarita and begged me not to let her make any more horrific life choices."

Damn, I'd forgotten about that. "You have a mind like a steel trap…hey, where did he go?"

Mac glanced around and did a palms-up. We'd been distracted by our verbal banter and somehow lost sight of Detective Black.

"Over here," a disembodied voice called from somewhere behind a row of rhododendron.

"Maybe he fell in the bushes," Mac hissed.

"Then shouldn't he be saying, 'I've fallen, and I can't get up'?"

"He's not eighty, Mom."

There was a scrape of wood on concrete as a door was dragged open. It seemed Hunter Black hadn't been waylaid by the shrubbery but instead was struggling with the door to the ancient shed. The thing looked ready to collapse in the next strong breeze.

"Is this the part where he shows us his collection of chainsaws and we are never heard from again?" I asked Mac.

"He's a cop. To protect and to serve, that whole shtick. Besides, if he was going to kill us he'd do it under cover of darkness." She eyeballed my purse, undermining her reassurance when she added, "On a totally unrelated matter, you still have that pepper spray, right?"

"Right here." All thoughts of grisly death scenes left me when I heard the roar of a massive engine firing to life. "Is that…?"

Hunter appeared, pushing the other shed door open to reveal the second most beautiful sight I have ever beheld, close behind the birth of my baby girl. "Judas Priest."

Mac blinked. "That's no old jalopy—it's a muscle car."

"Not just any muscle car," I breathed, moving over to put a hand over the growling hood. "This is a 2016 Dodge Challenger SRT Hellcat with a 6.2L V8 engine." And it came in pitch-black, my power color.

"It was delivered a few days after Al's passing," Hunter said. "He used to own one back when they first came out, and he'd been making noise about buying another one. I had no idea he was serious until the flatbed showed up. I just parked it in here and figured I'd hand the keys over to his next of kin." He tossed said keys in my direction.

I caught them reflexively, though my eyes were glued to the Hellcat. "Are you telling me it's never even been *driven*? Weren't you tempted?"

Hunter shrugged. "It wasn't mine to drive."

His sincere honesty kept me from saying something about how he should arrest himself on principle. I wouldn't have had the restraint not to slide inside such a sweet ride and take it for a spin up and down the eastern seaboard. It was all I could do not to scream *road trip* and burn rubber. Only the thought of our bare cabinets which could've given Old Mother Hubbard a run for her money reminded me I was a grown up and didn't have time to frolic.

But even driving Mac to school in the Hellcat was a boatload better than a morning of putt-putting down the streets of Boston in Fillmore, watching him belch smoke everywhere he went. I beamed up at our new neighbor. "Wow, this…this is incredible. Thank you."

His smile was slight, but his eyes spoke volumes. Again, the notion about still waters running deep played through my mind. I felt like a bubbling brook next to a vast river when I stood beside our new neighbor. But my daughter, who asked so little of me, had requested that I not get emotionally entangled with our new neighbor. I'd done it before, dated one of our landlords, and it hadn't ended well. And for her sake, as well as my own, I wouldn't pursue the detective. With considerable effort, I looked back at Mac. "You ready for school?"

Not one to wait for an engraved invitation, my mini tossed her backpack over the back seat and slipped into the passenger's side.

"Can I give you a ride somewhere?" I asked Hunter. Out of politeness, not because I wanted to spend more time with him. Not that he was even interested in me as anything more than a neighbor and someone to pay his rent to every month.

But he shook his head. "No, I'm heading back to the precinct in an hour. Enjoy the car, Mackenzie."

It was the first time he'd spoken my name, and the deep rumble of his voice had turned it into a sort of verbal caress. "I will. Um…I guess I'll see you later."

Our new neighbor didn't make huge gestures or any obvious clues as to his thoughts. He was a riddle hidden within a concealing fog. He simply said, "Looking forward to it."

Hunter stepped back, and I moved toward the driver's-side door, feeling an odd pang. Strange, I didn't know the man, not really, but leaving him behind felt…wrong somehow.

Sliding behind the wheel of the hellcat dispelled the bizarre feeling. "I could die happy right now," I told my daughter.

"Good. Then as your next of kin, I'll be the first to drive it," Mac teased.

I frowned even as I caressed the buttery steering wheel. "Where do you suppose Uncle Al got the money for this car? He wasn't exactly living the life of Riley in his apartment."

Mac shrugged. "Maybe he won the lotto or something. Come on, I'm going to be late for first period."

"Not if Helga and I have anything to say about it." I revved the engine once then shifted out of neutral, and the car shot forward. Panicked by the sheer responsiveness, I did a both feet on the brake thing and narrowly missed careening through the rickety garage wall.

"Maybe she doesn't like being called Helga," Mac suggested.

I was too busy catching my breath to respond. This car was certainly not Fillmore, and there could be no showboating with my offspring in the car. "No, she does, she's just flexing her muscles, letting us know what she's made of. But we can stand up to a little Hellcat guff, right?"

"Right." Mac nodded crisply, grin firmly in place. "Let's do this."

* * *

A few hours later, I parked in front of the third law office of the morning. The first two had been a bust, one claiming they didn't retain investigators and the other saying they had a full compliment. The second refused to see me because I didn't have a scheduled appointment. In layman's terms, I was SOL.

I figured I had time for one more before my lunch date with my mother. Though job hunting should under normal circumstances trump a ham and cheese, I knew better than to blow off this particular meeting.

Because Uncle Al had left the building to the two of us, we were co-owners, and as my mother succinctly put it, matters needed to be discussed. And meeting her at a restaurant was a hell of a lot easier than having her come to inspect the building firsthand. We'd had an unspoken truce ever since I'd left home at sixteen. We always met on neutral territory. That way neither of us had home field advantage.

But one thing at a time. It would be so much more satisfying to stroll into the café with a case file under one arm, knowing that whatever shenanigans Agnes Taylor decided to pull, I had the beginnings of a new career waiting for me. And in order to get that first case as an unlicensed PI, I needed to convince a lawyer to hire me.

At first glance, the law firm of Lennard Copeland & Associates wasn't all that impressive. It wasn't situated in one of the high-rise buildings overlooking Boston harbor. No, it was a small office with peeling lettering on the door sandwiched between a delicatessen and a rundown-looking bar. I drummed my fingers on the steering wheel for a minute, trying to decide if it was worth going inside. If worse came to worse, Lennard would tell me no, and I could brace myself with a drink before meeting with Mom.

With a plan in place, I exited Helga and made sure to lock the doors before pushing my way through the glass doors and into the law office.

A stoop-shouldered man sat at the reception desk. He had a coffee stain on his tie and liver spots on his expanding forehead, but he smiled brightly when I made my way inside. "May I help you, my dear?" His voice was accented with the honey of the Deep South.

"Yes, hi, I'm Mackenzie Taylor. I was hoping for a few minutes of Mr. Copeland's time. Do you know if he's available?"

The smile stayed in place and bright blue eyes twinkled merrily behind horn-rimmed glasses. "Why yes, I believe he does have an opening. If you'd follow me, please." He rose, the motion appearing painful, and my back spasmed in sympathy. It took a great deal of effort not to tap my foot in impatience as he shuffled around the desk and toward the door to the left of the water cooler. Then an arthritic hand reached for the doorknob, pushing the thing open a few inches. More shuffling, more pushing, shuffle, push, shuffle. And being a true gentleman, he held the door for me, which required still more shuffling.

Glancing around, I was surprised to see the room was empty, except for the two of us. Where were all the associates? Well, it was closing in on lunchtime. Still, it didn't seem right that Copeland abandoned the firm into his kind but clearly elderly assistant's care.

I offered a smile and a nod of thanks before taking a seat across from the cluttered walnut desk. A matching bookshelf stood behind it, overflowing with tattered law books. A hideous pea-green vinyl chair stood in the opposite corner with a cheap standing lamp behind it. I knew for a fact it was cheap because I had the same one at home. There wasn't much going on to instill confidence in Copeland's case-winning skills. Good thing I wasn't a client.

"Will Mr. Copeland be back soon?" I asked the assistant when I realized he was still in the room.

"He'll be in presently." My escort scuffed his way forward. I hoped the carpeting was tacked down properly. I didn't want the old guy to fall and break a hip. Way to kill a job interview before it even started.

I had an affinity for older people. Both my parents had been well beyond the average child-rearing age when they'd had me. I'd been a late-life surprise for my mother, who'd all but abandoned hope of having a child and had been disappointed in the one she had. When I lived with them, I'd followed the *children should be seen and not heard* edict, and years of sitting by the sidelines made me an excellent listener. It was a skill I retained, even after fleeing my mother's suffocating grasp. Seniors liked someone who stopped by to listen to their stories when their relatives were busy or had heard a particular tale one time too many. I could so relate, and it was easy enough to find common ground that I started conversations with complete strangers on the T who looked a little lonely and sometimes missed my stop. These habits were so deeply ingrained that Mac had dubbed me the Fogey Whisperer.

This particular senior was hard to read though. He didn't give much away, almost like he was a lifelong poker player. There was something about the look in his eyes, some secret that amused him. His expression was friendly and open, but it was almost deceptive, as though he were waiting for me to get the punch line of a joke he'd just told.

It clicked then. "You're, Mr. Copeland, aren't you?"

"My third grade teacher called me Mr. Copeland. I like the way you say it better, but you can call me Len." A dry sounding chuckle wheezed from him, and he extended a hand. "You're sharp, I'll give you that, Miz Taylor. What can I do for you?"

Here went everything. I took a deep breath and donned my brightest smile. "Actually, it's about what I can do for you. I was wondering if you needed a private investigator."

CHAPTER THREE

Around eighty percent of all cases a private investigator works are domestic and require nothing more than simple surveillance. Any PI who tells you he works only criminal cases is a liar.
From the *Working Man's Guide to Sleuthing for a Living* by Albert Taylor, PI

"You did it? You really got hired as a PI?" Mac's voice sounded both hopeful and wary over our static filled connection. "I'm not being *Punk'd*, am I?"

"You know that was cancelled. Besides, if Ashton Kutcher was here, you know I would have led with that." Overjoyed, I again looked down at the manila envelope, the details of my very first case as a private investigator—left out on the restaurant's clean white linens conveniently located for Mommy Dearest to notice.

"Like, you're getting paid and everything?" Mac still sounded skeptical.

"Hourly rates, plus expenses," I said proudly. Of course I left out the bit about being hired on a trial basis. Results were expected by both Len and the client.

"So what's the case?"

I made a disgusted sound. "What, no congratulations?"

"I'm not sure I should congratulate you. You don't have to bust up a black market trafficking circle or something, do you?"

"No, it's a child custody case." I didn't want to get into more details than that over the phone. Uncle Al's book had warned that the most successful PIs knew how to keep their mouths shut, and blabbing out the details of my first case in a crowded restaurant didn't seem the best way to start. "Really, all I need to do is take a few pictures with my phone, write up notes for my findings, and possibly appear in court, if Len thinks it's necessary for me to present testimony."

"Wow, Mom. That sounds important. Congratulations."

"Now was that so hard?" The restaurant door opened, and Agnes Taylor breezed in. "Shoot, I've gotta go. Grandma just showed up."

"Remember—like a kidney stone, this too shall pass," my daughter snickered.

I said good-bye to the smartass and stowed my phone as my mother approached. "Mom, how are you?"

In typical Agnes fashion, she ignored the question, instead surveying me from head to toe. "What on earth are you wearing?"

I looked down to the clean pair of jeans and dark leather jacket which had seemed the perfect PI ensemble with the added bonus of being comfy and provoking the maternal unit. "Clothes, same as you."

"Not the same as me." She indicated her tailored slacks and cream twinset. "I look respectable enough for a luncheon in this restaurant. How do you ever expect to meet a decent man if you go about dressed like you should be hanging off the back of one of those dreadful motorcycles?"

"Have you ever heard of the women's lib movement? I hear tell it was kind of a big thing in your day."

"Honestly, Mackenzie, we're not talking about equal pay for equal work here. You have a child and children need two parents."

I blew out a breath. No sense in pointing out that my child was the same age as I had been when I'd started living as an adult. "There's a biker bar not far from Uncle Al's place…"

She rolled her eyes then pointedly looked to the waiter who hovered nearby. "Tom Collins," she snapped. "And my daughter will have water with a twist of lemon. Make sure it's bottled, not tap. And no ice."

The young man nodded and scurried off. I looked at her. "Room temperature water with lemon?"

She lowered herself into her chair, setting her small purse beside her neatly folded napkin. "It kills the appetite. The holidays are coming, and you could stand to lose a few pounds beforehand."

There was a stabbing pain behind my right eye, and I glanced at the clock. I hadn't even been with her ten minutes, and I felt as though I were being lobotomized sans anesthesia. In other words, right on schedule.

"Now, about the building," Agnes began, but I cut her off.

"Mom, before we get into it I wanted to share some good news."

Her face lit up. "You're seeing someone?"

Immediately Hunter Black's face popped to mind, but no, he was our tenant, and Mac had made me promise not to screw it up. "No, I got a job."

"Oh?" Her eyebrows drew down. Leave it to my mother to be disappointed that she hadn't raised a gold digger.

"That's right." I forced enough cheerfulness for the both of us, imagining how Mac and I would celebrate my first case. Pizza with extra cheese and full-calorie soda to make up for the lemon water. "I'm going to be a private investigator. Isn't that great?"

She scowled. "What do you mean 'a private investigator'? You can't do that."

"I can, and I'm going to. In fact, this is my first case right here." I tapped the manila folder for emphasis.

The browbeaten waiter reappeared and deposited our drinks just as Agnes hissed, "Have you lost your mind?"

"I'll come back for your order." The waiter beat a hasty retreat.

I huffed out a breath, not really surprised by her lack of support. Why bother breaking a lifelong habit? "I need a job, mother. To support myself and Mac."

"You'd have plenty of money if you agreed to sell that accursed apartment building."

And round and round we went. "Mom, I've told you, we need a place to live, and Uncle Al's space is perfect for us. Let someone else snag the little house with a white picket fence and the man to bring home the bacon. We're doing just fine."

Her lips pressed into a thin line. Agnes Taylor was still a beautiful woman, when she smiled. Which she didn't do often. "That place is too much for you to handle. It needs work, and that's expensive."

I thought about the Hellcat in the garage. "Uncle Al was managing just fine. Mac and I will too."

"Mackenzie, please. Think about the example you're setting for your child. Do you want her growing up telling her friends that her mother spies on people having seedy affairs?"

I stared at the sad-looking lemon slice floating in my water glass. "Well it's better than telling people her mother is a browbeaten trophy wife who vents all life's disappointments on her daughter. You promised you would stop this, Mom. Five years ago when you begged me to let you be a part of Mac's life, you vowed that you would stop judging the way I choose to live. Stop forcing your screwy agenda down my throat."

My words didn't make a dent. "Lower your voice. We're in public."

I nodded once. "Thanks for lunch, Mom. It was memorable as always." I rose and scooped my file up. "I'll let you get the check. I feel like I've paid enough for the water already."

"Mackenzie, sit down." She seethed, but I turned and strode from the restaurant, mouthing a *sorry* at our waiter as I passed his hiding place.

"That went well." I breathed when I was once again out in the autumn wind. Why did I ever expect anything to be different with Agnes? Though she was half my size she was as immovable as a mountain. But I never failed to come away from a meeting with her with a lingering sense of disappointment. Seeing Helga parked at the curb lifted my spirits considerably, and I squared my shoulders and sat down inside to rack the file.

Len's client was Jessica Granger. She was a middle-aged pediatrician with two children—Evan, age thirteen, and Mary, age eight—and she was petitioning the court for sole custody of her two kids, claiming that their father, Paul, left the kids with his parents during his custody visits. Supposedly Paul had won joint custody because he had more flexible work hours and could really be there for his kids. My job was straightforward. Document Paul leaving Evan and Mary with their grandparents on several different occasions to provide support to Jessica's claim for sole custody.

It was early still, but I didn't feel like heading home to unpack one box and then coming back to see what went down when school let out. I parked across the street from Paul's parents' house and waited. And waited. Damn, I should have used the restaurant's bathroom before starting my surveillance. I really had to pee. Stupid lemon water. Having a kid myself, I was pretty familiar with the school schedule, so I doubted I would miss much if I drove to the nearest 7-Eleven and relieved the growing pressure in my bladder.

Fifteen minutes later I was back and fortified with a Slurpee and a few snack cakes, grinning at the imagined look on my mother's face when she saw my actual lunch, and settled in to wait.

* * *

Two hours later my butt was numb, and I had to pee again when a silver Lexus pulled into the driveway. Breaking away from the riveting game of *Angry Birds* that had kept me from losing my mind, I cleared the screen and opened the camera app, shooting multiple shots of the three doors opening. A man, a teenaged boy, and a young girl in pink tights and a blue coat exited the vehicle. Dollars to doughnuts they were Paul, Evan, and Mary. I couldn't help but smile at Mary, who skipped up the walkway, clearly delighted to be free from the clutches of the public school system. A wave of nostalgia rolled through me as I remembered Mac at the same age. Kids grew up too damn fast.

They all disappeared inside the house, and I shifted, trying to relieve the pins and needles feeling in my thighs. There wasn't much to document so far. Three people drive up to a house and go inside. My photos uploaded to the cloud automatically. I sent the best one to my email address just as an extra safety precaution and settled in to wait.

No more than five minutes later, Paul reappeared, got into his car, and drove off. Okay then, maybe he had to go get gas or pick up medication or something. I should probably stick around and see if he came back. This job needed to be executed thoroughly.

I scrolled back through the photos, checking to see which were the best. A light off to the side caught my attention, and I expanded the picture on the screen to see it better. I'd been taking high quality resolution, and though the large image was slightly distorted, it was still clear enough. A man sitting in a black Escalade was taking a photo at the same time I was, and the light that had distorted my image was from his flash.

I checked the street again, feeling a weird case of the heebie-jeebies. The Escalade was still there, parked in the driveway alongside Paul's parents' place. The windows were rolled up now. There wasn't much going on worth photographing on the street. I checked my photo again. Yeah, the guy had totally been taking a picture and not with his phone, either. The flash was much brighter than anything my little Droid produced, and though it was distorted, I could see a lens, one of those large detachable ones.

Snagging the file free from the graveyard of snack cake wrappers, I called Len's office. He picked up on the first ring. "Lennard Copeland's office. This is Lennard."

"Hi, Len, it's Mackenzie. Did you hire another PI for the Granger case?"

"No, sugar, I sure didn't. Why do you ask?"

I explained to him what I'd seen and checked the street again. "Is it possible that Mrs. Granger might have hired someone else on her own and not told you?"

He chuckled dryly. "When it comes to divorce and custody cases, I've learned that anything is possible. I can call her and ask if that would make you feel better."

"If you would. You can call me back at this number. I was going to wait and make sure Paul doesn't come right back."

"Very thorough. Color me impressed. I'll call you back in a spell," Len assured me and hung up.

Though my window was partly rolled down for picture taking purposes, I figured turning to stare directly at the black

SUV with the tinted windows would give the game away. I played with Helga's rearview mirror until I had almost a complete view of the vehicle. If the driver was a PI, it stood to reason he might have spied me too and had the same questions about me that I had about him.

My phone rang and I picked up without checking the screen. "Len?"

"Mom? Who's Len?"

"My new boss. What's up, hon?" From my vantage point I could see little Mary on a swing in the back yard. The teenager, if he was anything like my teenager, was probably hunkered down in front of one screen or another. Still no sight of Paul.

"Mrs. Burkowitz wanted us to come up to her place for dinner," Mac said, giving away no indication of whether she wanted to go or not.

Being the super mom I was, I read between the lines. "She's listening on your end, right?"

"Mmm, hmmm." Mac made an affirmative noise.

"And I'm guessing since you didn't say you would like to go that you'd rather skip it this time?"

"Yeah, I have a history test tomorrow, plus a ton of Spanish verbs to conjugate."

"Rough first day then?" I felt a little guilty for not being there for her, but I had to earn a paycheck.

"You have no idea." She sounded aggrieved. Mac didn't like being behind at school. It stressed her out big time.

And it was probably a good idea to set boundaries with the neighborhood Yenta early on. I already had one woman trying to marry me off to any guy who happened across my path. I didn't want to give Nona encouragement in that department. "Tell Nona thanks, but I have big unpacking plans when I get home." Translation: pizza, television, and Mommy-daughter time. "Ask if maybe we can do it this weekend."

"Oh, okay. I'll let her know. Have you cracked the case yet?"

"I'm chipping away at it. Be home soon." I hung up just as the car I was watching pulled out of the driveway and passed me.

I looked from the house across the street to the brake lights at the stop sign by the corner, torn in three directions at once. I could stay and let the pins and needles take over my whole body and see if deadbeat Paul showed up to spend a little quality time with his kids. I could go pick up that pizza and spend some quality time with my own offspring. Or I could follow the SUV and find out where it went, maybe get a better idea why the driver was taking pictures of the same family I was tailing.

I drummed my thumbs on the steering wheel. Len might call me back with answers. Then again, he might not. And pizza could wait.

Decided, I pulled out just as the SUV turned the corner.

Tailing a car wasn't as easy as one might think. In fact, if it hadn't been a supersized gas-guzzler that I was following, I wouldn't have managed it. The driver was aggressive, beating yellow lights that I got stuck at, and as the city traffic slowed to a crawl in the evening commute, I lost sight of my quarry more than once.

I must have told myself to give up and head home half a dozen times. And each time I decided I'd go on just a little bit longer. It made no sense, but life making sense was something my mother worried about. I just wanted one good look at the man driving that car.

When he broke away from traffic heading across Summer Street and went east on East First Street, I fell back a few blocks. This was Boston, and we were nearing the harbor. There wasn't too much farther east he *could* go.

The light faded as we headed farther into the Southie neighborhood. Would he turn into one of the houses up ahead, just head home for the day? If so, I'd have to think fast and find a place to park or, worst-case scenario, keep driving past. He seemed unaware of my presence so far, and I didn't want to clue him in now.

But the SUV didn't turn down one of the streets or find a driveway. Instead, it headed to the Conley Terminal. That eerie feeling in my stomach was growing, or maybe it was too many snack cakes. Either way, I was determined to ignore it and see this through.

The SUV stopped in front of a row of large shipping containers. When I saw his brake lights go on, I backed into the first turnoff I could and shut the engine off to kill my headlights. The sun was sinking fast behind me, and I was pretty sure I'd reacted quickly enough to keep the driver of the Escalade from noticing me.

Unfortunately, for discretion's sake, I had parked so far away that I couldn't see much of anything. And when I rolled the window down to hear, there wasn't much to hear, at least nothing out of the norm for a major seaport—just the *thunks* of cargo containers being loaded and unloaded, the shouting voices of workers, and the steady drone of equipment, occasionally pierced by the backing up of big machinery. A few crying gulls. Nothing unusual at all.

Until the gunshot.

I flinched in my seat, instinctively ducking down. For one wild moment I thought that the SUV driver had spotted me and was unhinged enough to fire at me. But there was no sound of breaking glass, no further noise other than the thundering rush of my heartbeat. I looked up just in time to see the Escalade reverse sharply and then speed from the terminal at a million miles per hour. Even if I'd wanted to follow him after that, I couldn't have.

I shook for a moment, full body tremors that had nowhere to go. Night had officially fallen, and I wondered if maybe my overactive imagination had made up the whole scene. What were some of the things that sounded similar to gunfire? Fireworks and old cars backfiring. One didn't usually see too many fireworks in October. And as for cars, it had been me and the Escalade. Everyone else was working far away.

No, there had been a gunshot, I was sure of it. But no one had gotten out of the SUV. I'd been watching it the whole time. Had someone been shooting at the driver? Was that why he sped off like a bat outta hell?

It was time for me to go home and maybe rethink this whole PI gig. I was a single parent. My job description shouldn't include dodging bullets. For Mac's sake as well as my own. I took one last look around and then turned the engine over. The headlights came on, illuminating a body lying face down in the weeds. And behind it, a silver Lexus was almost hidden from view.

CHAPTER FOUR

A client will tell you only what he or she wants you to know. A good PI will ask the right questions and get the whole picture. From the *Working Man's Guide to Sleuthing for a Living* by Albert Taylor, PI

I stared for a stunned moment at the Lexus, squinting at the Massachusetts license plate. That couldn't be Paul Granger's car. It couldn't. My hand shook as I held my phone up and dialed 9-1-1.

"What's the nature of your emergency?" a gruff male operator asked me.

"There's been a shooting at…" I looked around, swallowed and then gave the nearest intersection.

"The police are in route now. Is anyone hurt?" the operator asked.

Mighty fine question, one I should have looked into instead of sitting around like a big old moron. But I couldn't help it. "I'm not sure. There was a man, Paul Granger. He drove a silver Lexus, and I was following this Escalade, and maybe I should go check—"

"Ma'am." The guy cut me off. "Are you in any immediate danger?"

Now that the Escalade was gone, I doubted it. So why wouldn't my hands quit shaking? "I don't…no."

"All right. As long as you're somewhere safe, just hang on the line with me until the police arrive. Tell me your name." His voice was calm and efficient as he talked me out of what I was starting to realize was profound shock.

I had no idea what I said, but within moments sirens could be heard growing closer, and I saw the telltale flashing blue and red lights.

"Get out of the car and keep your hands up so the officers can see them," 9-1-1 Guy advised me.

"They won't shoot me will they?" I was pretty sure the answer was no but wanted to make sure before giving up the safety of being cocooned in Helga's relative safety.

"Not unless you give them a reason to," 9-1-1 Guy said.

Taking a deep breath, I popped the car door just as the first police vehicle roared into the terminal. I held my hands up as high as they would go, clutching desperately to the phone and the lifeline 9-1-1 Guy provided.

Two uniformed officers were out of the car in a nanosecond and had their side arms drawn, although thankfully not pointed at me. "Are you the woman who phoned in the shooting?"

"Yes," I said, afraid to put my hands down.

The woman who'd been driving approached. "Hands on the vehicle."

"Okay," I said, and turned and put my hands on Helga's shiny black roof. "I'm not armed or anything." Probably should have led with that.

She patted me down anyway, and I couldn't blame her. "What are you doing here?"

"I'm a PI," I said. "I was following someone."

"Licensed?"

"Not yet. I work for Lennard Copeland. It's my first day," I babbled.

9-1-1 Guy was saying something, but since I'd put my phone on the roof of the car, I couldn't hear him.

"Hey, Denton, you better come take a look at this" the male officer called from somewhere beside the Lexus.

"Stay here," Officer Denton instructed me. She had just finished checking Helga's interiors for weapons, and I noticed that she kept my little key chain of pepper spray. After last night, she was welcome to it.

Suddenly I thought about Hunter Black. He was a police detective, wasn't he? Why hadn't I thought to call him instead of

9-1-1? Probably because when I heard gunshots, all the adrenaline had made me sort of stupid. And just because he was a detective didn't mean he actually investigated random shootings. Or murder.

I shivered as the wind gusted in off the harbor. Had I really just witnessed a murder? I'd have to tell the police about the man in the Escalade and why I'd been following Paul Granger.

Or did I? Did Len's attorney-client privilege extend to me and my investigation? I didn't know.

Two more cop cars pulled up in front of the storage container and though all the uniforms looked over at me, none approached. But eventually a detective would ask me questions, and I needed to know what to say.

9-1-1 Guy was still on the line. I disconnected and then dialed Len's number.

"I think our client's husband was just shot," I said sans preamble. "At least I'm guessing it's him. How much do I need to tell the cops about our case?"

"Who is this?" Len asked.

I pulled the phone away, made sure I'd dialed the correct number. "It's Mackenzie Taylor."

"And you say someone was shot?"

"Yes," I told him. "Paul Granger."

"Did you shoot him?" Len's tone was mild as if he only had vague interest in the answer.

"No!" I said. "Of course not. I don't even have a gun. So, how much should I tell the police?"

"If you were a witness to a crime, you need to tell them everything you saw." Len sounded sharper this time around. More focused. "Tell them what you saw, and call me if they arrest you."

"Arrest?" I sputtered. "Why would they arrest me?"

"Oh, all sorts of reasons," he drawled, his tone cheery. "I'll be in the office late if you want to reach me."

"Len, wait!" I said, but he'd already hung up.

I blew out a puff of air and pocketed my phone. One of the uniformed officers headed my way. He watched me for a minute, probably having been told to keep an eye on the suspicious character by the hawt car. It didn't seem appropriate to smile, so I gave him a nod of acknowledgment. He scowled then turned to the side, his attention fixated across the lot. So, he was my babysitter.

I sent a quick text to Mac. *Something came up, eat dinner without me.*

Thirty seconds later there was a reply. *What did U do?*

Nothing!!! I typed back furiously.

A full minute of tech silence and then, *Need bail $?!?!*

No, I typed, then deleted it, wrote *Maybe,* but didn't press send. They couldn't arrest me. I hadn't done anything. I was a witness. And not even an eyewitness. I hadn't seen who pulled the trigger. I'd heard the shot and then seen the Escalade burn rubber. So I was an ear witness. Was that even a thing?'

Another car pulled in, this one an unmarked sedan, followed by a large white van. Three people in heavy coats scrambled from the van. The two men who climbed from the sedan approached the area where the uniformed officers had been stringing yellow crime scene tape. No ambulance, so it really had been murder.

I wrapped my arms around myself and stared at the ground. What had possessed me to follow the Escalade? I could be safe at home right now with a large slice of meatball and spinach pizza and watching something ridiculous with my kid instead of shivering in the frigid October night waiting for questioning.

"Mackenzie?"

My head snapped up at the sound of my name. "Hunter? What are you doing here?"

He raised one jet eyebrow. "I could ask you the same question."

"I can explain," I said and then winced. "Sorry. That didn't come out right. I mean…" I didn't even know what I meant.

"You look cold." Without asking, he took off his own coat and put it over my shoulders.

I sighed. The coat retained his body heat and the warmth slowly seeped into me. "Thanks."

"You were the one to call 9-1-1."

I nodded. "Yes. After I heard the gunshot and the Escalade took off."

"Did you get the plate number?"

"No, at least I don't think so. I might have caught it in one of the photos." I shifted to snag my cell from my back pocket.

Hunter moved closer so he could see the phone display. "This was earlier today?"

"Yes." I explained to him about Len hiring me and what had brought me to Conley Terminal. "See? Here's the Escalade. Shoot, you can't see the license plate though. Sorry." I made to stow my phone, but Hunter gripped my wrist.

"I'm going to need to hang on to this for a while."

"You're going to *take* my *phone*?" My tone sounded incredulous.

"Just until we get any evidence off of it." He pocketed my Droid, much to my dismay.

Damn it, my life was on that thing. Did I even have Len's number anywhere else? And how would Mac and I stay in contact throughout her school day? I didn't do well with separation from my offspring.

"I'll get it back to you as soon as possible," Hunter promised. "Do you need someone to drive you home? I can have an officer take you."

And risk him confiscating Helga next? No flipping way. I shook my head. "No."

"You'll be in for the rest of the night if we need to get in touch with you." It wasn't a question.

"Sure." Numbly, I moved back toward the Hellcat. If anything could douse my infatuation over my new neighbor, it was the fact that he was sort of cold while at work. I'd been looking for a rescuer, and he'd just been doing his job. He hadn't even volunteered to drive me home himself. Of course he had a dead body to see to, but still. It would have been nice if he'd made the offer.

Shucking his jacket, I lifted my chin and offered it back to him. "Here, you'll probably need this."

He took the coat, his eyes watchful. "You sure you're okay to drive?"

Not trusting my voice, I nodded briskly, then opened the car door and slid in before those watchful eyes could spot the mess of snack cake wrappers that had been my nourishment for the day.

After securing my seatbelt, I placed my hands at ten and two on the wheel and maneuvered Helga carefully between two cargo containers and back toward the exit, chastising myself the entire way. Served me right for jumping to conclusions. What had I thought, he'd heard my name over the police radio and had leapt at the chance to ride to my rescue? He was a cop—I was a witness who also happened to be his neighbor, end of story.

It was better this way. I had Mac, an apartment building to run, and a job that already had cost me half a tank of gas and my cell. I didn't have room in my life for a man anyway, no matter how delicious his leather coat had smelled or how squishy my insides went every time he locked those knowing midnight eyes on me.

Nope, from here on out, Detective Hunter Black and I were all about business. In fact, I should be grateful to him for reminding me that I was supposed to be a professional investigator, not some damsel in distress.

Well, maybe not *grateful*, I thought as I sat at a traffic light. But still, I needed the reminder. If I wanted to be taken seriously as a private investigator, I had to behave like I knew what the hell I was doing.

* * *

"So the police confirmed that it was Paul Granger who was shot?" Mac asked around her slice of pizza.

"If I knew seeing a homicide would pull your attention away from the computer, I'd hang out in sketchy neighborhoods more often," I teased her.

"Mom." She made a face.

"Sorry to disappoint you, babe, but nobody confirmed anything with me. Want a root beer?"

She nodded, her brows pulled together in thought. "It's too much of a coincidence that it was a silver Lexus that dropped the kids off, and then a silver Lexus is left abandoned at the crime scene when you followed the Escalade there. Why did you follow it, anyway?"

"No particular reason, just that it seemed to be casing the joint I was staking out." I poured soda from a two-liter bottle into the first of two Celtics glasses.

"Casing the joint? Staked out?" Mac fed her pizza crust to Snickers. "You're really getting into the PI lingo."

"If the fedora fits." I smiled saucily and handed her a glass. "Oh, I should get a fedora!"

"Mom, focus on getting paid before you buy a whole new wardrobe. I wonder if Pete could dig up info on the case." Mac drummed her short black nails on the counter.

I didn't bother to hide a grimace. Along with being an inventor of dubious morals, Pete the Pervert was also a hacker. "Mac, light of my life, please, for the love of java, let it go."

"But—"

"No buts. I want to hear about your first day at your new school."

She groaned and laid her head down on the counter.

"That bad, huh?" I took another slice of pizza.

"Can't you just homeschool me?" she begged.

I snorted. "You learned everything I had to teach you by the time you were seven."

She ticked some of my most marketable skills off on her fingers. "How to cuss, how to lie your way out of an awkward conversation, how to flirt your way out of a traffic ticket."

I choked a little and set my soda down quickly. "Yeah, well the flirting thing didn't go so well for me tonight. Hunter's the one who took my phone."

Mac blinked. "Hunter was there?"

"Yep. And all that sizzling chemistry was gone, so you have nothing to worry about."

"I wasn't worried." Now that the homicide talk was over, her attention had drifted back to her computer screen.

"You weren't?" I frowned. "I thought for sure that you said you didn't want me to get involved with him and make our living situation awkward."

"And you're not," she answered, gaze glued to the screen.

"Right." I set the other half of my pizza slice down, my appetite gone. Snickers stood on her hind legs, paws in the air.

"No," I told her sternly. She was cute, but I didn't want this to become a regular thing.

She barked at me.

"Mac, don't feed the dog from the table anymore. She's turning into a pest."

"Sure." My daughter's tone was absent.

"Does she have any actual dog food?" I peered around the half unpacked explosion that was our kitchen and dining area.

"Hunter left some. It's in the bottom of the pantry." Mac didn't even glance my way.

I rose. She was gone again, lost to cyberspace. After stretching out the kinks that had developed from too many hours sitting in the car, I nudged her arm. "Hey, you know what would be fun? If you came in and hung out with me in your new room while I go through stuff."

"You have an odd definition of fun." She waved me away.

"You sure you don't want to come? I haven't seen you all day." And after the one I'd had, I didn't want to be alone to think.

She blew air out between clenched teeth. "Mom, I have work to do. We'll hang later."

"Guess I'm on my own." Exactly what I'd been hoping to avoid. My mind kept going back to that cute little girl playing in her back yard after school. Was her dad home safe and sound, or was it really Paul Granger dead in that alley?

Mac had never known her dad. It was better that way.

Instead of dwelling on things better left in the rearview, I popped in my earbuds and then scrolled through my iPod selection, looking for the right sort of music to help blot out my thoughts and motivate me to pack up Uncle Al's office. Angry female rock? No, too judgey. Oldies? Nah, I needed some pep.

I settled on lost hits from the nineties and kicked it off with Chesney Hawkes' "The One and Only." Perfect.

I've always been a firm believer that every moment in life has a perfect theme song. Every connection, be it between parent and child, friends or lovers should have musical accompaniment like in the movies. My mother's theme song is Sir Elton's "The Bitch is Back," which pretty much summed up our whole relationship in a three minute and forty-one second musical interlude. Mac, who was born in August of 2000, owned Macy Gray's "I Try." It was either that or Christina Aguilera's "What A Girl Wants," but I never had been a fan of *The Mickey Mouse Club's* girls grown and gone wild. The song said more about me at that point in time as a sixteen-year-old single parent than it did about my newborn infant. Trying was the best I had to offer her, even a decade and a half later.

Uncle Al had been something of a packrat, though it could have been worse. His desk was jammed with receipts, old bills, newspaper clippings, and photographs. The kind of crap most people in the year 2016 kept on their phones.

A pang went through me as I thought about my phone. Stupid sexy neighbor cop man.

I sorted the hodgepodge of paper into three piles: crap to be tossed, important stuff to be saved, and curiosities to comb through at my leisure.

I had lost all track of time when someone tapped me on the shoulder.

"Hey, I think I made a good dent here," I said, thinking I was talking to my daughter and then let out a yell at the massive shape looming there. "Judas Priest! You scared me half to death. Again."

"Sorry," Hunter—no, Detective Black (I was going to stick with his official title so I didn't forget again)—murmured.

I looked him over and saw the strain on his face. Maybe it was kismet that Sarah McLachlan's "Building a Mystery" started the moment our gazes locked.

"I brought your phone back." Hunter held the device out to me.

I blinked, a little taken aback. "Did you get whatever you needed off it?"

"We got everything we could." Hunter scanned the office, his steady gaze assessing my progress. He moved back to the door and closed it before turning to face me. "If I say something, do you promise not to take it the wrong way?"

"No," I said. "But tell me anyway."

A ghost of a smile slipped over his face. "At least you're honest. Okay, I want you to quit your job as a private investigator."

I stared at him for what must have been a full minute. One would have thought I'd spend time coming up with a scathing replay, but all I managed was a choked, "Excuse me?"

"You're not prepared or skilled enough. Private investigation can be dangerous, as you witnessed firsthand tonight. Being a PI isn't like joining a spin class. It takes dedication and intuition, and even if you had those tools in your arsenal, you'd still be risking your life."

His words stung, mostly because they were true, but the fact that he would come into my home and say them to my face had anger blotting out the hurt. "What gives you the right to have an opinion on what I do for a living? Did I march into your home and tell you that your job was too dangerous?"

"I don't have anyone depending on me." He chucked his thumb at the closed door. "And I am trained as a police officer. You don't know what you're involving yourself in here, Mackenzie. You aren't prepared for the things you'll see."

My molars ground down, and between clenched teeth I hissed, "I am so tired of people telling me I'm not good enough."

Hunter frowned. "That's not—"

I poked him in the chest, effectively cutting him off. "You just said that I'm unskilled. And maybe I am, but that's something I can change with practice. Was I unprepared to witness a murder? Yes, but who exactly *is* prepared for that?"

He remained silent, those dark eyes fixed on my face.

I spun on my heel and marched toward the door, yanking it open so hard it smacked against the wall. "Thank you for your concern, Detective. Now if you'll excuse me, I have work to do."

Hunter studied me for a moment longer then shook his head. "I've made it worse, haven't I?"

I offered him a tight-lipped smile but didn't say anything.

He sighed. "Have it your way, then. But please, be careful."

My rage simmered as he moved past me into the hallway. I hated that he saw me as weak, fragile, even, and sneered when I remembered how much I'd wanted him to comfort me earlier. Best way to end an inappropriate infatuation? Find out that the individual you've been crushing on thinks you're a total loser.

Well, I'd show him. As soon as the door to the hall shut, I pounded my fist against the frame and whirled to face Mac.

"Problem?" she asked with a raised brow.

"Contact Pete the Pervert. I want to know everything about the shooting tonight."

Mac grinned and then began typing furiously. "I'm on it."

CHAPTER FIVE

"As a private investigator, your word is all that you have, so it better be solid."
From the *Working Man's Guide to Sleuthing for a Living* by Albert Taylor, PI

I kept Mac up far past her bedtime Skyping with Pete the Pervert and was able to access the details on the shooting I'd witnessed. Sure enough, the victim was Paul Granger, who was supposed to be at home with his kids. His parents had been questioned as well as his ex-wife, aka Len's client. Jessica Granger admitted that her divorce was messy, and that yes, she'd wanted primary custody of her children, which was why she'd retained a lawyer and sanctioned a PI. According to her statement, she hadn't recognized the man driving the Escalade or known why he was staking out her former in-laws' home.

Over coffee the next morning, I studied the pages Mac had printed for me, complete with my own interview with Detective Black. His report was brief and succinct. I was a PI who had been hired to find evidence for an ongoing child custody case and had followed a suspicious-looking vehicle to the crime scene, where I'd witnessed the murder. I hadn't caught the license plates with my grainy photos and hadn't bothered to note them either.

"Mistake number one," I muttered into my steaming cup of java. Note to self: take pictures of license plates from here on out.

"What was that?" Mac appeared fresh from the shower. She didn't look as if she'd spent half the night up to her cute little earlobes in the dark corners of the internet.

"You're sure you won't get into trouble for this?" I tapped the pages.

She shrugged. "Nah, Pete's the one who did the hacking. Besides, I'm a minor. It's not like they'll throw the book at me even if they did find out."

With my temper cooled, my guilt over asking my child to help me do my job grew and made my insides feel squishy. "Still, from here on out, we keep things above board."

She popped a piece of wheat bread into the toaster. "Mom, relax. We aren't going to get caught."

"Just promise me, no more hacking. It's not worth the risk."

She poured herself some OJ. "And what happens next time you get all hot under the collar over Detective Hottie?"

"Ignore me." I grumbled and refocused on the pages. "Is it just me, or does it sound like they are focusing all their efforts on Jessica Granger?"

Mac buttered her toast and then plopped onto the barstool next to me, Snickers hot on her heels. "You've seen crime-time dramas—it's always the spouse. Plus it doesn't help her case that she threatened to kill him in open court in front of a judge." She tapped the page with the judge's statement.

"Another stellar reason to stay single." I snitched the other half of her toast slice and dunked it in my coffee. "But it's not her. She has an alibi."

Mac quirked a brow. "Mom, you never even met Jessica Granger. How can you be so sure she wouldn't hire someone to off her ex?"

"Just a hunch."

"Well you can't take that to the cops." She fed her crust to the dog, who then started eye-humping my piece.

"Hey, what did I say about feeding the beastie from the table?"

Mac grinned. "That it's a bonding routine."

"Yes, but my exact phrasing included the word *don't*."

Snickers was tugging on the edge of my bathrobe and doing her little *grrr ruff* thing.

"What's the point of this?" I yanked my robe back.

"Just keep an open mind about her," Mac advised. "She knows you don't like her."

"Trust me, the feeling is mutual. I'm going to hop into the shower. Lock up when you leave."

"Will do. What's on your agenda for the day? Other than crime solving of course?"

"I plan to finish clearing out your room, then check in with Len and find out if there's anything I can do."

"My mother, the crime fighter. You always did love high-heeled boots. Hey, I forgot to ask, but how did it go with Grams yesterday?"

"You remember the end of *Braveheart*, where they're yanking out his insides? Like that only bloodier."

"Chin up. You only need to meet with her once a month."

"It's like the menstrual cycle from hell," I whispered in horror.

Mac laughed. "Only no menopause to get you out of it. Next time set it up on the weekend so I can run interference."

"Good idea. Have a good day at the office, dear." I dropped a kiss on her head, inhaling her strawberry scent, and shuffled off to the bathroom.

The hot water helped relax stiff and aching muscles, and I lingered longer than I'd intended. One of the tough things about the PI business, at least according to Uncle Al, was the irregular hours. I would have to build my schedule around other people's habits and lifestyles, and that would change from case to case. But there was an innate flexibility in that kind of schedule that appealed to me. Punching a clock was so last decade.

After I dried my hair I braided it to keep it out of my way, then donned jeans, sneakers, and an MIT sweatshirt I'd snagged from my last boyfriend. We'd split due to irreconcilable differences, since he had an opinion on everything and had somehow gotten the impression that I wanted to hear them all. His stance on toll roads was fine if boring, but I drew the line when he suggested Mac and I add more vegetables to our diet. As if ketchup wasn't good enough or something. He had taken the two of us on a tour of the MIT campus, and I had my fingers crossed that Mac would get in. Moving six weeks into the start of the new term had put her at a disadvantage, but I had every confidence she'd catch up quickly and once again be at the top of her class.

Once I got a system going with Uncle Al's office, I had boxes packed and ready for hauling down to the basement. I put my hands on my hips and stared at the massive pile. It was times like these that I thought maybe my mother was just a little bit right—it'd be nice to have a man around to haul heavy stuff down the rickety basement stairs. Of course then I'd probably be expected to feed him and pay attention to him and all that other nonsense people in romantic relationships had to deal with.

"And I have you for all that. Don't I, you raggedy little dust mop?" I cooed at Snickers.

She let out a low level whine and put her head on her paws, eyes on the door. Probably willing Mac to come back and save her from my company.

"I know. I miss her too." I hefted the first box and made my way out into the hall. I strode purposefully to the stairs, not allowing my gaze to drift toward Hunter's door. My mind wasn't nearly as obedient, and I couldn't help wondering if he was inside. Maybe still in bed after his long night of work, sleeping in the raw…

"Damn it," I muttered as I almost missed a step. "Down, girl."

"Mackenzie?" I heard Nona's nasal voice from the bottom of the stairs "Is that you, bubala?"

"Yeah," I grunted as I navigated the stairs to the bottom. In addition to the fuse box, the ancient water heater and a bunch of old hockey equipment, the basement of our house held the laundry facilities. Nona sat in a metal folding chair in front of a small card table with a game of Solitaire spread out in front of her, the dryer tumbling away behind her.

"I was just gonna knock on your door and see if you wanted a cup of coffee."

"Always." I set my box down next to the hockey stick corner. "Do you know who all this belongs to?" I asked, gesturing to the stuff.

"Oh, that's Hunter's." Nona collected her cards and struggled to get up. Moving swiftly to her side I offered her my hand, and she took it with a brief flash of her dentures. "Thanks, doll. I can't sit in that metal chair too long without my sciatica acting up."

"So Hunter plays hockey in his spare time?" I asked as I helped her up the stairs. She was winded by the time she made it to the first floor, and I paused to let her catch her breath.

"Oh, not anymore. I guess he played in college. I don't know much about it, but Al said he was real good, and he could have gone pro. You should ask him about it." Her tone turned sly.

I made a noncommittal sound. "I have a few more boxes to drag downstairs. Do you want me to pull your laundry out before I come up for coffee?"

"That would be terrific. I can only handle those stairs so often, you know. Damn knees ache like you wouldn't believe."

She headed up to her apartment, and I scuttled back into mine for the next load. By the time I was finished, the dryer had quieted, and I pulled Nona's warm laundry out into her small basket, trying not to stare at her supersized underwear.

I was on the top step when I heard Hunter's lock tumble. Frantically I looked for a place to hide, if not myself then the giant bloomers. Unfortunately, the hall was empty, and I didn't have enough time to dash either into my apartment or up the next flight to Nona's.

"Hi." Hunter looked fresh from the shower, that river of midnight hair slicked back in a ponytail. He sported the leather trench he'd warn the day before, this time with jeans instead of a suit. He looked scrumptious.

I, on the other hand, was sweating like a pig from my many trips up and down the stairs and in possession of what had to be the largest load of delicates on the face of the planet. "Um, hey."

To my horror, he moved closer. "I'm glad I ran into you. I was up half the night wondering how best to apologize."

I shifted the laundry onto my hip, trying to block his line of sight with my arm. I didn't want to draw too much attention to the laundry lest he wonder why I was acting weird about it. "Oh yeah?"

He nodded. "Yeah. I mean, you can be a PI if that's what you want. I just want to make sure you know some of the basics and minimize the risk."

I thought about the *Working Man's Guide,* full to bursting with Uncle Al's tips and tricks of the trade. "I have a mentor of sorts."

"Good, that's good." His dark eyes grew warmer, and he moved close enough that I could breathe in his unique scent. "So, am I forgiven?"

"Yeah. I'm a true redhead." He smelled almost…primitive. Earthy. Like pine, wood smoke, and male musk, aromas so foreign and alluring to my city-girl senses. I swayed a little, all my aggravation forgotten in a sensual fog.

His gaze dipped downward, and I blushed all the way to my roots when I realized how suggestive that last comment had sounded.

"What I mean is, I have a short temper, but I get over it quickly too. What's your superpower?" It was a stupid and inane remark, and I wasn't sure why I said it.

A slow wolfish grin spread across his face, and he leaned in close to whisper, "It's a secret."

My breath caught, and I almost collapsed right there in the hallway into a puddle of goo. The man had *game.* And judging by the light in his eyes, he knew it, too.

"Maybe I can take you out sometime? Dinner? Or coffee?" The dark promise in his eyes suggested other sorts of nocturnal activities.

I wanted to say yes. Something about him made me want to take a risk. Mac would understand—men like him didn't come along every day. Hardworking, honest, sweet, and sinful all wrapped up in a big sexy package. He made my blood run hot and my knees go weak. When was the last time that had happened?

I remembered exactly when, and that thought made me hesitate.

Nona's door creaked open before I could get a word out. "Mackenzie? You still coming up, doll?"

"I have to go." I chucked a thumb to the stairs.

Hunter reached into my basket. "Nona'll be wanting her bloomers."

I snorted. "I should have known better than to sneak something by a detective. I'm just glad you didn't think they were mine. Or Mac's." Though my daughter was a string bean, she could have pitched the underwear and used it for a tent.

"Anytime you want to show me your underwear is fine by me. Though I'd appreciate them more if you modeled them for me, Red." he murmured. "Think about dinner and get back to me."

I sighed as he turned and headed toward the front door. He wasn't the first person to call me Red, though it was a far better nickname than Carrot Top or the much-hated Ginger. Something about the way he said it, though, made a traditional nickname sound so much more…intimate. Alluring, even. Shaking myself free from the sensual spell, I hefted the laundry and headed up to Nona's.

Her apartment was considerably smaller than ours—one bedroom instead of two, no fireplace, and a tiny bathroom with a shower stall instead of the cast-iron tub downstairs. I'd peeked into the unoccupied unit across the hall, and it was as sparse.

I set Nona's laundry by the door. "Just so you know, Hunter was fingering your underwear."

She waved a hand in front of her face. "I think I'm having a hot flash."

"Join the club." I took the small mug of coffee she offered me. It was a sad little thing, almost a baby mug, and would barely contain six ounces of the elixir of life. Maybe one day it would grow into a full-sized mug, but for now it was the little cup that couldn't. I'd need four of them just to make the stairs worth it.

"So did he ask you out?" Nona lit a cigarette and eased herself down onto one end of her uncomfortable-looking sofa.

"He did." I drained my mug and looked around hopefully for more.

"Oh, where's he taking you?" The Yenta was relentless.

"I didn't say yes."

Nona frowned at the unexpected wrinkle in her plans. "Why not? He's nice, single, attractive. Has a steady job and is good with kids."

I frowned at this last bit. "How do you know he's good with kids? He doesn't, like, have any does he?" Maybe it was a stupid double standard, but I didn't want to get involved with a man who had children. I'd raised my daughter and wasn't looking to be the evil step monster to anyone else's.

But Nona shook her head. "No, doll, he's never had kids. But his sisters have a whole heap of them. They come by sometimes and play in the backyard. No matter how wild they get, he's always very patient with them. He'll be a good father someday in spite of, well, never mind." She waved this last bit off.

Intrigued, I opened my mouth to respond, but my cell phone started to buzz with a familiar number. "Excuse me a minute," I said and slipped out into the hall. "Hello?"

"Mackenzie?" The creaky voice sounded unsure.

I smiled. "Yeah, it's me, Len. I was going to come by in a little bit. What's up?"

"It's Jessica Granger. She sold several expensive pieces of jewelry on the day her husband was killed. The DA claims it was to pay for a hit on her husband. She's been charged with murder."

I blew out a breath. So the unlawfully obtained paperwork had called it right. "What can we do?"

"Simple," Len wheezed. "Prove she didn't do it."

CHAPTER SIX

You don't need much to work as a PI. Steady hands and stubborn will. Patience. Sense helps, but isn't required.
From the *Working Man's Guide to Sleuthing for a Living* by Albert Taylor, PI

Though I didn't want to admit it to myself, I needed help with my investigation into Paul Granger's death. As in technical help, aka computers. There were two people I knew who could find the information I needed on Paul Granger's life via the internet and only one person that would be willing to actually do the digging.

Unfortunately, school didn't get out until 3 PM.

I was waiting for Mac in the parking lot of the school when the bell rang for dismissal. She didn't see me at first—her eyes were glued to her cell. Several of the kids turned to watch her trek toward the bus, but no one spoke to her. Poor kid. There was only one public high school in Eastie, and most of the teens here had probably known each other since kindergarten. And not only was she the new kid, she was the mid-semester transfer new kid. When I'd lived with The Captain and Agnes, I'd had to do that a few times, and it was rough, especially as you got older and cliques grew tighter. Mac's MO tended to be *speak only when spoken to*, which didn't help her in the make-friends department.

I scrambled out of Helga and hurried over to intercept her before she climbed up the bus steps and disappeared. "Hey, little girl, want a ride?"

She did look up then, blue eyes round in mock innocence. "My mother told me never to ride with strangers. And they don't make 'em stranger than you."

"True, that." I took her backpack for her, groaning at the heft of it. "*Oof*, did you leave any books in the library?"

"It's my new netbook. You owe me fifty bucks by the way."

I cringed. "Sorry, I remember something in that heinous pile of orientation paperwork about a deposit. Must have slipped my mind. Where did you get the money?"

"Grams gave it to me."

I groaned. "Mackenzie Elizabeth Taylor 2.0, what did I tell you about borrowing money from your grandmother?"

"That it leads to the dark side and will forever dominate my destiny," she quoted dutifully. "I'm sorry, but when she came by to take me to lunch…"

I stopped. It was one of those comical types of stops that happen in movies. My feet just quit with the foreword momentum even though my top half was already in midstride. I nearly face-planted in front of a hundred teenagers. That would have made me a YouTube star by dinner.

"Mom?" Mac looked up, her expression concerned.

"Your grandmother took you out of school?" I spoke the words slowly, in case I'd somehow confused the message.

"No, she didn't sign me out or anything. She texted me this morning and asked if I had a free period. I do this semester, and you know I can leave campus for lunch if I sign out and back in. Why are you so upset?"

"I'm not upset," I grated.

"Mom, I hear your teeth grinding from here. Am I not supposed to hang out with Grams?"

No, you're not supposed to want *to hang out with Grams,* I thought, though thankfully didn't say it aloud. "I'm just hungry. All I've had to eat today is a couple of Pop Tarts that expired six months ago. If you ever wondered what frosted shingles taste like, I'm pretty sure that's the flavor."

"Hey, Mackenzie!"

We turned at the same time. Though when I saw the speaker, I knew he meant Mac, not me. Not only did he look barely old enough to shave, he had that weird aura that some favored children sported, all golden and glowing, as if nature provided him a constant spotlight. He was fit and showing it off, wearing athletic shorts in spite of the chill air.

"You're going by Mackenzie now?" I hissed

"It's on all the attendance rolls," she hissed back and then raised her voice and actually smiled at the kid who looked like Justin Bieber's little brother. "Hey, Todd."

Naturally he was a Todd. I rolled my eyes so hard one of them almost got stuck.

The kid did a flip thing with his ridiculous golden mane and dimpled at my daughter who actually blushed. It took every ounce of restraint for me to not go for his throat when he said, "Is this your sister?"

"No," Mac said, at the same time I said—

"Yes."

"Cool." Todd nodded as if that were all settled.

Mac gave me a dirty look, but I smiled placidly. The kid would probably be more himself if he thought I was an older sibling rather than a parental unit.

"So I was wondering if you wanted to be my lab partner for the rest of the semester. I just broke up with Bethany." He spoke as if the two items on his agenda weren't mutually exclusive. Maybe to him they weren't.

"Of course," I grumbled but was ignored.

"And now she doesn't want to work with me anymore."

"Some girls." Mac gave a strained-sounding giggle.

Oy vey. This was painful to watch.

"So what do you say?" He flashed those pearly whites at her.

I prayed she'd say no. I didn't want her within a mile of Golden Boy, who seemed to steal all the snark-coated thoughts right out of her head. But I had to stay out of it, had to be the sort of mother that my mother had never been. Accepting of my daughter's choices. Even if they were dimple-wielding meatheads that were using her to up their biology test scores. She was a smart kid, and I trusted her. I just had to keep telling myself that.

Repeatedly.

"Sure," she said and, oh Lord, actually bit her lip. "As long as Mrs. Fox says it's okay."

"Great. Okay, so I'll see you in class tomorrow." He flashed that dimple once more and then ran off.

Mac slid her blue-eyed gaze to me. "Don't, *sis*."

I held up my hands. "I didn't say a word."

"Let's keep it that way. So, food. Where to?"

I slung an arm over her shoulders. "Where did you eat with Grams? Top of the Hub?" I said naming a fine dining restaurant on top of Prudential Tower.

"No, we just went to a bakery and had cappuccino and scones."

"How about Santarpio's for pizza?"

"We just had pizza."

I looked at her blankly over Helga's roof. "So, what's your point?"

"Nothing, I just figured I'd mention it for the record. Hey, can I drive?"

"No. You're officially grounded after the *some girls* comment." She wasn't really, but I wanted my protest on the record.

Mac blew out an exasperated breath. "Did it sound as stupid as I thought it did?"

I reached over and squeezed her hand. "Honey, I know he's cute and all, but don't go changing who you are for a guy."

"Easy for you to say," she grumbled. "You're gorgeous."

My heart squeezed. "And so are you. But you have so much more going for you than I ever did. You're smart and capable, and you know enough about life to never let anyone take advantage of you. Plus you have a mother who would slay dragons for you. Or pesky quarterbacks with jock itch."

She snorted. "Subtle."

"I'm just saying, don't carry Golden Boy through science no matter how many times he flashes that dimple."

"Don't worry. He's an honor roll student, so I don't think he's after me for my brain."

I cut her a sideways glance. "That doesn't make me feel any better. You'll tell me if you want to go on the pill, right?"

"Mom!" She barked the word. "I don't even know his last name. Jeez, I'm not that stupid."

I said nothing.

One thing about Mac: unlike me, she knew when to extract her foot from her mouth. "Sorry."

I blew out a sigh. "Don't be. Getting pregnant in high school wasn't the brightest move I could have made. And it's not something I'd recommend to anyone, especially not you. You've got your whole life ahead of you. So if you do want to go on the pill, tell me."

She was quiet. "Did you know my father's last name?"

Oh no, I didn't want to go there. "Mac."

"I don't want to know." She shook her head. "If you say he wasn't good enough to be my father, then I believe you. I'm just curious."

And really, what could I say to that? "Yeah, I knew his last name."

She nodded, and we drove in silence, both pretending that was good enough.

* * *

"So how far did you get in your search into Paul Granger's death?" Mac cracked open a bottle of water and sat on the couch in front of her main PC.

"Um, Google?" I sat next to her so I could watch her type. "Oh, and I Facebook-stalked him, too. He was one of those sandwich people."

Because she was Mac, she knew right away what I was talking about. "Do people really think anyone is interested in their lunch? Okay, so you've covered the basics. But unless you're an idiot, you're not going to be spilling all your deep dark secrets on social networks. So, I'm thinking we need to find out a little bit more about his job and financial stats. Did you meet with the wife yet?"

I glanced at the clock. "Not yet. I'm supposed to meet up with her and Len at his office at six, but it would be nice to have accomplished something."

Mac was busy typing furiously. "Okay, well let's start with a standard background search. Name?"

"Paul Granger."

"And he lives in Boston. Get your credit card out."

I frowned at her. "Why?"

"Because for fifty bucks we can find out everything from a criminal record to marriages and divorces to neighbors, lawsuits, and judgments."

"Cripes," I breathed, looking over her shoulder. "Do me."

"Mom, focus."

"I just want to see."

Mac blew out a sigh and typed in *Mackenzie Elizabeth Taylor, Boston, MA*. We waited while the entire World Wide Web was scoured for my dirt in less time than it took to make a K-Cup of coffee.

"Nada." Mac sat back in her chair. "Way to keep it on the DL."

I frowned. "That's weird. Shouldn't it spit out something like address, phone number, anything?"

Mac leaned in close. "Depends on where they're getting their sources. If you have a valid driver's license, anything on public record should show up."

It was odd, but I didn't have time to fall through the internet looking glass. "Back to the task at hand. Here's the card." I handed it to her, fairly sure there would be enough room on it for the fee to clear. I'd just have to find another way to pay my mother back.

Mac punched in the numbers, and a few minutes later we were poring over the intimate details of Paul Granger's life.

"We already knew about the custody case. Len told me that's part of the DA's case against our client. She was in an ongoing legal battle over the kids, which speaks to motive."

"You sound all official-like, saying things like 'our client' and 'motive.'" Mac smirked.

"I watched a lot of *Matlock* as a kid."

My daughter turned back to the screen. "A costly battle from the look of this. He'd filed for bankruptcy."

I drummed my fingers on the table. "Weird. There was nothing about that in the file. He was employed and had flexible hours and all."

"What did he do?" Mac took another swig from her soda can.

I reached into my shoulder bag and thumbed through the file. "He worked for a small pharmaceutical company selling their drug to doctor's offices and such. Right Touch Pharmaceuticals."

"Any idea what they make?" Mac asked.

I did a palms-up. "I never heard of them."

Mac opened a second screen and typed in the name of the pharmaceutical company listed as Paul Granger's employer, then bust out laughing.

"What?" I nudged her aside to get a closer look at the screen. It was just a picture of a couple of moderately attractive people having a sunset dinner by the seashore. "What am I missing?"

She tapped the screen. "It's an ED drug."

I stared at her blankly.

Mac shook her head. "Erectile dysfunction? As in the little blue pills."

"Oh," I mumbled, feeling like an idiot. "Well, okay. So I guess he wasn't making any enemies at work."

"Unless the drug doesn't work." Mac crossed her slim legs—all-knowing Buddha disguised as a sixteen-year-old computer whiz. "That could make guys kind of mad."

I narrowed my eyes on her. "How would you know?"

This garnered an eye roll. "Mom, get real."

We were interrupted by a steady knock on the door.

"Shoot, what time is it?" I scrambled over to where I'd left my purse. "Mac, are you expecting anyone?"

She shook her head. I glanced at my cell. It was five thirty-five. "I've got to go. Let me just see who this is."

With the file in my mouth and struggling to turn my coat sleeve right side out with one hand, I opened the door with the other. The file hit the floor and papers scattered when I took in the sight of my mother.

With a massive amount of luggage stacked behind her.

A sense of foreboding filled me at the sight of all those suitcases. "Mom? What are you doing here?"

"I've left your father." Her tone was brisk as she whisked past me into the apartment as if she hadn't just yanked the rug out from underneath me. "I'm moving in."

CHAPTER SEVEN

Always expect the unexpected. And then some.
From the *Working Man's Guide to Sleuthing for a Living* by Albert Taylor, PI

I buzzed the intercom on Len's office building at six twenty-three. "Len? It's Mackenzie. Sorry I'm late. Something came up."

Something like my mother dropping a big old H-bomb and detonating my life. I'd lingered at the apartment as long as I could, trying to pump her for information.

The door unlocked with a low droning hum, and I made my way down the hall into Len's office.

Len was waiting in front of the reception desk. "Is everything all right?"

I nodded, not wanting to get into it. "Yeah. Is Ms. Granger here?"

"In my office. I was just getting her some water." He indicated the bottle in his hand. "Would you care for anything?"

I shook my head. "I'm fine, thanks." It was an outrageous lie, but he was asking about my physical comfort, not my mental state, so I figured I could get away with it.

Jessica Granger was a svelte, stern-looking woman with every professionally highlighted hair in place. She nodded in acknowledgement when I apologized for my tardiness but didn't comment.

My first thought was that she did look capable of murder. She was so calm and composed, not the hot mess I'd been expecting. If I'd been arraigned on murder charges, I would have been a total basket case. So what if, over the course of my investigation, I found out that she had been behind her husband's shooting? Would I still get paid?

It was a crummy thought considering the father of her children had just been gunned down, but my mother had moved into my apartment building, and I owed her money. Loan sharks were more forgiving.

Len shuffled to his desk and sat behind it. "Dr. Granger was just telling me she thinks she knows who killed her husband."

"Ex-husband," Jessica Granger corrected in a smooth, carefully accent-less voice. "Yes, I believe it was his mistress."

"His mistress," I repeated. "And do you know who that is?"

She blinked at me, eyelashes fluttering like Morse code. "Why yes, of course. Her name is Rose, Rose Fox."

I cast a sidelong look at Len, but he was keeping his own counsel. "Did you tell the police about Ms. Fox?"

"Mrs. Fox. And yes, her name came up."

"A widow?" I asked. She was so matter-of-fact about her husband's mistress. Maybe aloofness was her particular defense mechanism. Maybe she had huge crying rages in the privacy of her own home. Somehow I doubted it.

The good doctor shook her head. "No, she's married too. In fact, we met both Mr. and Mrs. Fox during one of our retreats."

There was a small notebook in my jacket pocket along with a pen. I uncapped the sucker, flipped opened the notebook and wrote *Mr. and Mrs. Fox on retreat.* It looked like the intro to a children's book. "What kind of a retreat?"

"It was for…people like us." She shifted in her chair, looking discomfited for the first time.

I shot an imploring glance at Len, but he just smiled. *Okeydokey then.*

"Mrs. Granger, may I call you Jessica?"

When she nodded I continued, "I'm here to help you, and I need a place to start. You say you knew Mr. and Mrs. Fox well? What was the nature of your relationship?"

"We…swapped."

"Swapped what?"

"Spouses. We traded spouses during the retreat. I was with Mr. Fox, and Paul was with Rose."

I shot another furtive look at Len. He raised his spidery eyebrows as if asking what I was going to do about it.

Nothing. I was going to do nothing except hopefully provide Hunter Black with enough evidence to arrest Rose Fox for murder and entice the DA to drop all charges on Dr. Granger.

"I'm going to need a little more to go on," I said slowly. "You met Mr. and Mrs. Fox on a spouse-swapping retreat. Did you know your husband was going to get romantically involved with Mrs. Fox?"

"We knew what we were signing up for, if that's what you're asking," Mrs. Granger said. "We'd done it before, swapped, for a weekend."

"Why?" The question slipped out before I could stop it. It really wasn't any of my business, and curiosity aside, I wasn't sure how it could pertain to the case.

She leveled a challenging stare on me. "Have you ever been married, Ms. Taylor?"

"No." I swallowed and tried not to squirm under her assessing gaze.

"Well let me tell you, marriages can turn stale if you let them. Len and I had decided to have an open marriage, to liven things up, but we had rules. I wanted full blood panels and a financial background check. And we only swapped with couples and only for a limited amount of time. It was supposed to be organized and contained, something apart from our day-to-day life."

"But that changed," I said softly.

Her hands, which had been folded primly in her lap, squeezed into fists. "Yes. Rose and Paul wanted more. They fell in love."

"And what did Mr. Fox think about this?"

"Robert was devastated, just like I was. It was such a shock to both of us."

I drew an arrow down and wrote Robert Fox beneath his wife's name. "Do you know what sort of car Robert drives?"

Her brown eyes narrowed suspiciously. "The police asked me the same question. Is that relevant?"

Len piped up for the first time. "A witness saw a Black Escalade speeding away moments after the shooting." I was grateful he hadn't identified me as being the witness.

"An Escalade? No, Robert drives a Prius. He wouldn't be caught dead in a gas guzzler."

Maybe not. Or maybe Robert Fox knew that and had borrowed one from a friend or a relative just to throw any investigators off the scent. I doodled a little picture of a car on my pad and asked, "Is there anyone else you can think of, anyone at all who had a grudge against your husband? Maybe someone at work?"

She actually rolled her eyes at that. "If anyone should hold a grudge it should have been Paul. They hadn't paid him in months."

"Why not?"

"He wouldn't say. We weren't on the best of speaking terms during the divorce."

Understandable. I scanned the notebook, wondering if there was anything else I should ask. Nothing sprang to mind so I looked up, forcing a smile. "I think that's enough for now. May I call you if I have any questions?"

She opened her small purse and extracted a crisp white business card. I almost didn't want to touch it for fear of leaving smudgy fingerprints. Gingerly I clasped it around the edges.

"I'll see you out," Len gestured for her to go first then held up one finger in my direction, indicating he had something more to say to me.

I waited only until the door closed behind Jessica Granger to return to the outer office.

"You did very well, Mackenzie." Len offered me a smile. "Both with the police and Dr. Granger."

My shoulders sagged in relief. "I'm doing my best to make my uncle proud."

"Your uncle?" Len raised an eyebrow.

"My Uncle Albert Taylor. He was a private investigator."

"I see. So he gave you the bug?"

"In a roundabout way. What can I do to help?"

"Exactly what you've started to do. Dig into Mr. Granger's past and come to me with any suspects who have an alternative motive for murder."

"Like the swinger husband who was devastated that his wife was leaving him?" I probed.

He pointed at me, squinting one eye. "Exactly."

I eyed him shrewdly. "You didn't really think the police were going to arrest me, did you?"

He worked his dentures a minute, and then smiled. "No, you're right on the money. I wanted to see what you were made of. Private investigation isn't for the faint of heart. And a smart PI knows how to work with the police, not against them."

"So I passed the test?" I asked him with a grin.

"With flying colors," he assured me. "Now let's leave it for the day. I'm all done in."

I waited on the front steps as Len shut the lights off and locked the office. "I'm surprised you're handling Dr. Granger's case. I thought you were a divorce attorney."

He let out a wheezy chuckle. "I'm whatever sort of attorney I need to be, at least in the private sector. Divorce, personal injury, wrongful termination, and even on the rare occasion criminal defense. I don't go in for all that highly specialized bunk. It pays to be well rounded."

"What do you think her chances are? Dr. Granger's I mean?"

Len paused by a white Cadillac that was larger than Helga and Fillmore combined. I decided to refer to the great white beast as Moby Dick, even if Len had already picked out a name, because nothing could be more picture perfect. "Well, that depends."

"On?" I raised my eyebrows.

"On whatever you find, Miz Mackenzie."

* * *

"Is it safe?" I poked my head from my bedroom into Mac's.

"When did you get home?" My daughter looked up from her open tablet and popped out one of her earbuds. How she could read and listen to music was beyond me. She lay on her stomach, feet crossed at the ankles, slime-green toenail polish clashing with her Celtics pajama pants and fair skin. Snickers sprawled across the bottom of the mattress and box spring I'd bought her when she turned eleven. The bed frame was stacked in a disassembled heap in the corner beside her dresser.

"Just now. Is the apartment clear?" Not wanting to run into my mother, I'd come through the back way, climbing over the small picket fence designed to keep Snickers in and through the dormant rhododendron bushes and into the small backyard. Thankfully the sliding glass door off of my bedroom was unlocked from when Mac had let the dog out earlier.

"Grams is upstairs talking to Nona, if that's what you mean."

I plopped down on the narrow bed beside her, ignoring the growling furball. Snickers, I was learning, talked a good game, but I doubted she would bite. Not that I planned to challenge her honor or anything. "I can*not* live with my mother."

"Sing it, sister."

"Babe, I'm a freaking pushover compared to my mother, and you know it."

"It's only until the furniture she orders arrives." Mac spoke as if that horrific idea was somehow supposed to make things better. "Then she'll take the empty apartment upstairs."

"But she'll be under the same roof as us. She'll know all of our comings and goings. And what about The Captain? She can't seriously mean to abandon him. Did she tell you anything? Like if they had a fight? Maybe he told her she was a horrible cook or something. It doesn't take much to set her off."

Mac shook her head, worrying her lower lip. "Do you think they're getting a divorce?"

"No, absolutely not." I shook my head so hard I could almost hear my brain sloshing around with vehement denial. "They've been married for thirty-three years, for the love of java."

Mac still looked worried, her blue eyes big.

"Trust me. Grams is just making a point. Once he apologizes, she'll move out of here faster than you can say guilt trip."

"But she bought furniture," Mac pointed out. "That isn't the kind of thing you do on a whim. She seems organized."

She did, and that scared me. But I had a murder to investigate and a teenager to raise. I had enough grim reality on my plate. "I'll talk to The Captain and see if maybe I can expedite her departure."

It would be uncomfortable, like all conversations I had with my father. Beyond "how's Mac?" he didn't seem to know what to say to me or I to him. And over every encounter, the fog of disappointment seemed to pervade until I beat a hasty retreat. The Captain didn't retreat so much as make strategic withdrawals to more defensible positions. But this was a full-fledged five-alarm emergency.

"We should try to be supportive of Grams." Mac rolled to her side, propping her head on one arm. "This is major for her. Did you know she's never lived on her own?"

I mimicked her pose. "No, I didn't. She told you that?"

"Yup, went right from her parents' house to living with Grandpa and being a Navy wife. She has to be scared."

I burst out laughing.

"Mom!" She smacked at me, her cheeks colored bright pink. "It's not funny!"

"I'm sorry," I wheezed. "But that woman hasn't been scared a day in her life. Angry? Passive-aggressive, hell yes. But actual fear? Nope, I'm not buying it."

"Well, you've got a blind spot when it comes to her."

More like I saw clearly. I didn't want to argue with her though, so instead I rolled off the bed and onto my feet. "I've got some more work to do. I'll let you get back to it."

"Wait." Mac leapt up, and Snickers bounded off the bed, not to be left out. "How did the meeting go?"

I thought about the uptight Dr. Granger admitting that she and her husband were habitual swingers. "It went. Len's impressed, which is a good sign since he'll be paying me. Now, I just need to come up with something worth paying for and I'll be all set."

"Are you keeping track of your expenses? Hanging on to your receipts?"

I offered her an exaggerated eye roll as I headed into the kitchen. "Yes, Mother. This isn't my first rodeo."

"What about your tax situation?" She folded her arms over her *Girl on Fire* logo. "Did you fill out paperwork for a W2, or is the lawyer cutting you a 1099?"

Our cupboards were sad, only the expired Pop Tarts and a bag of marshmallows the consistency of granite. Not wanting to chip a tooth, I left both selections there. "I should go to the store."

"What about health insurance?" Mac was like a dog with a bone. No wonder Snickers had taken to her. "Do you have eye care? Dental?"

"For the love of grief, kid. Would you let me worry about all this crap? Who's the adult here?"

"That's what I was wondering," my mother said from the doorway.

"Here we go," I muttered.

Agnes turned to her granddaughter. "Mac, would you please give the two of us a moment of privacy?"

Mac opened her mouth, took one look at her grandmother's stern expression, and then snapped it shut. "I'll be in my room."

As irritated as I'd been about the conversation we'd been having, I was sorry to see her go. Mac I could put off, distract, and redirect. I'd have to trap my mother in a closet somewhere to get her to leave off.

"Look, I know what you're going to say."

She raised one perfectly sculpted eyebrow and lifted her chin. "I'll bet you don't."

I cleared my throat and then raised the pitch of my voice to match her normal alto, and spoke in rapid succession. "You're always so concerned with how that girl perceives you. You have to be the cool mom, the anti-me. Well, it's time to grow up, Mackenzie."

She blinked and wouldn't hold my gaze. "You always have to think the worst of me. What I was going to say was that I can help you, if you won't be so proud."

I put my hands on my hips "I don't need a handout, Mom. I've been supporting Mac since before she was born. And besides, you have enough to worry about. What happened with you and The Captain?"

"Nothing," She broke eye contact, obviously lying.

We were on shaky ground. How closely did I want to look at my parents' marriage? As close as I needed to if I couldn't get her to relent. "Mom, go home. You don't belong here."

A flash of hurt crossed her face. It was gone so fast I wasn't even sure I'd seen it to begin with, especially when she straightened up to her full five-foot-two and somehow managed to stare down at my seven inches taller self. "Well, my furniture will be here tomorrow. I'll be out of your hair then."

"What furniture? When did you get it, how did you pay for it, and when exactly did you leave The Captain?"

She crossed her thin arms over her sweater set. "That's nothing for you to worry about. Now, did you say something about groceries? I'll give you a little money if you pick up the few things I need. The small refrigerator upstairs doesn't work so I'll have to store my things in yours. There's certainly plenty of room. You really should eat better. You're setting a bad example for Mac."

"Make me a list," I said, my smile tight. If she didn't want to tell me what the deal was with her and The Captain, I'd have to ferret out the information on my own. Good thing I knew a PI who worked on the cheap.

My mother pulled a silver pen from her wallet and looked around for a piece of paper. The small spiral bound notepad was still in my jacket, and I retrieved it for her. I checked the fridge again just to make sure—yup, we needed everything.

"What on earth are swingers?" Agnes Taylor asked. "Like trapeze artists or something?

Oops. I whirled around and grabbed for the notebook. "It's just a case I'm working on."

My mother held it aloft, a frown creasing her brow. "Rose and Robert Fox are not circus people."

My grabbing hand fell to my side as I stared at her. "You know them?"

"Only in passing. But they're a very elegant couple, not the trapeze artist sort. Your information must be wrong."

I looked at her in a new light. Of course she would be connected with a large part of Boston's elite. She'd always encouraged The Captain to pursue politics, though he'd never seemed interested. But that didn't stop her from hobnobbing with potential political supporters. "If you say so. Any idea where they live?"

"Beacon Hill area. Hold on, I have their address here somewhere." She rummaged through her purse and pulled out her phone. She handed it to me and then, almost as an afterthought, asked, "Why do you need it?"

I memorized the number and then offered her a wan smile and handed the phone back. "No reason. I have to go out now. To the store."

"But my list," she said.

"Text it to me," I called over my shoulder and shut the door in her startled face.

CHAPTER EIGHT

"When opportunity knocks, answer the door. But don't let it in until you see some ID."
From the *Working Man's Guide to Sleuthing for a Living* by Albert Taylor, PI

I'd turned around in my seat, ready to back Helga out of the driveway, when a blue sedan pulled to the curb behind me. The passenger door opened, and Hunter Black stepped out onto the curb. It was too dark to see who was driving the sedan, but he bent at the waist and spoke to the driver before slamming the door. The sedan pulled out, pausing at a streetlight, and I got the brief impression of a young blonde woman before the car merged into traffic. Hunter watched it go and then turned and headed for the front door.

Too late I realized he was going to walk straight past me. I'm not sure where the impulse came from, but I slithered down in the seat so he wouldn't see me. I waited, counting to twenty in my head and feeling like a jackass. Helga had tinted windows, and it was night. Why was I hiding from him? Because I was investigating the Granger case when he'd made it clear I shouldn't? Or because of the way he'd smoldered at me in the stairwell and then had been out with another woman?

Either way, cowering in the dark seemed like the way to go.

A knock sounded on the window, and I jumped, and then peeked up.

He stood there, a massive dark shape, foreboding in the streetlight.

Sighing, I straightened up and then rolled down the window. "How's it going?"

"Were you hiding from me, Red?" He tilted his head, his long dark hair falling over his shoulder like a river of night.

"No," I fibbed, hoping the low lighting would hide the flush on my cheeks. "I was looking for my earring."

"You aren't wearing earrings," he pointed out.

"Because I lost one." Was I a stellar liar or what?

Those lips twitched. "But you're heading out."

"Just to the store. My mother stopped by, and we're out of people food. I hear Snickers is all set, thanks to you."

"She's a sweetheart," he murmured. "I miss having someone waiting for me to get home."

"You want her back?" The words popped out automatically. I hoped he'd say no, as Mac seemed attached to the mutt.

He shook his head. "Nah, I'm not home enough to spend time with her."

"Because of your job?" I probed, wondering at the identity of the dark sedan driver. Nona had said he was something of a serial dater.

He wore that pre-smile, almost-amused look again. "If you want to know who dropped me off, you can just ask."

"Not my business," I choked out. The man read me like a sports column, with very little effort on his part. It was unnerving, especially because I knew diddly-freaking-squat about him.

The light caught in his dark eyes, reflecting back at me hypnotically. "Are you willing to make it your business?"

"Yes. No. I mean, that is…" I stumbled, my usual confidence heading for parts unknown. I took a deep breath and tried again. "I really don't think it's a good idea. What with us being neighbors, and then there's Mac and my mother, and I can't really afford a distraction right now."

"I understand." He held up a hand and my lips clamped together as if superglued, the heinous stream of babble locked safely in.

"For the record, that was my youngest sister, Kate. She's got some news and wanted my advice on how best to break it to our parents."

"Oh," I said, feeling stupid. "You didn't have to tell me all that."

He tipped his head to the side. "I wanted to. I want to make sure you know I'm a man who makes time for his family. Does that change your mind about going out with me?"

"No, but it certainly doesn't hurt your case." I grinned at him. It was sort of sweet the way he kept trying to convince me. I'd never really been pursued by a man before. "Look, can I be honest?"

He crouched beside the car so he could look me in the eye. "By all means, I prefer to date an honest woman."

"You scare me to death."

He blinked. It was as significant as another person gasping in astonishment. My bluntness had taken him off guard.

"I'm not my normal self around you, and I don't know why that is. All things being equal, you're tempting enough to make me want to figure out why, but you live right next door. If things didn't work out, it's not like we could avoid each other. Mac's already worried about weirdness. Add to that you're a cop, and you hate my job, and I'm sure it's not smart."

"I don't," he said then added, "I don't hate the job, though I'm not crazy about you doing it. Even after you're trained. But it's not because I'm some kind of misogynistic jerk. I don't want to see you get hurt, Red."

His brows drew together, and before I realized it, he was leaning into the car, cupping my cheek. It seemed only natural to tilt my chin, for my eyelids to lower, to part my lips in eager anticipation of his searing kiss. I knew down to the marrow of my bones it would be hot, too. Altering even.

"Ahem," a female voice said from behind Hunter.

I swore, lurching back into the steering column. Helga's horn blasted out. Meanwhile, Hunter smacked his head against the door as he struggled to stand and turn as quickly as possible.

"I finished the list," my mother said from behind him. "I was going to text you and saw that your car was still here. Who are you?"

"Mom," I said, still reeling at her sudden appearance.

"Hunter Black, ma'am." My neighbor was rubbing what had to be a rising lump on the back of his head, but he offered the other hand to Agnes.

She didn't take it.

"Mom, "I said again, this time with censure in my voice. It wasn't like her to be rude to anyone, other than me of course." "He's—"

"I thought you rushed out of there in a hurry. Of course it was to meet some man."

"Mrs. Taylor," Hunter began, but she rolled right over the top of him.

"Honestly Mackenzie, will you never learn? Sneaking out to meet some lowlife under my nose, same as when you were a willful teenager. I would have thought one unplanned pregnancy was enough for one lifetime for any woman."

"Mom!" I shouted. "He lives here."

She had built up a solid head of steam because it took her another seven seconds of ranting about my poor judgment and taste in men before the diatribe abruptly shut off. "What do you mean he lives here?"

Hunter pointed at the darkened windows of his own apartment. "That's my place right there. Albert rented to me a few months before his passing."

My mother blinked up at him, opened her mouth, but then closed it again without speaking.

"We just met the other day," I added before turning back toward Hunter. "My mother plans on moving into the upstairs apartment. She's a better watchdog than Snickers. I just thought I should let you know, so you don't try anything."

"I wouldn't dare," the detective muttered. "Mrs. Taylor, it was…memorable."

Just like his first encounter with me. He must have thought my entire family tree was certifiable. I wasn't sure he'd be wrong in such an assessment.

"I'll see you ladies later." With a nod to my mother he headed up the steps and let himself in through the front door. A moment later a light came on in his apartment. I wondered what it was like in there. Hunter didn't strike me as a stereotypical bachelor, with pizza boxes and empty beer cans scattered around his space. I bet it smelled great, with that hint of wood smoke and fresh air and the male spice that was uniquely his.

I was so lost in daydreaming that I didn't pick up on my mother's intent until Helga's passenger's side door was yanked open. "What?"

"Honestly, Mackenzie," My mother sounded all put out, like her making a scene in front of our new neighbor was somehow my fault.

"Mom? What are you doing?"

"Going to the store with you." She twisted around to reach the seatbelt. The harness snapped into place with a dire sounding click.

"I had another errand to run."

"Oh?" She pulled down the vanity mirror and was fussing with her perfectly coiffed hair. "What sort of errand?"

"One for work," I stressed. "So you should probably go in and stay with Mac. Since it's getting so late and all."

"Mac's fine. That man's a cop, you said. A detective? And Nona's upstairs too, so it's not like she's in the house all alone. She'll call if she needs anything." She flipped the visor back into place.

I tried to think of any way out of dragging my mother on a surveillance run. Especially a surveillance run involving a couple she knew. Somehow I doubted she'd approve of my plan to stake out the Fox residence and see what was up. And the thought of being trapped in the car with her for however long was close to unbearable.

The memory of witnessing a homicide was still fresh. Did I really want my mother to witness the same sort of horror? "Mom, I'm not dropping off a check at the PTO. This is for a murder investigation."

Her green eyes narrowed to slits. "And what makes you any more qualified to investigate than I am? Besides, two sets of eyes are better than one." She spoke deliberately as if she'd somehow rehearsed this conversation ahead of time.

I wondered if Uncle Al had ever been bullied into an unwanted ride-along. Somehow, I doubted it.

"I'm not getting out of this car, so just forget it." Agnes Taylor squared her shoulders and lifted her chin.

I never knew she had such a stubborn streak. *Maybe I can kill two birds with one stone here: find out what happened with her and The Captain maybe even talk her into heading back home where she belongs. That would be worth a few hours of discomfort.*

"You have to promise not to interfere with what I'm doing." I wagged my finger in her face as though lecturing a naughty child. I'd never been so stern with Mac—then again, my daughter was reasonable.

She looked so hopeful, even excited. "I promise. Are we going?"

"We're going." I let out a string of internal curses and shifted Helga into reverse. "Java help me, we're going."

* * *

"It's that one." My mother pointed at a large brick edifice on the opposite side of the street.

I parked along the curb in front of a darkened house and stared at the building. "You're sure?"

"I was here for a New Year's party a few years ago. It's a family home. They wouldn't have sold."

This was as close as I was going to get without using Mac for internet verification. That reminded me. I picked up my cell phone and texted her. *Do me a solid and look up Rose Fox on Facebook.*

A second later. *A solid as opposed to a liquid.*

Just look, smartass, I typed and added a little emoticon with his tongue sticking out.

A pause. Then, *What specifically about her?*

Pictures, relationship status. Stuff like that. She was having an affair, supposedly leaving her husband, but I'm wondering if that was public knowledge.

I'm on it.

An odd chill made me shiver.

"Something wrong?" Agnes asked.

I scanned the street before refocusing on the Fox house. Our position allowed me to see both the front and the side of the residence. There were at least two lights on upstairs, along with the flicker of what I assumed was a television on the main floor, and what looked to be a kitchen off to the side. No sign of a black Escalade, though there were several Cadillacs and a few Hummers along with a sprinkling of hybrids. Helga was the only muscle car in sight.

My mother shifted. "So what are you hoping to see?"

"Anything unusual." I kept my eyes trained on the front window.

"Define unusual," Agnes said tartly.

Binoculars. I needed to get binoculars. If it had been any other neighborhood, I would have gotten out and maybe walked the sidewalk in front of the property a few times to really get a feel for the place. But if anyone spotted me, I had no doubt the police would show up and arrest me for loitering in the prestigious neighborhood, and I had no money for bail. "I'll know it when I see it."

"How on earth were the Foxes involved in your murder investigation?"

I huffed out a breath. She wasn't going to stop until I gave her some information. Maybe I could use it to turn the tables. Deciding to leave the whole alternate lifestyle bit out, I summed up. "Rose Fox was having an affair with the victim."

"No." My mother breathed the word, her tone a mixture of appalled excitement and genuine curiosity.

"According to his ex-wife, yes." The hairs rose along the back of my neck, and I turned up the heat.

"Did Robert know?"

"Again, I only have her word for it, but yes, and he was devastated."

"You just never know what goes on inside a marriage." My mother refocused on the house. "They seemed like such a contented couple."

I guessed the swinging would do that for them. Keeping one eye on the house, I tossed out a line to see if it hooked anything. "So, do you know anyone else who cheated?" Dear old Dad, maybe?

"That's hardly appropriate conversation," my mother huffed like a bird whose feathers had been ruffled.

I decided to take that as a maybe. "You were all hot and bothered a minute ago when you heard about Rose's affair."

"I was not," my mother said waspishly.

I gave her my best *get real* look.

She sighed. "Maybe I was a little bit glad to hear that Rose Fox's life wasn't as picture perfect as she made it seem. To tell you the truth I always envied her a bit. Her home, her clothes. Every door in Boston was open to her. She has such deep roots, a sense of permanence. She's truly embedded in the community and is liked and respected." Her tone was wistful.

I stared at the Fox house. It looked as though it had stood there for a hundred years and would be there for another century. It was a far cry from the paper-thin carpet and beige walls of the various base housings I'd grown up in. It didn't matter where in the world we were, every place had a vibe of sameness, continuity. A total lack of personality. "You never said you wanted something like that."

The illumination from the streetlight high lit her face, and she offered me a wan smile. "What was the point? It's not like it was going to change. Even after your father retired our house always felt sort of…temporary."

For me it had been, but I didn't say so. "Does The Captain know how you feel?"

She shook her head. "I never told him. He provided so much, and complaining seemed almost ungrateful."

The more she talked, the more I realized I'd never truly understand her. "And leaving him high and dry after three decades of marriage isn't? Don't you love him anymore?"

She opened her mouth to respond then shut it and shook her head. "You don't understand."

I was ready with a comeback, but movement in the kitchen window snagged my attention—two silhouettes, one large and male, the other smaller and most likely female. I squinted, then on a flash of brilliance, pulled out my cell phone, hit the photo app, and zoomed in.

"What's going on?" My mother squinted as though that would somehow improve her eyesight.

"Judging from the overt hand waving and squared-off posture, they're arguing." About her dead lover perhaps? I took a photo, unsure how it would come out.

Agnes craned her neck so she could see my phone screen too. "Oh my, they're having quiet a row, aren't they?"

That was an understatement. Hands flailed, and even from the distance the wild gesticulation indicated severe upset. Still, we were both shocked when the man drew back his arm and smacked the woman.

Agnes's hands flew to her face. I shut down the camera app and dialed 9-1-1. "Hello? I'd like to report a domestic disturbance."

My mother tugged on my sleeve, shaking her head, her eyes round.

"What's the nature of the disturbance?" The operator had a thick Southie accent.

"A man and woman arguing." I waved my mother off, trying to focus on the conversation. "There's been physical violence."

"Address?" the operator said.

I rattled it off, then hung up and reached for the key. "We need to get the hell out of here. I don't feel like spending the rest of the night playing 20 questions with the police." Not to mention I didn't want to tip the Foxes off to the fact that they were being investigated.

"Mackenzie," my mother spoke in a shaking voice. "There's a man outside my window."

I whipped my head around, just in time to see a dark shape move away from the window and disappear into a row of hedges.

"He was right outside the car?" I asked.

She nodded. "I thought he was going to break in."

Pepper spray in one hand, I threw open my door and followed. If I'd been thinking, I wouldn't have done it, left my mother alone on a dark night in a strange, albeit nice neighborhood. But there was that creeping sensation I'd had since we got here. As though someone had been spying on us.

Because someone had. And I wanted to know why.

I broke through the hedgerow and sprinted across a backyard. A dog barked, and floodlights came on at my undignified crashing—nothing stealthy about me as I blundered on, over a low stone wall and back out to the street behind. The one where I'd abandoned my mother. Where the heck did he go?

I scanned the road and caught sight of him halfway up the next hill. He wore dark clothes, jeans, and sneakers, and he was in damn good shape because he was leaving me in the dust. There was no way I was going to run him down on my own. But I recalled that the street had no outlet, so unless he ducked into one of the houses, he would have no place to go.

I cut back through another yard so the people with the dog didn't set him loose on me. Helga's door was still wide open and my mother still sitting there with her mouth hanging open. I dove inside and roared off, leaving what I was sure was descent tread on the street behind me.

The guy was a runner, but I had a Hellcat, and I cut him off before he reached the rise where a black Escalade sat waiting. I spun the wheel, and my mother let out a shriek as the car performed one hell of a burnout before coming to rest directly in his path. A split second later he rebounded off the hood and went sprawling flat onto his back in the street.

My heart thundered in my chest as I flung the door open again.

"Is he dead?" my mother whispered.

"I sure hope not." It was unlikely, though I might have to call for an ambulance if he'd cracked his skull open in the middle of the street. Pepper spray in one hand, I approached slowly, hoping he wasn't armed because I was sure he was pissed. I would be if some crazy chick parked a hot car on a dime in my way when I'd been running at full speed.

I rounded the front of the Challenger, scanning for any sign of my stalker. Weird, I hadn't seen him pop back up and he hadn't hit the car that hard. Unless…

I spun on my heel and crouched in front of the car to see if he'd slithered beneath it. I only had time to make out a stubble-covered chin before he dosed me with his own vial of pepper spray. I stumbled back and went down hard on my keister, cussing a blue streak.

"Mom!" I wheezed through the burn. The sound of his running feet got further away. I spat, choked, and called out my last ditch effort. "Get his license plate number!"

But since it was my mother, she ignored my instructions, instead scrambling out of the car to rush to my side. "My God, Mackenzie, are you all right?"

The burn seemed to intensify. "No," I choked.

Sirens sounded. "Oh thank heavens, it's the police."

"Tell them he tried to carjack us," I panted.

I couldn't see, could barely draw breath, but my hearing was sharp as ever so I didn't miss the outraged squawking noise, as though a fat man had sat on a large bird. "What? You can't lie to the police."

I ran my sleeve under my running nose. "Sure I can, and you will too, or I swear I will never speak to you again. They can't know we were watching the Foxes. We were heading out, and he tried to carjack us, and he dosed me with pepper spray."

"Mackenzie."

I wiped enough of the goo off my face to look her in the eye. "This is my job on the line. I can't get a reputation as a nut job who runs around town imagining a perp in an Escalade everywhere I go."

"But I saw him too," her voice warbled, and I could tell her conviction was wavering.

"Please," I begged before rolling over and vomiting right there on the street.

"Oh all right," she groused. "But I want it on the record it was under protest.

"Noted," I wheezed just as the first cop car came to a halt beside us.

"This was sort of exciting." My mother rubbed my back in a soothing manner. "Almost fun, even."

I gagged and managed to sputter, "Yeah, fun. That's exactly the word for it," before upchucking once more.

CHAPTER NINE

There's something to be said for having an honest face in private investigation. If you don't have one, fake it.
From the *Working Man's Guide to Sleuthing for a Living* by Albert Taylor, PI

It took almost an hour for the worst effects of the pepper spray to die down. Without the distracting presence of Hunter Black, I experienced my latest dosing in all its scathing glory with the sound of my mother fretting in the background.

She was such a horrible liar.

"And then he came out of nowhere, yanked my daughter's car door open, pulled her out into the street, and sprayed her right in the face! Can you imagine?"

Though my eyes were still running, I could see the cop's face well enough to judge that no, he most decidedly could not imagine her farfetched story even before he muttered, "Wasn't she wearing her seat belt?"

"We were pulled over," I explained.

The scowl grew on his dark face. "In the middle of the street?"

"I thought I hit a cat. I intended to go out and check and see if it was all right."

"So you stopped your car in the middle of the street after hitting a cat and then were suddenly carjacked?" He didn't have eyebrow hair, but I could tell if he did, they'd be raised up under his hat.

"Maybe it's a scam," I offered. "Guy picks up stray cats and sets them loose in front of vehicles he wants to carjack."

"Mmm hmm. What did this cat-hating carjacker look like?"

"It happened so fast." My mother made a fanning motion with her hand as though she were a Victorian matron about to keel over in a crowded ballroom.

"His face was covered by a hoodie, though he was Caucasian and hadn't shaved in a while." There had been stubble, golden stubble, and a full mouth. I remembered because I wanted to knock all the teeth out of that mouth.

"So an unshaven guy wearing a hoodie set a stray cat in front of your car on the off chance you'd stop and unbuckle your seatbelt, and he could pull only one of you from the car and dose you with pepper spray? And then he just ran off, on foot?"

There was farfetched, but this was stretching into the outer reaches. Taking a deep breath, I pointed a finger at my mother. "She did it."

"What? That's ridiculous, I would never," Agnes sputtered.

"It was an accident. She meant to scare off the carjacker, but her aim was off." I knew for a fact that could happen.

"And why did you stop?" the officer probed.

"We were arguing. About my lack of a husband. And poor wardrobe choices." All good standbys.

"Mackenzie," my mother hissed.

The cop looked between the two of us. "And the carjacker just came upon you while you were arguing?"

I stumbled over to the car and withdrew the vile of pepper spay. "One dose down. I don't know if you have a way to measure that or not. The carjacker probably collapsed from laughter not far from here." I doubted they could actually measure such a thing, but if he tried, it'd back up my claim.

He looked from my bloodshot eyes and runny nose to Agnes, who wrung her hands fretfully. "You're lucky he wasn't armed."

"My mother, the hero." I smiled. "So can we go?"

He nodded, returning to his patrol car.

"That's it?" Agnes asked.

"Are you disappointed?" I headed back to the car. "Come on, I think we've disturbed the peace enough for one night."

We were barely a block over when she lit into me. "I can't believe you made me lie to the police. And what possessed you to tell him that I sprayed you?"

"He wasn't buying the cat thing. I could tell from his browbeaten look he has either a harridan wife or mother, and I decided to roll the dice with mother. Damn, I'm out of tissues. Do you have any?"

She whipped some out of her purse. Her purse tissues were the organized little packs that one could pick up in line at the grocery store. What passed for tissues in my bag were a hodgepodge of donut napkins and woodchip-riddled toilet paper snagged from public restrooms. It was the difference between blowing my nose with a cloud instead of attacking it with a sander.

"So that was a waste of time," she sighed as I headed back to Uncle Al's.

I gaped at her. "You're kidding, right? We know the Foxes are having severe marital difficulties, and whoever killed Paul Granger was lurking in their neighborhood. That's totally suspicious behavior."

My mother folded her arms over her chest. "I don't like this job of yours."

"Good thing you don't have to do it then. Still want to hit the market?"

"Too bad the liquor stores are all closed," she grumbled.

I must have looked like either a strung-out meth fiend or an extra from the *Walking Dead* because I received a lot of odd looks as we entered the all-night supermarket. If I'd been with Mac she would have teased me about my new head-turning look, and I would have played it up. With my mother I just put my head down and concentrated on filling my shopping cart.

Of course, since it was my mother, she had a commentary on that, too. "You really shouldn't buy so many processed foods. It's not good for Mac. Or your waistline."

I bared my teeth in what I hoped passed for a smile and snagged a bunch of bananas just to shut her up.

"Oh, look, kumquats." She scurried over to a display.

"Sounds dirty," I muttered and headed off to the bread aisle. Only carbs could save me now.

I was just putting the last frozen dinner in the cart when my cell phone rang. "Mom?"

"Mac? What are you still doing up?"

"I dug up that info you wanted about Rose and Robert Fox. It took longer than I expected. They must be the only two people on the planet not on Facebook."

I eyeballed Agnes scurrying toward me, kumquats brandished in victory. "I can think of at least one more. So what's the verdict?"

"Rose filed for divorce about a week ago. Quietly. It was in the county records, but didn't pop up on any radars."

"After what I witnessed tonight I'm wondering if that was what set her husband off." Briefly I summed up the domestic abuse as well as the guy in the Escalade that had spritzed me.

"So what are you thinking? That he works for Mr. Fox, like, does his dirty work?" There was the slam of a cabinet door on Mac's end of the line. "Did you get any peanut butter crackers by the way?"

"I'm on it." I veered down the snack aisle. "And about the guy in the Escalade, I don't know what to think. If he worked for either Rose or Robert, why was he parked a few streets over? For that matter, how come he used something non-lethal on me if he shot Paul Granger?"

"I still can't believe you went after him like that." My daughter sounded impressed.

"I'm setting a bad example for you, aren't I?"

"No more than usual. Besides, you're all badass as a PI. It'll be even better if we get paid. Oh and get me Pizza Rolls."

"Sausage or extra cheese?"

"Both," Mac answered and hung up.

I stowed my purse and maneuvered the cart back toward the frozen food.

"Did you get milk?" Now that I wasn't on the phone Agnes was back on my case at full volume.

"No."

"It's important to get calcium."

I picked up two gallons of Friendly's ice cream. "I got it covered."

"Honestly, Mackenzie." She threw up her hands in exasperation.

I'd had enough. "Mom, look. You're welcome to stay with us, but as long as you do, you don't get a say in what we eat, how I dress, how I parent, who I date, or anything else I choose to do. If you want to boss someone around go home to The Captain, *capiche*?"

"I'm only trying to help." She sounded both sulky and defensive.

I couldn't imagine a world where her nitpicky little comments could be interpreted as help, but having scored a victory, I didn't want to push my luck. Instead we headed toward the checkout line where a bored-looking teenager who was only slightly older than Mac scanned our items.

"I've got it." My mother practically hip checked me out of the way.

"No," I said firmly and handed over my credit card, holding my breath that there was enough room on it for the kumquats as well as all our normal junk.

"You don't let me do anything," Agnes kvetched. "You're flat broke and yet still too proud to let me pay."

"Next time," I said to pacify her.

"Well some of that was for me," she said, digging in her wallet for cash.

Why did everything have to be a big public scene? "You lent Mac money, so I owed you. Consider this payback."

"But that was for Mac," she protested.

"Who is my financial responsibility." I shot her an exasperated look. "I've got this."

"Stubborn," she grumbled.

"Pot call the kettle much?" I muttered.

"Pardon?"

"Never mind."

The girl raised an eyebrow at us but thankfully didn't comment.

The card cleared, and I bagged our items, barely containing my sigh of relief. I envied those people who had to just move some money around to pay groceries. Or shoes. If the PI gig didn't pay off, I'd end up selling plasma and my unwanted bananas on street corners. Still a better option than accepting money from my mother.

It was late enough that our trip home took half the time it normally would have, and soon Helga was secured in her garage for the night. My mind automatically shied away from the thought of selling the Hellcat. She represented everything I wanted my life to be—free, sexy, and fun. The thought of riding off into the sunset with Fillmore was just too damn depressing.

We humped the groceries across the front walk, and I instinctively checked to see if Hunter's light was still on. It wasn't. Probably a good thing, considering I didn't want to explain my current appearance.

"You like that man," Agnes spoke softly.

I knew what she meant, but did she really think I was going to open up to her after her earlier crack about unplanned pregnancies? Way to humiliate your only child, Mom. Deflecting her was probably my best move. "Of course I do. He's nice, and I feel safer having a cop for a neighbor."

She got that pinched look that I secretly called her constipation face. "Mackenzie Elizabeth Taylor, that is not what I mean, and you know it."

"Mom, please. Not tonight."

She looked me over from my rat's nest hair to my scraped knee showing through the new hole in my jeans and finally relented. "Oh, all right. But this conversation isn't over."

"Of course not," I grumbled. "I'm not that lucky."

* * *

I fell into bed, exhausted down to my bone marrow.

I'd agreed Mac could drive Fillmore to school, and she was gone when I stumbled toward the coffeepot, bleary eyed and grumpy. A fresh pot stood waiting for me like a long-lost friend. I inhaled gratefully and then turned toward the counter where I'd stashed my *Bruns* mug.

It was gone.

Frowning, I opened the cabinet above where we'd stockpiled our meager few dishes and was surprised to see the pantry goods from the night before arranged there. No dishes.

I turned and gaped at the sight of the living room. Not a single box in sight. The place was completely unpacked, every book lined up on the small bookcase built in next to the bay window seat, every cable for Mac's computer coiled neatly and secured with a zip tie.

Unfortunately, the organized room only showcased all the stuff wrong with the place—cracks in the walls from where the foundation had settled, scuffs on the hardwood floor, dents and dings in all the wood trim, water stains on the ceiling, not to mention the heap of boxes blocked the draft from the failed seals on the windows.

I swallowed hard and whispered, "Java preserve me."

That was just what I could see. Who knew what else might be wrong with the house's innards? The roof, the electricity, the water heater? I'd never been a homeowner before, and loathe as I was to admit it, my mother might have been right. This house could have been too much for me to handle.

"Good morning!" Agnes bustled past me, an armload of neatly stacked towels balanced precariously in front of her.

"Were we robbed by very neat burglars?" I glanced about like a drowning woman seeking a life preserver.

"Of course not." My mother set the towels down on one of the barstools.

I shivered as a gust rattled the windows. "What happened to all of the boxes?"

"I collapsed them and stacked them in the basement." She proceeded to unfold the already folded clean towels, arranging them first by color then from pale to bright.

"And where are my dishes?" I waved desperately at the cabinets. "And my coffee mugs?"

"Over the dishwasher. It's much more efficient that way." She snapped out a towel to its full length.

Gritting my teeth, I moved stiffly towards the cabinet. The mugs were there, so the bloodbath was staved off for a little while at least.

"You could at least say thank you." Snap went the linens, making me flinch.

"Thank you?" I was stiff as all get-out from the antics of the day before and wasn't a morning person in any sense of the word. Her frenetic tidying frayed my last nerve. The coffee was piping hot, though, and strong enough to crank start a Model T. I gulped, actually glad for the scalding down my esophagus. It gave me something to focus on other than her glaring.

"Yes, I unpacked all your things and am creating a system for your household. When someone does you a favor Mackenzie, it's customary to offer at least a verbal show of gratitude."

"Why?" I set the mug aside and braced my hands on the counter. "Mom, why did you do this?"

She looked at me as though I were the one out of my ever-loving mind. "Well, someone had to."

The front door buzzed, and she dropped the last towel onto the stack and hurried out of the room. "That will be my furniture delivery."

I returned to the love of my life, aka the hot pot of java. With coffee, all things were possible, including figuring out what Agnes Taylor was up to.

Of course the personal sleuthing would have to wait. I had a list of doctor's offices to visit so I could find out more about Paul Granger and the drugs he peddled. After the antics of the night before, I was fairly certain the Foxes had something to do with Paul's death, but spending a day covering my bases wouldn't hurt.

The sound of a crash from the outer hallway broke me out of my mental planning, and I hurried forward to see what was going on.

Agnes Taylor stood in the foyer, hands on hips, chewing out the no-necked goons carrying…

I blinked. "Is that a piano?"

"Yes, or it was before this oaf dropped it." Agnes glared viscously.

"What's it doing here?" As far as I knew my mother had never once sat down in front of a piano.

"I bought it, of course."

Upstairs a door creaked open, and Nona's head, sporting green curlers, peeked out over the railing. "What's all the racket, doll?"

"Oh, Nona, wait till you see!" Turning her back on me, Agnes headed up the stairs to talk to her new neighbor.

I didn't want to be a stick in the mud, I really didn't. She was so enthusiastic, so much less caustic. But there was no freaking way that thing would fit in the tiny upstairs apartment. "Mom, there's no way you're going to fit that thing in your apartment."

The movers paused, the bald one looking to the one with the porn mustache and then at me. "All sales are final."

"It won't fit," I insisted.

"That's what she said," Pornstachio snickered.

Another door opened, and Hunter Black emerged from his apartment. "What's going on, Red?"

"My mother bought a baby grand piano for her apartment." I gestured helplessly to the thing.

"So I see."

"I'm trying to explain to these, um, gentlemen, that there is no *freaking* way they'll be able to actually put it in there."

More snickering, but at least they kept the lewd sidebar to themselves.

"Sure it will. You just need to take the door off the hinges." Hunter headed up the stairs.

A moment later I followed.

"Nona, Mrs. Taylor," Hunter greeted the women waiting in the hallway. Nona was her usual Yiddish spouting self, but my mother didn't respond. At least not until I heard her screech, "What are you doing?"

I rounded the newel post just in time to see Hunter's broad back disappearing into her new pad. I gripped her arm before she could pursue. "He's just trying to help. Worry about the mouth breathers hauling all our new stuff in. Where did you get the money for all this, by the way?"

"Al's accounts. You got the car, and I got his bank balance." Her tone sounded distracted as she bent to the side to peer past me. "What's that man of yours doing in there?"

"He's not my man. We haven't even kissed. Hunter's just being neighborly. Tell her, Nona."

"Oh yeah, he's a good egg." Detective Black's number one fangirl rode to the rescue. "With Al gone, it's good to know we've got a young man who knows how to get things done around here."

"Mackenzie," Hunter called from behind the door.

"Yeah?" I stepped forward to peer around it so I could see him. "What's up?"

"In my apartment there's a toolbox. I need a mallet and a Phillips-head screwdriver. Would you grab those for me, please?"

I opened my mouth to tell him he didn't have to do this but then clamped my lips together. He was offering me a shot to see inside his apartment. "Sure. Is your door unlocked?"

"Should be."

I turned and headed for the steps. The piano still took up the majority of the space in the foyer, and the movers had returned to the van to grab a glass-topped table. How much crap had she bought?

Shaking off the unsettling notion that my mother truly intended to leave The Captain for good, I reached Hunter Black's door. Taking a deep breath, I turned the knob and pushed my way inside.

I hadn't realized I'd been expecting anything in particular until I got a good look at the apartment. Like mine, Hunter's space sported hardwood floors, though his were a much lighter shade, almost a blonde color. All the woodwork around the windows and doors was the same dark stained hardwood. Except his place had no dings and dents, no visible scuffs or stains from leaks gone by.

There was no stereotypical bachelor pad pleather sofa or big-screen TV. In fact, there was no sign of a TV at all. Just a small round kitchen table and two chairs with an all-in-one PC sitting on top. Instead, a huge pool table dominated the area beside the fireplace. Beneath it sat the advertised toolbox.

I pulled out the items he'd requested then paused. I couldn't explore the way I was dying to, but I probably had time to check out at least one of the remaining rooms. So, bedroom, bathroom, or kitchen?

The bedroom seemed too intimate somehow. If I went in there I'd be crossing a line, and if he did come see what was keeping me I'd be better off not getting trapped in his bedroom. The bathroom, well it was a bathroom and other than poking through his medicine cabinet, there wasn't much I could learn. Easy enough to pretend my own bathroom was out of order at some point and come back over to use his at a later date. That left the kitchen.

At first glance, it wasn't much different from my own. Same blue-patterned linoleum, same ancient fridge and stove. His sink had been upgraded from the ceramic country-style basin in my place to a modern double-sided stainless steel sink. His plates were the neat square kind that some fancy restaurants used, cobalt blue, no pattern to personalize them, but at least they all matched. His mugs told me nothing. They were all lined up like good little ceramic solders. Cutlery, just as nondescript.

His fridge held eggs, milk, salad greens, and bottled dressings and a marinating steak. No wine or beer, nothing other than some bottled water. Maybe he was a recovering alcoholic, or just not a drinker?

No cookies in the cabinets, though he did have a box of green tea. A health nut maybe? He was in stellar shape. It made sense that Hunter would be one of those my-body-is-a-temple types. *Sign me up to worship.*

"Mackenzie?" my mother's voice called from the hallway.

That was my cue. After taking one last glance around to make sure I hadn't left any telltale evidence of myself behind, I strode toward the door, tools in hand.

Something stopped me at the last moment, and I turned to survey the space again. What was it?

My gaze flitted from the partially visible kitchen to the main living area. The computer was on a screensaver—nothing personal, just the little Windows icon bouncing off the sides.

He'd been working on his computer.

No, I couldn't. Could I?

Apparently I could because before I knew it, I was tapping the screen, bringing the snoozing machine to life.

The home screen was a family picture, or at least who I thought must be his family. The first thing I noticed was Hunter with his arm around a petite blonde with mischievous eyes and a ready smile. He held her tucked into his side, and she barely reached his shoulder. If not for the other people in the photograph I would have believed she was his girlfriend or maybe an ex-wife.

On his other side, a middle-aged woman who was even shorter than the blonde rested her head against his shoulder. Her hair was the same light color, though it had paled out somewhat. Next to her a ruddy-faced bald man with twinkling eyes and a nose that looked like a potato had her arm tucked through his. Beside him were two other women, visibly older than the woman beside Hunter, but all had the same strong resemblance and three children, two girls and a baby dressed in little boy clothes, all blond with the same ruddy complexion.

All the people resembled each other strongly. Except for Hunter, who stuck out like a sore thumb. From his bone structure and the fall of his unbound hair, I guessed he had at least some Native American blood. He was dark to their fair, huge to their compact builds, brooding to their effervescence.

Hunter Black was adopted.

CHAPTER TEN

A smart PI goes in, gets his information, and leaves. Chasing the target could get you killed.
From the *Working Man's Guide to Sleuthing for a Living* by Albert Taylor, PI

After handing over Hunter's tools, I beat a hasty retreat back into my apartment. Damn, why did I have to go snooping? Or sleuthing as Uncle Al would have called it. Either way I was burdened with information about my sexy new neighbor that I had no right possessing. It wasn't like he'd told me he was adopted. Hell, maybe being adopted wasn't that big a secret, but it raised all kinds of questions. Did he know who his birth parents were? Did he even *want* to know?

Maybe I was just jumping at shadows. It could very well be that he'd picked up some sort of recessive gene that had skipped the rest of his family—the large, Native American gene that was buried under a heap of hearty Irish stock. The only way to know for sure was to ask him.

Snickers trotted to her water bowl and pawed at its empty bottom, then gave me a dirty look. *Jing jing.* Fill 'er up. I took a cup to the faucet and ran the tap, still mulling over my discovery. If I mentioned the computer he'd know I'd peeked. Had he expected me to look? He could have retrieved the tools himself. Maybe he sent me in there so that I could be nosy.

Maybe I needed to get a life. Speaking of which, I had a job to do and doctors' offices to visit. I headed for the shower, trying to focus on the snooping…er… *sleuthing* I would eventually get paid to do.

The movers had finished with my mom's stuff by the time I headed out to the car. Hunter was either locked back in his apartment or had gone to work because I saw no sign of him.

"You have to come look!" my mother called from the upstairs landing.

"Later. I need to go out." Fearing a repeat of last night, I quickened my steps until I was out under the brilliant October sky.

The first doctor's office on the list Mac had compiled was a twenty-minute drive from the villa. I parked in the three-level garage that serviced the building and strode in looking like I knew what the hell I was doing.

Technically, I did know. I was going to ask to speak with Dr. Bernard Dole about Paul Granger, who had visited this particular office along with three others in the week before he was killed. And since I hadn't been able to get in contact with anyone from Right Touch Pharmaceuticals, I was going to ask about the ED drug Paul had peddled.

Dr. Dole shared a practice with three other MDs. The waiting and reception area was painted a cheery buttercup yellow with the standard unremarkable art prints on the wall and uncomfortable-looking composite and blue vinyl chairs that looked more like modern art than seating. Ancient issues of *Time* and *National Geographic* were stacked in tidy piles on the end tables, and harpies on *The View* blared out at a billion decibels from the flat-screen mounted on the wall.

There were two other people in the waiting area, both male, one an octogenarian and the other about two decades his junior who looked the part of the quintessential silver fox. The relatively younger man gave me a slow up and down then flashed even white teeth. Gross—he was The Captain's age if he was a day.

I offered a tight smile and made my way to the receptionist desk.

The African-American woman with bleached blonde highlights slid the window back so she could talk to me. "Do you have an appointment?"

"No. I'd like to—"

"Then you'll have to make one." She slid the window shut and turned back to her computer.

I rapped on the glass with my knuckles, lightly, not wanting to seem rude. She eyeballed me a minute and then opened the window again.

"Hi, my name is Mackenzie Taylor. What's yours?" I offered her my brightest smile, hoping I could maybe win her over with charm.

She didn't look charmed. "I'm Ruth. And I have work to do."

She made to shut the window again, but I reached forward, catching it halfway across the track. "I'm so sorry to disturb you, Ruth, but I need to ask about Paul Granger."

"We can't discuss patients with anybody. Now getchya hand off my window,"

"He wasn't a patient," I ground out. The woman was crazy strong. "He was a pharmaceutical rep. Sold an ED drug for Right Touch Pharmaceuticals. Any of this sound familiar?"

She raised an eyebrow at me. "You mean the leg-humper?"

"Um…maybe?" At this point could I rule anything out?

She stopped trying to slam the window in my face. "Hey, Kimmy, someone's askin' about the leg-humper."

A small Asian woman with chartreuse hair pulled back into a severe ponytail rolled her office chair back so she could see me. "You know the leg-humper?"

"I know a bunch of them," I said." There was a picture of Paul in the file Len had given me, and I dug it out to show to them. "This the guy?"

"Oh yeah, that's him." Ruth crossed her arms and leaned back. "Came in here every month, trying to convince one of the doctors to buy his lousy drug. They never would though."

"How come?" Hastily, I stuffed the picture back in the file folder and dug out a pen. "Didn't it work?"

"You'd have to ask the doctors about that." Kimmy blew out a breath, causing a section of her yellow-green hair to lift away from her face. "All I know is he'd come in here, start schmoozing all the men and pawing at the ladies. Didn't matter if they were eighteen or eighty, he was on them like white on rice.

We had to call building security to remove him more than once. He cornered me in the parking garage once, and I dosed him with pepper spray."

Having been dosed twice in the past week, I almost felt sorry for Paul. "Did you report him?"

Kimmy shook her head. "He begged me not to, said it would cost him his job. And he wasn't scary as much as annoying."

I uncapped my pen. "When was this?"

She frowned in thought. "Not too long ago. Ruth, was it before or after the guy with the hernia had a heart attack in the office."

Ruth's hands flew to her keyboard even as she muttered. "Oh it was defiantly after, the same week. Let's see, that was September seventh." She tapped what looked to be a calendar.

Hmmm, after the Grangers had filed for divorce. And he was already looking to cheat on his swinger mistress? I turned back to Kimmy. "Do you really think he would have gone through with it if you were interested? Some guys are all talk."

"Oh no, he was interested all right," Ruth spoke before Kimmy could get a word out. "I caught him whackin' it in the ladies restroom once. Damn fool didn't even realize he'd turned right instead o' left. That man had an itch he wanted scratched in the worst way."

Behind her, Kimmy nodded. "Yes, I think he really was serious, especially that one time. There was something a little desperate about him. Like an addict, you know?"

I blinked. "A sex addict you mean?"

"All men are sex addicts," Ruth interjected. "My Melvin would do nothing else but bend me over the counter if I let him. But that leg-humper man had *a problem*."

"Would Dr. Dole have a few minutes to answer a few questions?"

"Who'd you say you were?" She narrowed her eyes at me.

"Mackenzie Taylor. I'm a private investigator."

"Why you asking all these questions about the leg-humper? Is he in some kind of trouble?"

Probably best to be honest without revealing the whole truth. I didn't want to start rumors. "Not anymore. Is the doctor available?"

Kimmy leaned over Ruth's shoulder and pointed at a block on the calendar. "Yes, as a matter of fact. He's getting ready to leave for the hospital. I'll see if he'll agree to meet with you."

"Thanks so much." I smiled at her and then at Ruth. "You've been such a help."

Kimmy moved into the back, and I chatted with Ruth for a few minutes about the Celtics' upcoming season. The woman knew basketball almost as well as she knew men.

The door to the back office opened, and a tall man wearing a white lab coat emerged. He was carrying a briefcase and had a brown trench coat draped over his arm. His eyes were obscured behind thick lenses, and his hair was brown with gray sideburns.

"Dr. Dole?" I asked, extending a hand.

He took it, his handshake limp. "You must be Mackenzie. Kim said you had a few questions for me. I'm in something of a rush, but if you want to walk with me to the parking garage, I'll answer whatever I can."

Handshake notwithstanding, he seemed like a nice man, the kind of doctor you'd trust through good times and bad. He held the door for me when I remembered Helga needed to be sprung from the overpriced parking garage.

Rushing back to the window I rapped on it smartly. When Ruth slid it open I held up my ticket. "Do you validate?"

Her eyes narrowed, but she took my ticket and stamped it. "Girl, don't run around looking for validation. You're better than that."

"Tell that to my credit card company," I said and headed out.

* * *

"So what can I do for you, Ms. Taylor?" The doctor had a faint tinge of South Boston peppering his speech. It made him seem much more approachable than Jessica Granger's clipped consonants and perfectly accent-less manner. I smiled up at him as we waited for the elevator.

"I'm interested in your take on Right Touch Pharmaceuticals and specifically the ED drug Paul Granger was trying to sell."

"You mean Alphadra?"

I hadn't known that was what it was called but nodded. "That's right. Does it work?"

"Depends on who you ask," the doctor said. "I don't recommend it to my patients because it has some nasty side effects."

"What kinds of side effects?" I probed.

The elevator dinged and the doors opened, revealing an empty car. Dr. Dole continued as we stepped inside. "Most notably priapism, a prolonged and painful erection that lasts more than four hours and must be treated medically. It claims to work faster than the other ED drugs available, but it doesn't play well with other drugs. There have been studies indicating an increased risk of heart attack and stroke with prolonged use, more so than in the other options."

"Did all the doctors in your practice agree with your assessment?"

The doors opened, and he gestured for me to step out first. "After you."

I did and fell into step alongside the good doctor.

"To answer your question," he began, "no. But none of us will recommend the drug either."

"Why not?"

"We're a small practice in the grand scheme of things, Ms. Taylor. And we decided as a group that it wasn't worth our reputation to recommend Alphadra, at least not as it was. Your Mr. Granger was really persistent though. He insisted one of my colleagues, Dr. Yates, saw potential in the drug."

"So that's what you discussed with him during your meeting last week?"

"I'm afraid so. Right Touch had armed him with new data claiming the side effects were minimal as long as the patient is not taking any other drug long term. I agreed to look it over and come to a decision at our next staff meeting."

"And did you?"

He nodded. "Yes, but I believe the results of the study were falsified. Specifically, that Right Touch handpicked men in their early thirties to mid-forties who were otherwise in prime health."

I frowned. "What's wrong with that?"

"There were no overweight men, no men with existing chronic conditions like diabetes, rheumatoid arthritis, ADHD, alcoholism and so on. All had relatively low blood pressure indicating that they exercised regularly. In other words, the ideal physically fit man, not the average patient who walks through my door. I believe Right Touch hoped to increase their sales through underhanded means."

"Did you find anything at all off about Paul Granger, personally?"

We'd entered the parking garage where Dr. Dole rummaged for keys and then inserted them into the door of a battered blue Ford Focus. "You mean, other than the fact that he was a liar and a pushy one at that?"

"Your receptionists seemed to think he was a little too pushy around women."

"I never noticed that. Then again, I tried to spend as little time with the man as humanly possible. Now, if you'll excuse me, I need to make rounds."

"Thank you for your time, doctor. I truly appreciate it."

He ducked down and folded his lanky frame into the car. I stepped back, watching as his reverse lights came on and he backed out of the space before heading down to the exit.

My phone was in my jacket pocket. I pulled it out and moved into the empty space so I could get a signal. I wished Len texted, but the lawyer had informed me the night before that he didn't go in for any of that "newfangled gadgetry." I'd have to set Mac on him.

On the other end, the phone rang twice before Len picked up. "Copeland here."

"It's Mackenzie. I may have found out a few things about Mr. Granger as well as the Foxes."

"Would you care to meet up for lunch? There's a great Jewish deli on the corner, and I was just on my way there."

My stomach rumbled at the thought of a corned beef on rye, but I was flat broke. "It might take me awhile to get there. I'm across town."

"I'll order for you, whatever you like, my treat."

Those were the magic words. I gave him my order, glad I didn't have to head home to throw lunch together.

Heading back over to Helga, I texted Mac. *How's your new lab partner working out? Abs or glutes?*

She hit me back just as I reached Helga. *You think you're funny, but you're not.*

I am freaking hilarious. Off to lunch, Len's buying, I typed, feeling important.

There was no reply, and I figured she'd had to stow her phone. Damn public education, taking my daughter away for six whole hours every day. On second thought, she probably needed a break from my antics since I could be a handful at times.

Pocketing my phone, I reached for the car door handle just as a hand was clamped over my mouth.

CHAPTER ELEVEN

A smart PI goes in, gets his information, and leaves. Chasing the target could get you killed.
From the *Working Man's Guide to Sleuthing for a Living* by Albert Taylor, PI

I acted on pure instinct, trying to scream around the hand covering my mouth. When that didn't do any good, I struggled against the hold, trying to break free. So vehement were my efforts that it took me a minute to realize that the thug who had grabbed me was calling me by name. "Mackenzie, it's okay, it's me."

I froze, trying to place the voice. "Hunter?" I asked, though with his hand still clamped over my mouth it came out more like "Mmpher?"

"Don't scream, struggle, or ask any questions," Hunter murmured in my ear. "Just get in your car, and drive home. I'll meet you there in an hour."

I wanted to ask why he was acting so oddly, but he met my eyes and gave a brief shake of his head.

"I'm meeting someone for lunch," I muttered instead. "Can I do that?"

"No."

A shiver went through me. "Am I in danger?"

"Trouble, not danger. Promise me you'll go right there, or I swear I'll drive you there myself and handcuff you to my bed."

My mouth went dry as my gaze flew to his. If he was bluffing, I couldn't tell. "I promise."

He strode off casually as though he hadn't just accosted me in a darkened parking garage and threatened to…

All of a sudden I was sorry I hadn't snooped in his bedroom. He was a cop. Of course he had handcuffs. But did he have…other things?

Best not to think about that.

I got inside Helga, reversed out of the space, and headed down the ramp toward the exit. After handing over my validated ticket, I made a left and headed for the villa.

The closer I got though, the more my temper flared. Who the heck did Hunter Black think he was, popping up out of nowhere and telling me that I couldn't go to lunch? Sure he was an officer of the law, but I was 99.9 percent sure his authority didn't extend to my eating habits.

I should ask a lawyer, just to be safe.

The midday traffic was light, and I made it to the deli Len had indicated. The sun shone on the little outdoor patio, and I spied Len sitting at a picnic table, his suit rumpled, his tie pulled loose. He waved when he saw me.

"Can a police officer tell a person whether or not he or she can go to lunch?" I asked Len as I took a seat in front of the corn beef sandwich and, bless him, cardboard coffee cup.

Good sport that he was, Len didn't inquire why I wanted the information, he just shook his head. "Not unless you're detained for questioning or under arrest."

"How about handcuffing them to his bed?" I asked before sinking my teeth into a sandwich.

"Not without the other person's consent. Does that help?" Len raised an eyebrow.

I smiled and then took a swig of coffee, not wanting to lie. If Hunter ever did handcuff me to his bed I was fairly sure a big, stupid part of me would be okay with it.

Len waited patiently while I downed half my sandwich, polished off the coffee, then wiped my hands on a napkin before saying, "So tell me what you've found out."

Extracting the file from my bag, I flipped to the folder with my notes to help me summarize all that I'd learned, starting with the conversation with Dr. Dole and working my way backwards.

Len listened, nodding thoughtfully as I told him my findings, though he frowned about my second run-in with the mysterious man who drove the Escalade. "So you still didn't get a good look at him?"

"No, and I didn't report him to the police, either."

"If he worked for the Fox family, I think he would have confronted you or run toward their house, not park a street over and rabbit when you noticed him. That doesn't sound like killer for hire behavior, especially the part about the Mace."

"It was pepper spray," I corrected. "And I thought the same thing. Not that I'm ungrateful about him not shooting me."

"You need to be more careful," Len advised. "You're not law enforcement, so don't take unnecessary risks to catch a suspect. Are you armed?"

I paused with the other triangle of sandwich at my lips. "Only pepper spray."

"Do you own a gun?"

I set the sandwich back down, my appetite gone. "No. Is it a job requirement?"

"Absolutely not. In fact, if you are uncomfortable with guns, I'd recommend you stay that way. If you want to learn, hire someone experienced to teach you enough to be proficient and get a concealed carry permit. Your greatest weapon is the information you gather. I've worked with some hotheaded PIs in the past who think they're Dirty Harry. It never ends well. What's your next step?"

I blew out a sigh. "I wanted to speak with someone over at Right Touch Pharmaceuticals, but no one has returned my calls. I guess I'll keep going down the list and talking with doctors and staff who work at the offices Paul visited. See if I unearth anything else."

I nodded, taking his advice to heart. "I should probably go. Thank you for lunch."

He studied me a moment. "You can submit your expenses any time, and I'll advance you and just bill the client later."

"Do I look that pathetic?" I asked with a rueful smile.

"Not pathetic, my dear. More…hard-pressed. I noticed you didn't agree to lunch until I offered to buy, which I will be billing our client for, by the way. You're doing a thorough job investigating, and I want to make sure you get a fair shake."

Between Len and Uncle Al, I couldn't have asked for better mentors to help ease me into my new career. "I've been kinda worried about the expenses, not the cost as much as what I can and can't charge."

"You compile a list, bring them to me, and we'll go over them before submitting them to the client. And since you're working for me, I'm happy to advance you the hours you've already put in on this case." He reached into his pocket and withdrew a wad of bills.

"Cripes, Len," I yelped. Standing quickly, I bent down and blocked the fistful of bills from anyone in the deli. "You shouldn't flash that kind of cash out on the street. Someone will target you for a mugging."

He shook his head. "I keep forgetting I'm not in a small town anymore. You're right. I'll be more careful in the future."

"Oh? How long have you been in Boston?"

"About five years."

I stared at him. Five years was more than enough time to become acquainted with the safety precautions deemed necessary by city dwellers. I thought back to walking him to his car the night before. "Please tell me you make a habit of locking your car and your front door."

He shrugged. "When I remember about it."

"You're killing me, Len. But thank you for this. What prompted your move anyhow?"

"My sweet Madison passed, and I couldn't bear to stay in our lifelong home without her."

How sad. "But why Boston? Do you have family here?"

"We never had children of our own. My brother-in-law was looking to retire so I sold my home and bought his practice. It keeps me occupied—gotta keep the mind engaged or old age will chew it up and spit it out."

My nose wrinkled at the image, but I understood the sentiment. "Well I better head home before the cops are out looking for me." One cop in particular.

"Stop by the office tomorrow, and we'll go over those expenses." Len urged.

My heart went out to my employer who was such an interesting combination of wise and foolish but above all exceptionally lonely. "I will. And you should come by Uncle Al's place for dinner some night. Meet my daughter and avoid my mother. It'll be a real insider's glimpse."

Len's face lit up. "You cook?"

"Hell no, but I order takeout with the best of them."

"I'd like that."

With a final farewell, I sprinted to Helga and prayed to the traffic gods for mercy so I'd beat Hunter back to the villa.

It was ten past two when I walked up the front steps, wishing I had somewhere to hide. My palms were sweating, and my knees didn't seem to be working right. Len had assured me that the law was on my side, so why did I feel as if I was about to get hauled into the principal's office for flushing cherry bombs down the locker room toilets?

Note to self: you're in the right, so stop being such a wuss.

That conviction only lasted until I strode through the front door to see Hunter Black sitting on the steps to the upstairs, obviously lying in wait.

He didn't say anything as I shut the front door. The tension built as I strode closer, chin lifted as though ready to do battle. At the last second I dove for my own door in a desperate bid for freedom.

"Not so fast."

Hunter moved like lightning. He had my key out of my hand and spun me to face him, pinning both my arms above my head. His expression was neutral, but those midnight eyes blazed with righteous indignation.

"You pick, Red. We doing this at your place or mine? Or right here in the hall for all I care, but I doubt you want your mother to see what comes next."

"I…" I had to swallow. My throat had dried up like a grape left in the sun. "I'm not sure what you mean."

"You promised me you'd come home."

"I did. I'm home now."

From the other side of the door I heard scratching followed by a soft whine. Hunter's gaze fell to the door.

"She's been in there alone all morning." I was a horrible, awful, desperate person to be playing the poor doggie card. I mentally promised Snickers I'd feed her pizza crust from the table every night if she'd just distract Hunter long enough to let me escape. She could even sleep in my bed as long as she stayed away from my shoes.

"Your place then." Hunter made the call and inserted the key into the lock.

Snickers barked, at me, not Hunter, then trotted towards my bedroom and scratched at the door. Hunter propelled me forward by the arm, following in the dog's wake.

"Hey," I struggled to break free of his hold. "Can you at least tell me what I did that was so horrible that I deserve the perp walk?"

Hunter didn't pause at my bedroom door, just let himself in as though he had every right. The room looked as though a tornado had touched down, with clothes shoes, CDs, and other personal flotsam strewn every which way. It was apparent that my mother's tidying hadn't extended to my space.

After releasing my arm, Hunter made for the French door that led to the back yard, opened it, and let Snickers out before turning to face me. "Do the words interfering with a police investigation mean anything to you?"

"I didn't—" I began, but he held up a hand.

"How about obstruction of justice? Lying to a police officer."

"I didn't lie to you! I promised I would come home, and here I am."

His eyes narrowed. "Maybe not to me. But how about the uniform who responded to your attack last night?"

"I wasn't attacked." I frowned. "You have faulty information."

He moved in closer, a dangerous panther prepared to spring. "No? A man didn't try to carjack you and your mother in the Beacon Hill district last night?"

"Oh, that."

He crowded in closer, so I was forced to look up to see his face. "What were you doing there anyway, Red. Hmm? There are grocery stores a hell of a lot closer than Beacon Hill."

Cowering really wasn't my designer knockoff handbag of choice. I squared my shoulders and looked him in the eye. "If you must know, I was doing surveillance. And I wouldn't have to except that you arrested our client without investigating any of the other suspects."

His hands clenched into fists so tight his knuckles turned stark white. "So it's my fault some thug carjacked you?"

"I wasn't carjacked." I said, wondering if there was any way out of this without winding up in handcuffs. "I did something stupid and made up that story as a cover."

"Did you spritz yourself again?" he asked.

Lying was a temptation, but it didn't seem to help where Hunter was concerned. And whatever punishment he did concoct would probably just make it worse. "No, a guy spritzed me after I tried to run him down. Let the dog back in before she scratches up the glass."

Without taking his eyes off me, Hunter stepped back and opened the door. Snickers trotted in, and he shut it again in one tense motion.

"I'll tell you if you promise not to go ballistic on me."

"I promise," he said.

"That was fast. No caveat or addendums before you agree?"

"It's obvious you've been hanging out with a lawyer. No, and I'm a man of my word, so when I say I won't get angry with you, you can count on it."

"You're already angry with me. I can tell because there's this vein in your forehead, kind of like a Klingon vein. You know, Klingons from *Star Trek*? Well it's standing out all angry and—"

"Mackenzie." That was all he said. My name sans any real emotion attached to it. One word, three syllables. It was enough to cease my babble mid-stream.

"Tell me," he prompted, "everything."

So I did, not because he insisted, or because he was a cop, but because I needed to tell someone the whole entire story. My daughter was my best friend, but it wasn't fair to burden a sixteen-year-old with the grim reality of our financial circumstances, plus I didn't want to worry her.

But Hunter was already worried, and what was more, he wouldn't relent. I had zero doubt that if I stopped speaking he'd come up with some very creative ways to make me talk.

"Dr. Granger is innocent, of murder at least," I finished. "I'm sure of it. Why would she hire a PI to tail her husband if she'd already hired someone else to bump him off?"

"So a witness could truthfully claim she wasn't there." Hunter sat down on my unmade bed. "She still could have hired someone."

"You're so stubborn." There was a lacy purple bra about six inches from his butt. No way to move it without drawing attention to it.

"I'm stubborn?" He raised one dark eyebrow. "How do you figure?"

"Because you won't even entertain the possibility that someone else could have killed Paul. From what I saw last night, Robert Fox has a vicious temper and serious rage issues. And the victim ruined the guy's marriage. Plus the staff at the doctor's office called Paul the leg-humper."

"That's unique." Hunter looked like he was thinking about smiling.

"And it indicates that besides his gorgeous and frosty wife and wealthy mistress, he'd chase anything in a skirt. That's the sort of guy that'll piss people off, women and the men they're involved with. Would you like it if some sex fiend was macking on your girl?"

I didn't know what possessed me to ask this last part. Stupid, broken brain-to-mouth filter.

Hunter's gaze intensified, his seamless shift from cop mode to potential lover almost unsettling. "No."

Message received. My hands clenched in the comforter, my heart thudding against my rib cage like it wanted to leap out and run screaming down the street. Oh, I was playing with fire with him. I knew it, but I couldn't seem to stop.

Hunter broke eye contact first. "But I also wouldn't off a man due to petty jealousy. Murder requires a strong motive or psychotic personality. You're sure it was the same guy, the one you were tailing and the one who spritzed you?"

"Since I didn't get a good look at him either time, no. But it was the same Escalade."

"Why are you so sure?"

"There's a dent in the front quarter panel." I pulled out my phone and opened my gallery. "See here? I noticed it because it looks like he hit some sort of small animal. If it was a deer or another vehicle it would have been bigger."

Hunter frowned so I enlarged the photo so he could get a closer look. "How did you pick up on this?"

"I used to work at a body shop," I told him, "when Mac was a few months old. I liked cars, and the guy who ran the place had a soft spot for me. He gave us room and board above the garage, and I did the paperwork for him. He had a heart attack about a year after, and his family decided to sell the shop, but I did pick up a few things."

"You were just a kid." Hunter searched my face. "Where was your family?"

I rose, unable to hold that penetrating gaze a moment longer. "Look, the day is zipping by, and I have a few more doctors' offices to visit, so are we done here?"

Out of the corner of my eye I saw him stand and move toward me. "One of these days you're going to trust me with your secrets."

"We just met." It was a token protest, but I was desperate to achieve a little distance. "Besides, it's not like you're opening up to me."

"I let you into my apartment, didn't I?"

"It's not like it's oozing with personality."

"I'm sure you learned something interesting. You were certainly in there long enough."

I blushed, but didn't answer.

He tipped my chin up with his forefinger. "What can I say to convince you to give up private investigation?"

I thought about Mac, proud of my cool new job. I thought about Len, sitting by himself in his law office. And I thought about Uncle Al and his unpublished manuscript. The man had loved the business, and I had begun to love it too. "There's nothing. I want this more than I've wanted anything since my daughter was born. It feels...right. I don't want to keep crossing swords with you over this. What can I say that will help you accept that I'm doing what I want to do?"

Hunter tilted his head, his dark, unbound hair falling over one shoulder. "I don't know. Promise me you'll be careful and that you'll call me if you get in over your head."

"Only if *you* promise not to get mad about every move I make."

"Not every move. I've got to get back to work." He headed toward the door, the French door that led to the back courtyard. He opened it and then turned. "Oh, and Red?"

"Yeah?"

"Nice bra."

It was only after he left that I realized I hadn't asked how he'd found me in the parking garage that morning.

CHAPTER TWELVE

The trick to doing something sneaky is to look like you have every right to do what you have no right doing.
From the *Working Man's Guide to Sleuthing for a Living* by Albert Taylor, PI

"Nona invited us upstairs for dinner and a movie," Mac said when I dragged my weary carcass back through the door at quarter to six. "Wow, Mom you look awful."

"Thanks, kid." I ruffled her auburn hair and dodged a swat. "Is your grandmother going to be there? I have had my fill of passive-aggressive for the day."

"I don't know. Did you find out anything new?"

I'd been to what felt like every men's health clinic in the greater Boston area. "Only that you should have your prostate checked on a regular basis. Good thing we don't have one. The process is downright unpleasant."

"Well, women have the whole mammogram boob smush," Mac pointed out. She set her laptop aside and patted the sofa until Snickers jumped up next to her and rested her furry little chin in my daughter's lap.

I flopped down in the matching armchair. "I'm starting to realize the entire medical process is highly undignified. Good thing I don't have much dignity. Did Nona want us to bring anything?"

"She didn't say." Mac stroked the dog's head, and Snickers let out a contented sigh.

I watched my daughter for a minute. "Is something wrong, hon?"

"We have this biology assignment—" she began.

"And you want Todd of the rippling abs to come over," I guessed. "Don't worry, Mommy will pack up all her S&M gear."

Mac rolled her eyes. "No, it's not about Todd or his abs. Or your kinky sex life, which I would prefer to remain in the dark about."

"I was joking," I said, though without too much conviction. Sure, it had been a joke, but then the image of Hunter and his handcuffs had popped into my brain, giving the idea a whole new dimension. "So what's the assignment?"

"It's genetics. We're supposed to bring in photos of our biological families, as far back as we can, so we can dissect traits and figure out which we've inherited. I have stuff about you, and Grams and the Captain and Gram's family, but that's only one side." She peeked those baby blues up at me.

Baby blues she didn't get from me, since my eyes were green. Damn.

"Is there any way…I really just need pictures." Mac spoke hesitantly, so very *un*-Mac like.

Damn, damn, damn. "When do you need it by?"

"Monday." Mac looked relieved. Had she been expecting me to say no?

"I can't guarantee anything. Mom might have tossed out all my old stuff. And it'll probably just be him. I doubt I had any pictures of his family."

"Did you ever meet them?" Mac leaned forward, dislodging a put-out puggle. "Because maybe if you describe things about them, I can write those down and do the project that way."

She sounded so hopeful, and I could have cheerfully strangled whatever biology teacher had come up with the project. It was just the excuse Mac needed to go digging in dirt better left unturned.

"I'm starved. Let's head up to Nona's." Though it took more effort than I thought I could muster, I managed to heave myself up out of the chair.

"Okay, let me just go get my phone. It's charging in my room." Mac bounded up.

"And let the dog out," I called after her.

She trotted off, full of youthful exuberance. It was all I could do not to collapse onto the floor. Why did the biology project have to come up now? Didn't I have enough crap to juggle?

I'd always known I'd have to give Mac information about her dad. For health reasons if nothing else, she'd need medical history stuff. But I'd wanted a little longer when she was just mine, and that I didn't have to share her with a father who didn't even know she existed, even a memory.

This project didn't seem fair on a bunch of levels. What about children who were adopted? That thought, like so many others, brought Hunter to mind. Would he be at Nona's? I was sure the Yenta had tried. I wanted to ask about his family, maybe even ask his advice about how to handle the Mac situation.

That thought was accompanied by the scent of burning break pads and the sound of tires screeching to a stop. Since when did I ask anyone's advice about how to deal with my daughter? Hunter and I barely knew each other, so why was I leaning on him more and more?

Maybe because he offered the freedom of unburdening myself, a freedom I hadn't known in my entire adult life. Who was I supposed to talk to about worries I kept from Mac, my mother? The Captain?

Not likely.

"Ready?" Mac asked.

She'd pulled on a black V-neck sweater and wore the gold heart shaped locket my mother had given her for her sixteenth birthday. I'd been smug when I'd seen the gift, knowing that Mac would much prefer the new cell phone I'd gotten over such a girly trinket.

"Yes. You look beautiful."

"Get real," she said, though without venom.

We headed up the stairs, and Mac knocked on Nona's door. There was music coming from inside, Sinatra if I didn't miss my guess, and something that smelled like spaghetti sauce.

Nona opened the door. "Hello there, dollies. I hope you're hungry. I made manicotti. My first husband was an Italian stallion, and he taught me how to make fresh pasta. Ruined me for any other pasta. And any other man, if you catch my drift." Nona wiggled her spidery eyebrows.

"Ew," Mac said. "I think I'm too young for this conversation."

"Sounds like a lot of work." I set my bag by the door. "The pasta, not the husband."

"Oh, they both were. What can I get you ladies to drink?"

"I'm easy." I said and then cut a glare at Mac. She made a choking noise but refrained from commenting. "Whatever you have is fine."

"I'll help." Mac followed Nona into the kitchen. It wasn't big enough for the three of us, so I wandered into the living room.

Mac came back and handed me a plastic tumbler filled with what looked and smelled like iced tea. The apartment smelled like herbs and sauce. My stomach rumbled loudly.

"Didn't you eat?" Mac, always the mother hen of our dynamic duo, frowned.

"Well, I ate half a sandwich." Snickers had snagged the other half out of my bag while I was dealing with Hunter.

"Since when do you eat half of anything? You're not *dieting* are you?" Mac looked horrified by the prospect.

"Chocolate forbid. Going on a diet would be too much like admitting Grandma's right and that I need to slim down and find myself a man. Besides, my pants fit, so I don't see the point."

Mac shook her head, her expression torn between vague dismay and awe. "Mackenzie Taylor, the only woman over thirty who still eats carbs."

Setting the tea on Nona's glass-top table, I made a show of putting my hands on my ample, carb loaded hips. "And I look good doing it, too."

"Attagirl." Nona shuffled in. "You know in my day people didn't get all worked up about what sorts of food they were eating. They were just grateful to have food. Now my second husband, he was an investment banker, and oy vey, what a glutton. If he was awake, he was putting something in his mouth. Most of it wasn't kosher, either."

I'd been taking a sip from my glass, and ice tea spurted out my nose. I coughed a few times.

"Are you all right, doll?" Nona asked. "Want some water?"

I nodded, still sputtering. Mac patted me helpfully on the back, her whole body shaking with silent laughter.

"Criminy," I wheezed. "She keeps on like that, and I'm sure to rupture something. Do you think she realizes how it sounds?"

"Not everyone's mind camps out in the gutter," Mac observed.

"More's the pity." I intercepted Nona and took the water from her just as the doorbell rang.

"Are you expecting someone else?" I asked even as I thought, *please don't be Hunter, please, please, oh pretty please do not be Hunter.*

"That will be Agnes." Nona said.

"Damn," I hissed low so only Mac could hear me. "Well, that'll teach me to be careful what I wish for."

Always the skeptic, my daughter raised an eyebrow. "Will it? Will it really?"

"Probably not," I admitted just as my mother entered Nona's apartment carrying a giant bowl.

"Sorry I'm late. I got caught up unpacking." My mother kissed Nona on the cheek like they were lifelong friends instead of brand spanking new neighbors.

The thought of neighbors and spanking in the same sentence made me cringe.

Mac frowned up at me. "You're all twitchy tonight. What's your damage?"

"I love it when you use my nineties catch phrases." I said.

"Mom, I'm serious. Is something going on that I should know about?"

Maybe, but this was neither the time, nor the place. "I'll talk to you when we get home."

"Girls, there you are." My mother set her bowl, which sadly contained just salad greens, on the table, then turned to us.

"I was just telling Nona that after dinner you should all come see the apartment now that I'm all moved in."

I flinched again, and Mac shot me a dirty look before replying, "Sure Grams. We'd love too."

My mother smiled at her and then frowned up at me. "Your hair is a mess, Mackenzie. Don't you own a comb?"

"Yes, I do. It's the using it part I can't get my head around. Someone should make a YouTube video to demonstrate."

Agnes rolled her eyes. "Always with the jokes. Mac, why don't you see if you can give Nona a hand? I'd like to speak to your mother a moment."

I gripped my daughter's arm. "If I'm not back in ten minutes, wait longer."

She shook her head, but when she moved toward the kitchen, her grin was in place. Mission accomplished.

Agnes pulled me over to the front of the living room. "Did she tell you about her project?"

"Yes."

"Well, what are we going to do about it?"

I stared down at her. "Mom, we aren't going to do anything. *I* will track down a copy of my high school year book and give her the descriptions she needs to complete the project."

"But you still haven't told her about her father?"

"No, it hasn't come up before." That was only partly true. Mac had brought it up a time or two, more in the last few months, but there'd never been a pressing need before.

"This is precisely why I've been telling you to find a husband. A girl needs a father, and if you had a suitable substitute in place this wouldn't be an issue."

"Mom, it's a genetics project. A stepfather wouldn't be any help with that. And she would still have questions about her birth father. All kids do." I didn't even address the idiocy of her suggesting I chain myself to some man for life to give Mac an edge up on her homework.

Another shiver went through me. *No, self, chains are not sexy, so just stop thinking about Hunter for two freaking seconds.*

"Dinner's on the table, dollies." Nona called.

"Praise java," I muttered and took my seat. The meal, as delicious as it was, couldn't end fast enough.

* * *

"Well, what do you think?" Agnes asked, standing in the middle of her new apartment, arms held out grandly to make sure we were taking it all in.

"It's pretty, Grams," Mac said in a faint voice.

"Very colorful," Nona added. "And trendy."

"Mackenzie?" my mother prompted.

"Still taking it all in," I murmured.

The same way you would a particularly brutal car accident. Modern art hung on the white walls, large splashy canvases that looked more like crime scene photos than paintings. The new piano stood in the middle of the room, gleaming under the clip on gooseneck lamps Agnes had somehow managed to fasten to the ceiling to create hideously high-intensity spotlights. A large gilt mirror stood in the corner by the glass-topped dining room table so that anyone who sat there and ate would be forced to look at themselves while doing so.

Only parts of the space had that über-chic look. The rest was tattered and worn, threadbare. And obviously stolen.

"Is that my chair?" I asked, pointing at a chair that was an exact match for the one in our apartment downstairs. "And the rugs?"

"You weren't using them. And anyway, I'd like to get something a little more modern in here. White fur, maybe."

I shivered in revulsion. Not that I could say anything about her stealing furniture. Technically, anything that had been Uncle Al's was half hers to do with any way she liked. I just wished she'd do it somewhere else.

"We should all get together and play cards," my mother exclaimed. "Or start a book club."

"I'm already in a book club." Nona says. "We like those dirty books with all the spankings. Oh, is that my phone? I've been waiting to hear from my daughter." She headed out the door towards her own apartment.

"Sweet java, have mercy," I mumbled.

"So how about it?" Agnes looked hopeful.

"We need to be going," I spoke loudly, so she couldn't misunderstand me. Well, any more than usual. "It's getting late."

Agnes glanced to a hideous chrome clock over her pilfered boxed TV. "It's only eight o'clock."

"And I have work." Despite my exhaustion, it felt really good to say that.

"You're not going out again tonight, are you?"

"I wasn't planning on it."

"Oh." Maybe it was my imagination, but Agnes seemed almost disappointed that there wouldn't be another round of late night shenanigans. "Well, I'll pop by in the morning."

"Pop by?" I repeated.

"Maybe you can come down for a movie tomorrow," Mac offered. "You and Nona. It's our turn to host, right, Mom?"

"Er, um…" I said, unwilling to commit.

"Oh that sounds terrific. What can I bring?" My mother pounced on that idea like it was a poor, helpless mouse.

"Whatever. We usually have popcorn and candy, things like that, like a real movie experience without concession stand prices. See you."

I waited until the door to our own apartment was completely secured before rounding on my offspring. "What the hell was that?"

"What?" Mac had moved back into the living room and was booting up her laptop.

"You just invited Nona and my mother to movie night. That's our special night."

"Special? What's so special, the part where you slub around in pants with elastic waistbands or the food orgy that makes them necessary?"

"Come," I said with a lilt in my voice. "Let me sing you the song of my bloated people."

"Mom," Mac said. "She's lonely. They both are. What can it hurt?"

I envisioned our normal carb and sugar fest done Agnes Taylor Style. The popcorn would be smart, the candy sugar free, the movie dialogue filled with interruptions to the tune of

"What's he doing now? Why's she going in there? I can't believe they're doing that on film."

"Mac, come on. Things have been totally nuts since we moved in here. I've been dosed with pepper spray twice, and now my mother lives upstairs and can 'pop by' whenever she wants." I made air quotes around the horrific phrase.

Mac rose and put both hands on my shoulders. "Mom, relax. I know you have this insane fear of commitment, but it's one night, not every weekend for the rest of our lives."

"It's the gateway night," I complained. "You think you're only in it for one night then bam, it becomes a routine. You heard her. If we don't watch our step, we'll be signed up for bridge and a book club. Do you think she's going through menopause? And where the hell is The Captain? Why isn't he pounding on her door, demanding she come home and make Salisbury steak or chicken pot pies?"

"Have you called him?"

"I've been a little busy, what with the murder investigation and all."

Mac reached into my shoulder bag and plucked my cell free. "No time like the present."

"No wait!" I lunged, though it was too late.

My daughter had reflexes like a cheetah, and the phone was already ringing when she handed it to me.

"Hello?" a gruff male voice answered.

"Um, hi, Dad. It's, um, me."

"Mackenzie," he said as though there was anyone else on the planet who called him Dad. Although most of the time I referred to him as The Captain, since he was more comfortable in that role than he was being a father.

"How are you?" I asked, testing the waters.

"Fine."

"And Mom?" I asked.

"Fine."

I held the phone away from my face so I could gape at it. He wasn't going to tell me? His own daughter?

If that was how he wanted to play it. "May I speak with her, please?"

There was a great deal of throat clearing and then he said, "She's not here at the moment."

"Where is she?"

"I'm not exactly sure." My father's gruff voice didn't sound uncertain, more like irritated at the inconvenience.

As usual, my temper got the best of me. "Well I am. She's here."

"With you?" He sounded incredulous.

"No, Dad. She's upstairs in one of the apartments in Uncle Al's villa. She bought a piano and some hideous art, and she's acting like whatever is going on between the two of you is permanent."

Silence.

"Dad? What happened?"

"It's none of your concern," he said.

"None of my concern?" I realized that at some point in the conversation I'd begun to pace the length of the room but couldn't seem to stop. "Did you not hear the part about Mom living right upstairs from us? And in what universe is my parents being separated none of my concern?"

"We're not separated," he snapped. "We're getting a divorce."

CHAPTER THIRTEEN

Burden of Proof—the duty to prove or disprove a fact or idea. From the *Working Man's Guide to Sleuthing for a Living* by Albert Taylor, PI

Another crappy night of sleep and I was up and out of the house early the next morning. Armed with a giant coffee and fortitude, I drove out past Cambridge to my grandmother's old farmhouse situated on the outskirts of Boston.

My father and Uncle Al had grown up in the farmhouse, and I'd stayed with Nan there most summers as well as my sophomore year of high school. The Captain had been stationed in Italy, and he and my mother had offered me the choice between staying with Nan or coming with them. In the end, even time in Europe couldn't compete with the idea of being free from my parents for an entire year. It was an option they'd both bitterly regretted.

I pulled Helga up into the shale drive and parked under the giant red maple that was a sight to behold in October. The swing where I'd spent many a summer day was long gone, but the memory of it still made me smile. Nan had been a terrific lady, fun and feisty, a real true blue Yankee to her core. I'd spent hours with her in her garden, weeding, plucking potatoes, cucumbers, lettuce, onions, and carrots from the earth, which she'd then turn into a delicious meal in a process that was nothing less than magic. Being back in her space, I could almost hear her voice.

"It's all about the love, Mackenzie. You put love into everything you do, or you shouldn't bother doing anything at all."

"That's not what my mom says," I'd replied as I licked mashed potato off a beater.

"Stuff and nonsense. Your mother wouldn't know passion if it bit her on the rump."

She'd always referred to Agnes as that pretentious, social-climbing tartlet, a phrase that was as descriptive of her character as it was of my mother's. I wondered if she'd be pleased that my mother wasn't living in her home any longer, but thought that she would be more upset that her only surviving son's marriage of thirty-three years had failed.

Feeling Nan's spirit with me for the two unpleasant tasks I'd come here to handle, I lifted my chin, squared my shoulders and made my way up the steps to the front door.

The Captain pulled it open before I could knock. "I thought I heard a car."

"You did." I offered a halfhearted smile. If I were a guy, we could do the whole manly handshake thing, but the damn double standard that ruled my father's world wouldn't go for that, so we stood there in uncomfortable silence.

"Would you care for a cup of coffee?" he asked.

If it had been anybody else, I would have cracked a joke about my coffee addiction being worse than crack or heroin and called him an enabler. Instead I just nodded and stepped past him into the house.

My father led the way down the dark pokey hallway that spread out into Nan's bright, sun-filled kitchen. The cabinets were white, and each had a different piece of fruit stenciled by the knob that Nan had painted herself. My father went to the pear one and pulled down two coffee cups.

"Milk and sugar?" he asked politely.

"Yes, thank you." I slid my coat off and draped it over the back of my chair by the farm table.

He fixed the mugs and then handed one to me, keeping the other for himself. I was fairly certain that my caffeine addiction came from him.

"So, things going well?" He didn't look at me, his sharp blue gaze fixed on his coffee. My father was a tall man with big, broad shoulders and a nose that looked like a piece of Play-Doh someone had stuck on as an afterthought. Uncle Al's had been the same way. The two men had looked like twins, even though there had been six years between them. Thankfully my nose and Mac's came from Agnes's side.

"Yes, Mac has a genetics project for school."

He sipped his coffee and nodded. "So you said on the phone."

"And I wanted to see you. See how you're holding up."

"Mackenzie, I was in charge of a Nimitz-class aircraft carrier with a crew of five thousand. My life's not about to fall apart because my marriage is."

"I know that," I said. "But I'm asking more about the emotional side."

"I don't deal well with emotions. You know that."

I did, all too well. "Dad, look. Mom's putting on a brave face, but I can tell she's missing you." I could tell nothing of the sort, but I wanted to butter him up. "Do you think maybe if you two talked you could—"

He slid his chair back abruptly. "No, Mackenzie. Stay out of it."

I stared up at him, utterly stunned.

"You needed some pictures, you said?" Without waiting for me to respond, he made his way toward the stairs. I left my practically untouched coffee on the table and followed, my head spinning.

The room that had always been mine was exactly how I remembered it. After Nana died and my father retired, Mom had talked of turning it into a yoga studio, but never got around to it. Typical Agnes, talked a good game but lacked the follow-through to do much other than live vicariously through her husband and daughter.

Which made their separation doubly weird. What had The Captain done that she actually left him?

I couldn't quite manage to voice the thoughts that kept tumbling around in my head. *Did you cheat on Mom? Did* she *cheat on* you*?* For one thing, I didn't want to know that much about their sex lives, and for another I doubted either of them would answer. I'd never heard my father crack a lewd joke or even laugh at one. If someone else did, he usually stood around looking gruff and uncomfortable, which, when I thought about it, was pretty much his MO.

Another reason he was my polar opposite.

CDs I'd forgotten all about stood in a little cube container on the white nightstand. Cheap bead necklaces hung from a white sculpted hand that Nan had made in some pottery class, with my sterling toe ring resting in the palm. The lamp had been draped with a purple-and-white polka-dot scarf, and funky bucket hats hanging off the frame of a standing oval mirror attested to the horrific perm my best friend had given me halfway through the school year.

If only that had been my worst decision. Funny, I couldn't even remember the aspiring stylist's name now. Everything that had happened after had erased her from my memory.

My father, probably sick of watching my mental stroll down memory lane, moved past the twin bed and white duvet to the closet door. He crouched down and pulled out a box while I stared in horror at the clothes. Tattered jeans and oh, java, save me from the Great Wall of Flannel that had been my tribute to all things hipster. Thankfully, my fashion sense had bounced back from such a low point.

"In here," he said, handing me the box.

After all the reminders of the insecure teen I'd once been, the last thing I wanted to do was go pawing through old photos and yearbooks in front of The Captain. But it seemed ungracious to just mutter a thanks and bolt. "You should come over for dinner and see the place now that we're settled." *Thanks to Mom*, but I left that part out.

He shifted, looking as ill at ease as I'd ever seen him. "Well, I don't think—"

I scrambled to think of a decent enticement. "Mac will be there. You haven't seen her since the summer, and she can grill you for questions about Nan for her project."

I could see him hedging, and inspiration struck. "Oh, and my new boss will be coming over. He's a lawyer, but a real decent guy despite that."

He blinked, clearly surprised. "You got another job? Working in a law office?"

"Come over, and I'll tell you all about it." I wouldn't, not really. The Captain would likely burst a blood vessel when he found out his only daughter was an aspiring private investigator, just like his "deadbeat brother."

"All right," he said, surprising us both. "What time?"

"Seven thirty?" I asked, figuring that if the meal didn't go well, at least everyone would have the excuse of school or work the next day to make a hasty exit.

"Sounds good," The Captain said and then picked up the box for me and headed down the stairs.

"Where'd the car come from?" he asked as we exited the house, heading for Helga.

"Oh, she was part of the inheritance."

"Albert must have been doing well for himself." My father set the box on the passenger's seat and then stepped back.

"I got the feeling he loved what he did." I said.

The Captain frowned. "What makes you say that?"

"Nothing. Just a hunch."

"Albert was no better than a Peeping Tom, following cheating spouses and stirring up trouble." He squared his shoulders with military precision.

"He helped people, Dad. Found lost kids and reunited them with their families. You should be proud of him." I never understood the animosity between my father and his only sibling. Sure they were different, but blood was blood. "Nan was proud."

"Your grandmother had no idea what he did. It was better that way." The Captain didn't back down, instead choosing to retrench. "I'll see you tomorrow. Give my best to Mac."

Dismissed, I slunk around the side of the car, settled in behind the steering wheel, and turned the engine over. Just to unnerve me, my father watched me back out of the driveway. He looked lonely, standing there by himself. No men to order around, no wife to nudge him back inside for a hot cup of coffee. My father wasn't the sort of man who did well on his own.

Helga, sweet little ride that she was, came equipped with Bluetooth, and I ordered her to dial Mac. She answered on the first ring with a, "Ground control here. That you, Major Tom?"

Sometimes I loved that kid so much it hurt.
"Affirmative. One mission down, one to go. We have a couple of parents to trap."

* * *

I swung by Len's office on my way back into Boston for the promised paperwork tutorial and to invite him to dinner. Bad enough I was planning to spring my parents on one another, but that was a fib of omission. If Len wasn't actually in attendance, that would have been a flat-out lie.

Luckily, Len was eager for the invite. "Oh, what should I bring?"

"Um…" It was slowly dawning on me as I was inviting all these people over for dinner they were under the misguided notion that I'd be preparing some sort of meal. "Whatever you want, Len."

"How about wine. I have a right nice wine cellar here. Red or white?"

Depending on how the evening went, we might need both. "Surprise me."

Len hummed as he got down to brass tacks and pulled up a complicated-looking spreadsheet. "Okay, so when it comes to your expenses, anything that falls under the cost of doing business qualifies. Gas, food you buy while out on a case, even phone and internet service, you want to bill for."

"How about my cell phone?" I asked, surprised that the PI gig would be so lucrative.

"Absolutely, as long as you're using it for purposes pertaining to the case. I find that the more meticulous your record keeping, the less likely a client will be to challenge. If you have car trouble, charge the cost of repairs not covered by warranty. If you travel for a case, charge the cost of the room, plus any taxes and fees. Best to steer clear of any adult movies if you plan to present the invoice to the client though." He winked.

"No *Debbie Does Des Moines*. Got it." I winked back.

"Do your best to keep it within reason. Most clients won't put up a fuss, but occasionally it'll happen."

"What about background checks?" I asked, recalling the one I'd shelled out fifty bucks to obtain on Paul Granger.

"Absolutely. Though I hope you aren't using one of those hokey internet searches," Len cautioned. "You can do it yourself with more accuracy for a lot less. Plus you still have to verify that the information you found is legitimate as well as current."

"So how do I go about that, then?" I asked, feeling a little overwhelmed.

"A lot depends on what the client is looking for. Some things, like criminal or civil charges, are often a matter of public record. You can check federal or state sources for financial purposes like tax liens, judgments, and bankruptcies as well as notices of default and assets people try to hide."

"Wow." I'd decided about halfway through that I should write down what he was saying.

"Of course these days you want to check with social media as well. I had a case last year where a woman was scamming a charity even though she had photos of a massive in-ground pool and hot tub and admitting to having a pool service on Facebook. That judgment is still pending, but you can bet your boots the people running the charity look a little closer now than they did before at their applicants."

I wrinkled my nose. "That's heinous and disgusting."

"People do worse. The point is that the more information you have about your subject, the better, but all you really need is a few pertinent details."

"What about adoption cases?" I asked.

"Depends on the case. In Massachusetts, any records before April of 1974 are open and can be obtained with a few forms. Why do you ask?"

"No particular reason." Hunter was in his thirties like me, so that wouldn't be any help. "I better go. I want to try to corner someone at Right Touch Pharmaceuticals if I can. The weekend staff might not be as cagey. And I think maybe I should look into any history of violence with Robert Fox."

Len pointed at me. "You're one smart cookie, Mackenzie. Come back to my office, and I'll front you money for your first few weeks' expenses."

Other than a tank of gas for Helga and a crumpled convenience store receipt with snack cake filling smeared on it, the only other expense I had so far was the internet search. But I felt kind of silly for using it now that Len had explained more of the ins and outs of PI work.

Len handed me two fifties.

"That's way too much," I protested. The man was an unbelievable soft touch.

"You'll earn it quickly," he said.

Though I was too proud to take money from my mother, I agreed with Len. No one would work harder for that hundred dollars than I would. "Thanks for the tutorial. I feel more confident going forward."

"We all need to start somewhere. I've worked with enough bad PIs to know you're going to make a terrific one."

His confidence was humbling. "And on that note, I better get to it."

My phone rang right as I pulled out into Saturday traffic. "Hello?"

"Mom." It was Mac, and she sounded out of breath. "We found him."

"Found who? What are you talking about, babe?"

"The guy in the Escalade. We have a photo." The pitch of her voice was practically giddy.

"Who's 'we'? And why are you so sure it's the same guy?"

"I called Pete, and he came over to help me. We've been going through the traffic cameras surrounding the warehouse all morning, but finally got a clear shot of his face and his license plate. Do you want me to text you the photos?"

"Yes, absolutely. I pulled over into a laundromat parking lot. "You guys aren't going to get in trouble for this, are you?"
"No, we covered our tracks. Texting the photo now."

"I have to hang up. I don't think I can talk and read a text at the same time."

Mac said good-bye, and I waited for the damn text. As soon as I verified it was the same guy, I'd pass the photo to Hunter and let him go and question the man. Of course since I hadn't seen his face there was no way to be one hundred percent sure I even had the right man. Maybe I'd use some of my newfound detective skills to track the creep down, just to make sure.

The first image pinged through with the Massachusetts license plate. I jotted it down in my little notebook while waiting for the second image to load.

It finally did, and I stared at it, unable to blink, or draw breath. No, it couldn't be.

The box of stuff I'd picked up at The Captain's was still secured in the passenger's seat. Ripping the lid off, I dug through photos of friends long forgotten until my fingers brushed the spine of my yearbook.

My hand shook as I pulled it free and opened it to the sophomore class. A small white rectangle slipped out onto my lap and I picked it up and turned it over. It was one of those photo booth prints that had been popular back before everyone had camera phones. A series of four images with the same two laughing faces.

I ignored mine and stared at the other. Young, tanned, blond guy, with all-American good looks and mischievous blue eyes. Captain of the sailing club, the debate team, and the swim club—the high school heartthrob. Something in my chest squeezed tight.

My gaze shifted back to the photo Mac had obtained. Same strong jaw, though now covered with stubble. Same sharp nose and full lips. He wasn't smiling in the highly pixelated image, but I recognized him all the same.

The man who drove the Escalade was Mac's father.

CHAPTER FOURTEEN

"The first rule of lying—stick as close to the truth as possible. The second rule—don't get caught."
From the *Working Man's Guide to Sleuthing for a Living* by Albert Taylor, PI

My phone was ringing again. Ignoring my daughter's image flashing on the screen, I opened up Google and typed in a name I'd done my best to forget over the last sixteen years. Brett Archer.

Several thousand hits came up. The first several talked about some former track and field star, so I knew even without looking at the photos I had the wrong guy.

"I only run when I'm being chased by something," Brett had said to me and a bunch of our friends one day at our lunch table. "A grizzly, a mountain lion, maybe a mob boss."

"You plan on delving into organized crime, do you?" I'd teased him.

"I'm keeping my options open," he'd muttered and kissed me.

Blinking, I pulled my attention back to the present. Ignoring all the websites that didn't end in *.gov*, I hunted for any mention of Brett in public record. I found his driver's license, complete with a photo of the older Brett, stubble and all. The RMV image also offered an address that I scribbled down. No criminal charges but an eight year old record of marriage to a woman whose name didn't ring a bell. Two years after that, a petition for divorce had been filed. I couldn't find a record of employment, and he seemed to be the last holdout on social media because there was no way to friend or follow him that I could see.

Mac could have done more, but there was no way I was going to ask her.

I shifted my focus to maps and typed in the address listed on his license. It was down near the harbor in Southie.

I drummed my thumbs against the steering wheel as I debated what to do next. The Brett Archer I'd known wasn't a killer, and there was nothing in any of the surface intel I'd dug up to indicate he had a motive to off Paul Granger. The way I saw it I had three options: call Hunter and tell him what I'd found, investigate Brett myself, or sneak home and eat a pint of ice cream until I came up with a way to tell Mac that her father was part of my ongoing investigation.

Both plans A and C had their high points, but my jeans were feeling a wee bit snug, and I didn't really want to talk to anyone about what I'd discovered. Decided, I shifted into drive and merged with traffic.

The drive didn't take too long, and soon I was parked across the street from Brett's house. It was a shingle-style duplex, finished in dark gray naturally weathered shingles. Very quintessential New England. Too bad I wasn't here for the architecture.

The address I'd found listed Brett as side A. There was no garage and no sign of an Escalade anywhere on the street. A big blue Cadillac DeVille was parked in the driveway by side B, though.

Talk to people. The same advice Uncle Al listed in his book time and again. A good PI knocked on doors and asked questions. If I wanted to know about Brett, I should speak to his neighbors and hope they were in a chatty mood.

The concrete steps leading up to the small stoop on side B were crumbling a bit, and the railing looked like a tetanus hazard. Careful to choose my footfalls, I slowly made my way up the walk. When I looked up again, an older lady with white hair wearing a garish floral dressing gown was standing just inside the storm door, watching my slow progress.

"Whatever you're selling, I don't want any," she informed me in a thick Southie accent marred with two packs of unfiltereds a day.

I hopped over the last step and offered her my most winning smile. "Actually I'm here about your neighbor. We went to high school together, and I was wondering if I could ask you a few questions."

She didn't invite me in, but didn't slam the door in my face, either. "Can't say I know him very well. He's only been here for a few months. He's single if that's what you want to know."

I hadn't realized I did want to know until she'd said as much. "Does he have any kids?" More importantly did Mac have any half brothers or sisters running around?

"Not that I've seen." She shook her head, and I let out the breath I hadn't realized I'd been holding.

"Do you know where he works?"

"He doesn't, so far as I can tell. At least nothing legitimate. Doesn't keep a regular schedule at all. Though he's got people from all over tromping in and out of here at all hours of the day and night. They don't stick around long at least, and thankfully they aren't loud. These walls are paper-thin. My best guess is he deals drugs. If you ask me, you're better off letting the past lie."

"Thanks," I said and turned to go, just as an Escalade pulled up to the curb behind Helga.

I swore long and loud. For the second time that week I was tempted to duck down and hide from a man, but there was nowhere to hide.

I turned back to his neighbor. "May I use your restroom?"

She scowled. "That's your guy now. You change your mind about talking to him?"

"Yes, and I don't want him to know I was here either. So is it all right if I come in until he goes into his place?"

"You don't got a gun, do you?" she asked. "I'd hate to be robbed at gunpoint in my own home."

"Just pepper spray," I admitted.

"All right. You look harmless enough I suppose." She unlatched her door, and I practically ripped the thing off the hinges before diving inside for cover.

The storm door led to a small mudroom and into a kitchen at the back of the house.

"You want some tea?" my hostess, whose name I still didn't know, asked grudgingly.

"I'm fine, thanks." There was a small window to the left of the storm door, and I pulled it aside to get a clear view of the street. The Escalade's driver's side door was open, and I saw Brett emerge, his head down, a cell phone glued to his ear. The conversation ended, and he snapped the phone shut. He didn't look over at his neighbor's house. His gaze remained focused on the sidewalk.

I watched him for a minute, searching for signs of the carefree boy I'd loved. He'd filled out, especially in the shoulders, and he moved with the same confident stride I remembered. How could I not have recognized him?

And how could *he* not have recognized *me*?

Brett stalked up the stairs and into his own place. I closed my eyes, imagining him dropping his wallet and keys, maybe going through his mail. Maybe he was tying off his arm and looking for a vein. Or, maybe he was unlocking the woman he kept chained in the basement for a round of tickle the pickle.

I didn't want to think of Brett as a criminal, but I needed more information.

"Loo's first door on your right," my hostess gestured.

"I actually just didn't want him to see me." Dropping the curtain, I turned away from the window and asked, "Does he live alone?"

The sour neighbor was perched at her kitchen table, a cigarette hanging from her mouth. She didn't bother to remove it before answering. "Sure does. He had a girlfriend for a while with a great big dog. Pooped all over the yard and neither of them bothered to clean it up."

"But she's gone now?"

"Oh yeah, left before Labor Day."

So, Brett was in there alone, doing whatever it was he did that got him involved with murders. What sort of man had Mac's father become?

Speaking of the devil seed, my phone lit up yet again with her face. "I better answer this," I told Brett's sour neighbor, "before my daughter sends out a search party."

She didn't look impressed as she stubbed out her cigarette. "I've gotta poop. Lock the door behind you when you leave."

"Will do," I called faintly. She was a tough old bird, oversharing notwithstanding.

I slid the green phone icon over and held it to my ear. "Mac?"

"Oh my God, what happened to you?"

"My phone died," I fibbed. If Brett happened to be looking out his front window, he probably had the same view of his neighbor's stoop as I had of his. There had to be a back door around here somewhere. "I had to wait for it to recharge."

"Bull," Mac called me on the lie. "If your phone died, it would have gone straight to voice mail instead of ringing through. What's going on? Are you in danger? Should I call Detective Black?"

"No!" I paused halfway through the kitchen and scanned the area, looking for any alternate exit and finding none. "Mac, please. I'm fine, nothing to worry about, okay?"

"It's not okay." She had steel in her voice. "You tell me everything."

"No, I don't." No door, but the kitchen window was large and missing a screen. The place reeked like an ashtray. Placing the phone between my ear and shoulder, I used my hands to shove the window up. Cold air rushed in.

"Mom, you text me like seven trillion times a day. You ask me when you're thinking about buying a new nail polish."

"This is different." The ground sloped up toward the window so the drop was only a few feet. If I went out legs first, I was pretty sure I had enough upper body strength to dangle until I could successfully drop to the ground. Then it was just a matter of cutting between houses and heading back to Helga. "My job requires me to keep secrets sometimes. Other people's secrets. Now I'm fine, but I have to go. Love you."

I hung up and stowed the phone before crouching low and slinging one leg over the windowsill. After securing my grip, I ducked my head through and then followed with my remaining leg. The track cut into my palms as my full weight was suspended from them, the force of gravity yanking me down urgently. My palms started to sweat, and my grip grew precarious.

"That's it," I huffed, trying to straighten my legs so I landed on my feet. "No more snack cakes. For at least a month."

"Now that's just crazy talk," a male voice said from behind me.

Surprised, I yelped and tried to turn and see who it was, moving my palms to the right. My precarious hold had enough of my antics, though, and decided to give up the ghost. With a yell, I tumbled backward and hit the ground hard.

No, not the ground, but something equally unyielding.

Brett?" I panted, scrambling off of him. "Are you okay?"

He blinked and then turned his head to meet my gaze. "You always knew how to make a grand entrance. Or exit in this case."

"What are you doing here?" I asked before I thought it through.

He sat up, blond hair roguishly tussled, and quirked a brow. "In case it escaped your notice, we're in my back yard."

"Technically, it's your neighbor's back yard. And I hear you don't clean up after your dog."

He grinned. "It was my ex's dog, and therefore her crap to deal with. I see you've been chatting with Doris. She's a pip, isn't she?"

"Not the word I'd use." I could see why his girlfriend had left him—he hadn't matured at all since high school.

He gave me a slow once over. "You look great, Mackenzie. Haven't aged a day."

I snorted. "Must be all the preservatives in my diet. Better than Botox."

"Can I ask why you felt the need to climb out her window instead of using the perfectly acceptable door in front?

My jaw dropped. "You knew I was here all along, didn't you."

He picked up a tendril of my hair. "It's like a beacon on a sunny day. I knew it was you the second I pulled up."

"And the other night, when you dosed me with pepper spray? Did you know it was me then?"

Brett stood in one fluid motion and pulled me to my feet. "Sorry about that. I couldn't take the chance you'd recognize me and give my name to the cops. You do like chatting with them, and my client is paying me a lot of money to keep this investigation under wraps."

I let go of his hand. "Your client. Please tell me you're not a contract killer."

That goofy lopsided grin stole across his face. "Of course not. I'm a PI like you."

* * *

Brett, it turned out, wasn't a PI like me, mostly because he knew what the hell he was doing. "I knew you were tailing me the second you started." He opened the side door to his house and ushered me inside.

"Was it that obvious?"

"Don't feel bad. It takes practice to tail a car right. And it's defiantly easier to go unnoticed without driving a sixty-five-thousand-dollar vehicle."

"I should have thought of that." I grimaced and checked the scrape on my left elbow that had impacted the ground.

"Let me see that." He pulled me toward the window and bent my elbow until he could examine the scrape.

"It's not bad," I said through clenched teeth, trying to ignore the stinging sensation.

"This needs to be washed out. I have some disinfectant and bandages in my bedroom. Hold on a sec." He sprinted off in what I could only presume was the direction of his bedroom.

While he was gone, I looked around the space. It was what I thought of as lived in. No art, but plenty of photos. I recognized Brett's older sister and brother in a group shot, a picture of his parents at a barbeque, Brett aboard a sailboat, looking all wind tousled and happy. A lump formed in my throat. Mac would love to go sailing, to know another set of grandparents, aunts and uncles she didn't have on my side.

I had to tell him. I had to tell them both.

But not yet. No, I needed to find out whatever Brett knew about the Granger case because I was laying odds on the fact that when I fessed up about Mac, he'd never speak to me willingly again.

Brett returned with a large black knapsack, which he unzipped. I watched as he extracted hydrogen peroxide and gauze, but stepped away when he reached for my arm.

"I can do it."

"Let's call it even since I spritzed you the other night. Who was with you by the way?"

"Agnes. Ouch, that stings."

"Sorry." Blue eyes flicked up to me, the expression there telegraphing his surprise. "The battle-ax is a PI too?"

I laughed. "I forgot we used to call her that. And no, she was more of an unwanted ride-along. I tried to shake her, but she's relentless."

He was quiet as he finished bandaging my arm. "So what happened to you?"

I stared at the carpet. It was a hideous mauve shad that was so not Brett's style. "The Captain got reassigned, and I went with them." It was the simplest version of the truth, and I'd promised myself I wouldn't lie to him.

He looked hurt. "You couldn't call? Or write? Hell, look me up on Facebook?"

"You aren't on Facebook."

He snapped his fingers and pointed at me. "So you *did* look."

"Sneak." I batted the finger away. "Just recently. So, who hired you to follow Paul Granger?"

Brett studied me a moment and then leaned back against the doorframe. "His employer. Or more accurately, his employer's insurance. It was a workers' comp claim."

I blinked. "Seriously? But he was visiting all those doctor's offices, pushing his ED drug."

"No, he wasn't. He hadn't made a sale in months. He filed for workers' comp on a supposed back injury, and that's when Right Touch hired me because they suspected he was faking the injury."

"And was he?" And was scamming a small pharmaceutical employer motive for murder?

Brett shook his head. "I don't know one way or the other. He was a shifty bastard and never let me see him doing anything that could have disabused the claim—never picked up his kids, or anything heavier than a briefcase. My gut tells me he was lying though. No man with severe back pain could be having the kind of sex that guy was."

"You saw him at it? With his wife?"

"And the mistress, Mrs. Fox. I have enough trouble keeping one woman happy without a back injury, you might remember."

I ignored that last bit, as he was obviously fishing for a compliment. "Who do you think killed him? Mr. Fox?"

"I really couldn't say. Guy wasn't a peaceful sort. He made enemies wherever he went. Tends to shorten a man's lifespan."

"So you're done with the case now?" I asked.

He folded his arms over his chest. "That one, yes. It ended when he died."

"So why were you checking up on Mr. and Mrs. Fox?"

His lips thinned and his eyes narrowed. "I walked right into that one, didn't I?"

I crossed my arms over my chest. "Since I got a snoot-full of pepper spray, I think I at least need to know the reason you were lurking in their bushes."

"I wasn't lurking. I was doing surveillance, and a better job of it than you, might I add. You need to be more careful if you don't want to get made."

I lifted my chin, unwilling to back down.

He blew out a sigh. "Okay, if you must know, I wanted to make sure Rose Fox was all right. I'd been following Paul long enough to know Robert has a temper and uses his fists on his wife. I couldn't call the cops in before without risking my case, but after Paul was killed, I had a feeling the Foxes were going to have it out. And I was right. But you beat me to the punch, so to speak."

Brett's words were tinged with regret. Because he hadn't called the authorities before? Or was there something else at play?

Before I could ask, my cell phone buzzed. Dollars to doughnuts that was Mac again.

Squaring my shoulders, I looked my unwitting baby daddy in the eye. "I should go."

He blinked. "Just like high school all over again. You're going to run away again?"

The buzzing phone sounded angry. "No, I'm not, but there's somewhere I need to be tonight, someone waiting for me."

"Husband?" Brett asked.

I was halfway out the door when I looked back at him. "Never married, but you already knew that, didn't you?"

He grinned and reached into his back pocket, extracting a clean, white business card. "You're learning quick there, hot stuff. Don't be a stranger."

I took the card and then sprinted for Helga. The buzzing quit as I turned the engine over and I sent a quick text to Mac. *On my way home.*

A message came through while I was backing out, but I ignored it, heart pounding like crazy.

Brett or Mac? Which one should I fess up to first?

CHAPTER FIFTEEN

Conflict of Interest—When a private investigator has a duty to more than one individual or group, but both parties' varying interests make it impossible to act impartially for either entity.
From the *Working Man's Guide to Sleuthing for a Living* by Albert Taylor, PI

I'd forgotten about movie night until entering my own apartment to see my mother in my kitchen, trying to work a blender filled with what looked like daiquiri mix.

"Did you have a nice day at work, dear?" My mother asked the same exact question she'd asked my father every single night throughout my childhood.

"What are you doing?" I eyeballed the blender with deep mistrust. The last thing my secret-keeping self needed was a healthy swig of alcohol to loosen the old tongue.

"Don't worry, it's virgin. That way Mac can participate too," she said as she wrestled with the gadget.

I moved past her into the living room where Mac was typing away in a fervor. "Hey, kid."

"Grams," Mac said without looking up. "Would you please tell my mother that I'm not speaking to her at the moment?"

I blinked and looked over my shoulder at the amateur bartender, who shrugged.

"Why?" I asked Mac. "What did I do?"

She didn't respond, though the clacking of her keys grew in intensity.

I plopped onto the couch beside her. "Okay, stupid question. I didn't pick up when you called a few times, didn't tell you where I was, what I was doing, or when I'd be home. You were worried. I'm sorry for that."

Her gaze flicked to me briefly before she refocused on the screen.

I glanced into the kitchen. Agnes had been staring, but she hastily returned to her blender mishap.

"Mac, come on."

"Where were you?" Her question was smooth, level.

"It had to do with the case," I hedged.

She stood up and walked past me into her bedroom, slamming the door as only a pissed-off teenage girl could.

I leaned back into the couch and closed my eyes.

There was some rattling and then the whir of the blender. *Way to go, Agnes*.

A cabinet door opened and shut and then something cold and smooth was pressed into my outstretched hand.

"Thanks," I said taking the straw between my lips and sipping. After a minute I frowned down at the glass then back up at my mother. "I thought you said these were virgin?"

"I had one of those little liquor bottles of rum in my purse. You look like you needed it."

I raised the glass in a mock toasting gesture. "All she had to shout was a 'You're ruining my life,' and she'd be my clone."

"Why do you think I carry little liquor bottles in my purse? Déjà vu."

I laughed in surprise. "Was that a joke? I don't think I've ever heard you make a joke before."

Agnes puffed up like a wet chickadee. "I'll have you know in my day I was quite the kidder."

That made me snort daiquiri through my left nostril. "Oh, that stings!"

She scurried back into the kitchen and handed me a paper towel, which I used to wipe off the blotch on my shirt.

"Honestly, between the drink and all the pepper spray I don't know how much more my sinuses can take."

Agnes sat down in the spot my daughter had vacated. "So, where were you?"

"Mom!"

"What? I was on a case with you last night."

"Not on a case. We were doing surveillance. Poorly."

Her eyes narrowed. "Says who?"

"Another PI. He's someone I used to know, actually."

"Oh really. Who's that?"

My gaze slid to the closed bedroom door and back.

It took her a minute and then her mouth fell open. She snapped it closed with an audible click. "No, it can't be. Are you sure?"

"Positive. I spoke with him."

"Did you tell him about Mac?"

I shook my head and sipped from my drink.

I could see her struggling with the information the same way I had. "And he's an investigator too?"

"Small world."

"A little too small." Agnes hesitated. "Are you going to tell her?"

I sighed and leaned back against the couch, gaze fixed on the ceiling. "I think it's time. I don't want it to be time but I don't want to keep lying to her, either. I'm not sure if I should tell her first or if I should talk to Brett and prepare him."

Agnes didn't say anything, and I straightened so I could see her more clearly. She'd set her drink down and was wringing her hands.

"What? What is it?"

"Have you ever regretted something, a choice you made that you thought was right at the time but later on changed your mind?"

I snorted. "Story of my life, Mom."

She shook her head. "You don't have regrets though. I see you. You did what you thought was right, keeping the baby and raising her into an intelligent young woman with a bright future. You make plenty of mistakes, Mackenzie, but when it comes to the things that matter, you always choose the right way."

I blinked at her, unable to say anything. Was my mother actually *complimenting* me?

"Anyhow, I have a long list of regrets, most of them to do with you."

"Tell me something I don't know," I spoke in an acerbic tone.

"I mean our relationship. You were my baby, my only child. I'm not sure when this…bone of contention got in the way, but it did."

"How many tiny rum bottles went into your drink?" I asked skeptically.

"I only had the one." Her tone was dry. "I'm not drunk, just seeing things in a different light."

"Things?" I asked.

"My life. The world around me. Your father couldn't accept that."

"And that's why you left him?" The question was low, quiet. "Why you're divorcing him?"

"Partly. Your father and I were a great team, but we never had what you would call a happy marriage. All couples have their issues."

"But all that history," I countered. "You and Dad together. How can you just give up on it?"

"I'm not giving up. I'm moving on. Besides, we're getting off the subject."

I'd forgotten there was one. "So, what's the regret you were talking about?"

"When you turned up pregnant, you said you didn't want to ruin your boyfriend's life."

I nodded. "The one decision we agreed on."

"No, it wasn't. I wanted you to tell him about Mac. He had a right to know."

I stared at her for a full minute before saying, "Are you freaking *kidding* me with this?"

She blinked. "No, I—"

"Don't even." I stood up so abruptly that the entire coffee table rattled. "Don't you think I have enough to deal with without hearing that you think one of the fundamental decisions of my life, one you'd agreed with me about to my face, was a mistake?"

"I'm not trying to upset you," she said.

"No, you aren't trying. You're succeeding in upsetting me." I was too tired and emotionally tattered to deal with her right now. "Movie night isn't happening. You should go."

"Mackenzie."

I shook my head. "Mom, I'm tired, I'm hungry, and I have zero patience right now. Go home."

"I'll stop by tomorrow. Maybe we can all have a nice Sunday dinner?"

Crap. I'd forgotten all about Dad coming, but was in no mood to go another round with her over the fact. "Sure."

She rose and headed to the door, but paused. "I didn't tell you that to make you feel badly. I just wanted you to know that I'm supporting your choice now."

The door clicked behind her, and I stared at it for a full minute, not knowing what to make of her words.

Hefting the box of photographs and high school memorabilia I'd left by the door, I headed down the hall. Mac's door was shut, and my hands were too full to knock, so I depressed the long thin old-fashioned handle with my elbow.

Mac lay curled on top of her comforter, Snickers curled up against her back.

"Hey," I said.

She rolled to look at me, and my heart broke when I saw the tear tracks. "Ever heard of knocking?"

I raised a brow. "Ever heard of teenage cliché?"

She made a disgusted noise and sat up. "Thanks for dropping by. Feel free to leave whenever."

I had the oddest sense of history repeating itself and realized that I was having almost exactly the same conversation with my daughter as I had with my mother, only this time I was on the other side. Genetics were freaky like that.

"Look, I'll give you all the space you want, but I promised you I'd get you the stuff you needed for your project."

Her gaze fastened hungrily on the box. "What is all that?"

I set it down on the foot of her bed. "Mostly junk. Notes I passed with my friends, random pictures, my old yearbook and other tidbits. You're welcome to keep whatever you like."

Her hands trembled as she reached for the lid, but she paused. "Don't you want to keep any of it?"

I stepped back. "No, I have all the keepsakes I want." Like her baby blanket, the first book I'd read to her, her first pair of boots, and a monkey butt ton of pictures. The contents of the high school box belonged to a different era, a different Mackenzie.

I turned towards my bedroom, but a small voice called out, "Mom?"

"Yeah, kid?" I glanced at her over my shoulder, hoping for an olive branch.

"This is a lot of stuff. Would you…that is, will you go through it with me?"

"Sure thing," I said and smiled. My long night was far from over.

* * *

"And that was Mr. McNutt. Your dad swore up and down that his first name was Buster." I tapped the photograph of the health and PE teacher before passing it over.

Mac raised an eyebrow. "Buster McNutt? His parents must have hated him. Who's that?"

We'd decided to spread the trophies of my misspent youth out in the living room. Instead of parking it on the couches, we sat across from each other on the floor, the box's innards dotting the landscape between us. It was cold, and my backside was asleep, but my daughter was smiling again which was all that mattered.

I craned my neck. "That's Jimmy Hogan. He was in the sailing club with your dad."

Mac studied the image of a large blond teenager who had a scar bisecting his left eyebrow. "He looks like a jackass."

"Not just any jackass. He was the king of the jackass mountain—always had something lousy to say, flushed cherry bombs down the toilets, stupid stuff like that. I never knew what Brett saw in him, friend-wise, but he's a loyal guy."

"Brett." Mac picked up another picture, one I thought was swiftly becoming her favorite. It was of the two of us at the homecoming dance. I had on a green sheath dress with spaghetti straps and had my hair piled on top of my head, fastened in place with one of my grandmother's classic combs. It had been a marvel of modern engineering and a testament to extra hold hairspray. "He's so good looking. You both are."

"Don't sound so shocked." I reached into the bowl of popcorn by my side and plucked out a few kernels.

"I am shocked. You date such plain guys."

"Hey!" I threw the fistful of popcorn at her. "I do not."

She lowered her chin and gave me her *get real* look. "Mom."

"Okay so maybe I do go for more of the average men. They're nice, stable, and worship the ground my designer knock-off heels tread upon."

"And they bore you." My daughter reached across the pile for my sophomore yearbook. She had me there.

"The pretty ones are trouble," I cautioned, thinking of her new lab partner and a certain detective. Although pretty was the wrong word for Hunter Black. He was visually arresting. The pun made me snort.

"I don't really look like either of you." Mac was studying our yearbook photos. "Maybe around the nose a little."

"You have my hair. Same color as your dad's mom, my nana. And you have Brett's eyes. Same exact shade of blue. And Gram's stubborn chin."

"So what happened—" Mac set the yearbook aside "—when you told him you were pregnant? Did he, like, freak out or demand you get an abortion?"

"You've been watching too much television. Something you also get from me. Write that down." I pointed to her notebook.

"I'm serious. How did he react?"

Suddenly all the fun had gone out of the game. "It's getting late."

Mac rose as easily as only a sixteen-year-old could. I rocked a bit, swearing as my back spasmed. It was the same muscle group that had made itself known earlier when I was hanging out of Brett's neighbor's window. Too much abuse in too short a time span.

"You okay?"

"Fine," I grated, though I was anything but. Oh, for the love of java. Eventually I made it to hands and knees. A hand appeared in my peripheral vision.

"I'll help you up, if you tell me." Mac waggled her fingers in my face.

"You'll help me up because I gave you life." Was I actually sweating? Maybe I had better scale back on the snack cakes for real. I flailed for her hand, and she gripped it but didn't pull.

"Mom, just tell me. What's the big secret?"

I tried pulling myself up without her help, but my screaming back muscles weren't having it. "This is not how I wanted to do this," I grumbled under my breath.

"What was that?"

"Okay, I promise I'll tell you, just help me up before anything else goes hinky."

"Swear on something you love."

"Your life?" I panted.

"Helga. And your coffeepot."

Damn it, she was playing hardball. "Fine, I swear on both Helga and Mr. Coffee that I will tell you after you help me get up."

"Right after," Mac insisted. "No putting it off until I'm twenty-five."

"If this whole tech genius gig doesn't pan out, maybe you should go to law school." I was a little in awe of her closing a loophole I hadn't even considered. Of course I was stiff and under caffeinated and having the back spasm from hell, but still.

"Promise me, right after."

"I promise within five minutes."

She glared down at me.

"I have to pee. Can I at least pee first, maybe get a pain reliever?"

"Immediately after."

I gave a weary exhale. "Agreed."

Mac helped me up, and I stood as erect as possible, stretching my aching back.

She waited, arms folded across her chest, one toe tapping. There was no way out of it.

I looked at the ground, at her Converse sneakers with the little mutant head she'd drawn on the toe portion in pink neon. Up and down it went, up and down. "I didn't."

The head froze. "You didn't what?"

I looked her in the eye and finished. "Tell him. I never told Brett I was pregnant."

I gave her a moment to digest that—my bladder was screaming— and shuffled down the hall to use the facilities. Snickers leapt off the bed and followed me.

After flushing and washing, I snagged the bottle of Extra Strength Tylenol and headed back into the living room. Mac was in pretty much the same position she'd been in when I departed.

There was still some daiquiri in the glass my mother had poured for me earlier. After popping two pain relievers in my mouth I knocked the drink back, almost choking because the mixed cocktail had begun to unmix. Ick.

"Did he rape you?"

My head snapped up. "What?"

"Did Brett, I mean did my dad—"

"No Mac, of course he didn't."

"Then why didn't you tell him?" There was pleading in her tone—pleading for understanding the why behind my choice.

I shrugged helplessly, knowing the truth would hurt her but unable to lie about something so important. "It's complicated. And he wasn't…well he wasn't ready. Neither of us was, but my life had to change, his didn't. And it would have the second I told him." I left out the part about why I'd felt so sure he wasn't ready and the real reason I hadn't told Brett, the fact that I'd walked in on him with another girl when I'd been on the verge of telling him.

She stared at me for a full minute and then moved down the hall.

"Mac," I called, hating that I'd hurt her, unsure of where I'd gone wrong or what I could have said or done to spare her pain.

Her door slammed. After a moment there was a whining sound, followed by scratching. The puggle was at Mac's door begging for entry.

I shuffled forward, tried the handle, and wasn't surprised to find it locked this time. "Come on girl, you can stay with me tonight."

The dog gave one more powerful sniff as though she could suck Mac out through the crack beneath it before trotting after me into my bedroom. I left the door open in case Mac emerged and was prepared to fall face first onto my bed when I looked at the wagging tail dusting the floor by the door. "You have to go, don't you?"

Snickers waited.

I sighed and then moved over to open the French door so she could relieve herself.

The night breeze was cold, and I stepped out onto the patio. The yard was large by city standards, almost a quarter of an acre. Ivy had taken over the broken crumbling fountain, which made for eerie shapes at night. The fencing was small pickets, only enough to keep a medium sized dog contained. Maybe I should get some chairs out here. Mac might like that.

If she ever spoke to me again.

There were no lights and no streetlights, just the soft glow from a harvest moon. I stared up at it for a minute before picking up on a small shuffling to my left. Thinking it was Snickers, I headed in that direction, only to find Hunter Black sitting on a bench on his patio, his gaze also trained up at the night sky.

There was something odd about his posture. It wasn't relaxed like a man kicking back after a hard day of work. No, it was more intensely brooding, as if he'd come out here to be alone.

I was about to creep off back to my own area of the back yard when he looked up.

"Sorry," I said. "Just letting the dog out. Is everything all right?"

"No." Hunter shook his head.

Though he hadn't invited me I sat next to him on the bench. "Want to talk about it?"

"I don't, but I don't have much of a choice. You know that woman you interviewed yesterday, the one you told me Paul Granger assaulted in the parking garage?"

"Kimmy. What about her?"
Hunter put a hand over mine. "She was murdered."

CHAPTER SIXTEEN

Garbology 101, aka Dumpster diving for pros—sifting through trash in an attempt to find information. Aka the holy grail of private investigation.
From the *Working Man's Guide to Sleuthing for a Living* by Albert Taylor, PI

"Morning," I said to Mac's closed bedroom door as I stumbled past heading for the source of vitality that made all things possible, aka my coffeepot.

Snickers paused hopefully by Mac's bedroom door and gave a pitiful whimper.

"Your dog misses you," I called over my shoulder. "Punish me all you want, but leaving her with me is basically animal cruelty."

No response. Not that I'd expected one after the great reveal of the night before, but goading her was better than thinking about what Hunter had told me.

Poor Kimmy.

I spaced out as I watched hot brown liquid drizzle slowly into the pot. It had taken me a full minute of staring at Hunter Black's rugged profile to translate his words. "I just talked to her yesterday."

"I know. Ruth told me when I questioned her."

"How?" I'd croaked.

"Same as Paul Granger, execution style with a small caliber bullet. It was at her home, made to look like a B&E gone bad, but even though the place was trashed, there was nothing missing."

"And you don't think it's a coincidence." I'd started to shiver.

Hunter slowly shook his head. "I don't."

Snickers came bounding over to him, and he'd scooped her up into his lap. She gave his hand a few enthusiastic licks, turned three times, and plopped down. Big men weren't supposed to appreciate little dogs, but he'd looked so at ease with the little beastie.

"I dropped by to tell you earlier," Hunter murmured.

"I was out." I kept it short and simple and hoped like hell he wouldn't ask me where.

He didn't sigh, didn't make a peep.

"It can't be Dr. Granger." I said. "Maybe Paul, but she had no motive to kill Kimmy."

"I'm not a judge, Mackenzie. I follow the evidence."

"So do I," Or at least, I'd been trying to. "Kimmy told me Paul came on to her in the parking lot one night after work. She dosed him with pepper spray. So she wasn't having an affair with him, and Dr. Granger would have no reason to kill her."

He'd run a hand over his jaw. "Unless she lied to you."

"Why would she?"

"Maybe she was embarrassed or didn't want it getting out that she'd been having an affair with him. Did you ask her in front of anyone else?"

I'd thought about it. "Ruth was there the whole time. She's the one who called Kimmy over."

"People lie for all sorts of reasons. It could be that she was afraid she'd be linked with his death."

I'd shaken my head. "You didn't see her. She was disgusted by him."

"I'm not going to argue with you. You're better off tracking down your mysterious Escalade driver."

"I already found him." The words had come out before I'd thought them through.

"What?" Hunter had sat up abruptly, disturbing the dog, who'd hopped down.

My teeth had sunk into my lower lip. Damn it, I hadn't meant to say that. "Yeah, he's another PI who was also following Paul Granger. He was hired by Paul's employer because Right

Touch Pharmaceuticals thought Paul was faking his disability claim."

"I need to talk to him. Do you have his information?"

"About that…"

Even in the low light I'd felt his intense gaze on my burning cheeks. "What aren't you telling me, Red?"

So, *so* much. "Well I sort of know him. The PI. Not recently, but from a long time ago. He's, well it's kind of funny actually."

Hunter had waited.

I'd blown out a sigh. "He's Mac's father. Only he doesn't know he's Mac's father, so if you'd just not mention her to him."

"Is he dangerous?" Hunter asked. "Are you afraid he might hurt you or your daughter?"

"What? No, nothing like that. I just never told him."

No one could do quiet like Hunter.

"You think I'm horrible, don't you." I didn't phrase it as a question. "My daughter's not speaking to me because when I saw him earlier, I knew I had to tell her, to tell them both, and now she thinks I didn't want her because I told her I wasn't ready for a kid. She doesn't understand that she has been and will always be the very best thing in my life."

He hadn't responded.

The wind had picked up, and I'd risen, wrapping my arms around myself, temper flaring. "Well don't just sit there and listen. Say something!"

"Aren't women supposed to like it when men listen?"

"When they *actively* listen. And engage in conversation. Otherwise it's me just ranting like a lunatic."

Slowly, carefully as though he'd been worried about spooking a wild animal, he'd gotten to his feet. "It's okay, Red. She doesn't hate you."

"Well she should. I sort of hate me. I mean, I'm still freaking fabulous but—" I'd run out of words and just shaken my head.

Warm palms had gripped my shoulders and he'd stood there like a great barrier against the world's dark underbelly. "You made a tough decision. I told you before I'm no judge."

I'd sniffled. "If you'd gotten your girlfriend pregnant at sixteen, wouldn't you have wanted to know about it?"

"My situation was different. Much different, from what you're describing. But yes, I think I'd want to know."

"So, I have to tell him. Now. Because I know my kid, and if I don't tell him, she'll show up on his doorstep and tell him herself. Better I prepare him and he takes out whatever gut reaction on me." I'd been trying to put up a brave front, but the truth was I'd been terrified of telling Brett.

"It's all wrong." I had shaken my head. "He was supposed to be this great academic, have this huge future with piles of money, a place on Nantucket where his family would be all mint juleps and tennis whites all summer. The kind of life my mother always wanted. How is it he's doing the exact same thing I'm doing?"

Hunter hadn't said anything, and this time his silence had felt lighter, reassuring. He hadn't had any answers, but he had been there with me, there for me all the same.

I'd stepped back. "I should go in."

"I won't mention you when I talk to him. It's not my place to spill your secrets."

"Thanks, much appreciated." I'd turned, but he caught my arm.

"Do I still scare you?" he'd whispered.

More than ever, but in a much different way. Mac had been right. I liked relationships I could control, ones I never had problems walking away from when the time came. Though I barely knew Hunter, something instinctively told me he wouldn't tolerate that, would never cede control to me. I'd licked suddenly dry lips and murmured, "I'm not sure how to answer that."

"Honestly." He pulled me closer, so close that the wood smoke and pine scent of him cocooned me. "That's the only way you should ever answer me. With honesty."

He wanted the naked truth? Fine. "Yes. But it's more about me than anything to do with you. You've been…"

"I've been what?"

Perfect. I'd thought. Supportive, protective, everything a man ought to be. Sure we'd had our showdowns, but even arguing with him had gotten my blood pumping, reminded me that I was a woman, and I had needs. Needs that hadn't been met in a very long time.

It was as though central casting had yanked the image I had for a perfect mate directly out of my head and teleported him into reality. Telling Hunter that wasn't an option. Instead, I'd gone with a lame, but still honest response. "Great. You've been great."

"I'll show you great," he growled and lowered his lips to mine.

I'd been cold half a second before, I knew it, remembered it. His warmth had rolled over me like a liquid wave of heat as he kissed me senseless. He'd cupped my face tenderly, almost as though he were being extra careful not to leave a mark, even as his mouth had devoured my own.

I'd melted into him, all my strong-woman bravado washed away in the current of passion that roared to life. Oh this was bad. Anything that felt so amazing had to be bad.

My lips had parted, hungry for more. Damn my hedonistic hide. Willpower, had to get me some of that.

Hunter had ended the kiss first, though he didn't release my face. I'd sucked in much-needed oxygen and tried to think of something to say.

His thumb had traced my bottom lip. "Good-night, Red."

And then he'd disappeared inside his own apartment.

* * *

The sound of Mac's bedroom door creaking open pulled me from my reverie. I had so much to tackle, and most of it should have been done yesterday. Or sixteen years earlier. Either way I was behind schedule, and why was my coffeepot taking so long to yield the sweet nectar of life?

"Hey." Mac stood in the little gap between the counter and the kitchen.

"Hey yourself." I studied her. She didn't look any the worse for wear, but that was a sixteen-year-old for you. I'd lost track of how many times I'd scrambled up the old oak to my bedroom window after spending all night with Brett, changed my clothing, and gone down to breakfast with Nan without missing a beat.

I waited for Mac to say something, but she was looking at me as though holding back until I said something.

We waited, eyeing one another, the only sound the bubbling hiss from a coffeepot as old as Methuselah.

"You're the best thing that ever happened to me," I blurted at the same time as she said "I'm so sorry, Mom."

We rushed to each other like it had been choreographed, and I hugged her close. She tucked her head beneath my chin the same way she had when she'd been five and perched on my lap.

"What do you have to be sorry about, huh? I'm the screw up, not you," I murmured, stroking her auburn hair.

"But if not for me—"

"I wouldn't have a reason to get out of bed every morning. I'd probably still be living with Mom and The Captain. Well, if they were still together. The point is that I'd be totally lost without you."

Mac shook her head back and forth. I wasn't sure what she was trying to communicate— remorse maybe.

"You know what you need? Some coffee."

There was a small sniffle, but when she pulled back, her eyes were dry. "Sounds good."

"It's a date then. Go, get dressed."

"For coffee?" she asked.

"Yeah I'm pretty sure the pot is busted, and I have a giant to-do list, and going out sans caffeine is a public health issue."

"I thought we were broke," Mac protested.

My shoulder bag was on the counter, and I fished out the bills Len had spotted me. "Not totally broke. And come on, we're taking Fillmore on his first stakeout."

Mac had turned back down the hallway but paused. "How come we're not taking Helga?"

"I have it on good authority that she's too noticeable. Go get dressed, and meet me outside in ten. I need to run up and see Grams for a second."

Mac disappeared into her room, and I dug through the mountains of laundry until I found a black tank top and clean pair of jeans. I threw a white men's button-down shirt over the top and then tied it at the waist, before sitting down to do the socks and sneakers bit.

Mac was speaking to me again, that boded well. I wasn't about to take my sixteen-year-old daughter on an actual surveillance, trip, but I thought maybe I could practice my tailing skills and give her a real in-person look at her father at the same time. After, I'd drop her off back home to set up for the dinner shindig while I got back to work.

But first I had to set the other half of my parent trap.

Fully dressed, I snagged my leather jacket and shoulder bag and sprinted up the stairs to knock on my mother's door. No answer. I dug around in my pockets until I retrieved the small notebook and pen and scribbled her a hasty invitation to dinner. Then, for good measure, I headed over to Nona's door.

"Mackenzie, how you doing, doll?"

"Fine, Nona. Sorry about the movie night getting cancelled."

Nona waved it off. "No trouble. My sciatica was flaring up anyhow."

"Sorry to hear that. I'm having a little dinner get-together tonight and wanted to invite you. If you're feeling up to it, of course."

"Oh, that sounds nice. What time and what can I bring?"

I was tempted to ask for the entire dinner, but refrained. "Whatever you want to bring will be great. Come down at seven thirty." Inspiration struck, and I added, "Maybe you can get together with my mom and plan what to bring."

"Will Hunter be there?"

I flashed hot and then cold again as I thought of our kiss. "I'm not sure. I haven't seen him yet today."

"Oh he's out with his sister. I saw her pick him up when I went out to get the paper. If he comes back, I'll ask him for you." She winked at me.

"Nona, you're a trip, you know that, right?"

She shrugged. "I've been called worse. See you later, doll."

Mac was waiting for me on the front porch. "What were you doing?"

"Inviting the upstairs neighbors to dinner. My boss is coming too, and The Captain."

"They're coming here," Mac repeated. The chill autumn wind brought out the pink flush in her cheeks. "For dinner. Tonight."

"That's right." I unlocked Fillmore's driver-side door, squashed myself in behind the wheel, and then reached over to unlock Mac's side.

"Mom." She had an incredulous look on her face as she plopped in her seat. "You know they're expecting actual food to be cooked and served to them."

"Mac, I told you, you can't waste your time worrying about other people's expectations." Fillmore had always had a rough starter, but the week of sitting idle hadn't done him any favors. He choked and wheezed and grumbled like the little old man he was before finally throwing up his hands to do what I wanted. "Besides, considering the way your grandparents are ignoring each other, it might not last too long."

"But," she protested as I pulled out onto traffic, "we've never hosted a dinner before."

The sad little Jetta putt-putted along. Helga had ruined me for other cars. "Where's your adventurer's spirit? I'm trying to do a good thing here. The least you can do is support me."

"The least I can do is commit you," Mac grumbled as we reached the coffee shop. "You better keep the engine running if we don't want it to die on us. What do you want?"

"Coffee with extra coffee and a side of coffee. Oh, and see if they'll top it with coffee beans." I handed her a twenty.

When she disappeared inside I called Len. The machine picked up at the office, but I doubted he was in. He'd given me his home number, and I rummaged around in my shoulder bag until I found the scrap of paper where I'd scribbled it.

"Lo?" Len wheezed.

"It's Mackenzie. I spoke with one of the detectives on our case last night. There's been another murder. One of the employees who worked for the men's clinic."

"This could be good news for our client, but only if they can tie the murders together. She has an alibi for last night."

"Oh?"

"An administrative meeting at the hospital. She called me this morning to tell me they've asked her to take a leave of absence for a while."

Damn it. It made sense. No one wanted his or her kid being treated by a pediatrician who was fighting a murder rap, but still… "What should I be doing?"

Len answered my question with one of his own. "What does your gut tell you?"

"To find out information on the victim and find out if there was a connection to anyone besides Paul Granger. And find out who would want her dead."

"Exactly what I would suggest." There was a smile in Len's voice. "We can discuss anything you find after dinner tonight."

I hung up with him just as Mac reappeared carrying two giant cups of coffee. Even with the windows rolled up, my mouth began to water.

Supplied and ready, I headed back to Brett's neighborhood. Mac fiddled with the radio as we drove down the street. "There's nothing good on. Freaking auto-tune BS."

"You know, I have never once doubted that you are my child. No hospital mix-ups for you." Taking a page out of his book, I backed into an empty driveway three houses down with a for sale sign on the lawn.

"What if someone sees us?" Mac slunk down in her seat.

"They'll think we're just waiting for a real estate agent to show up."

"And if an actual agent shows up?" She raised a brow.

"Then we say we were driving past and wanted to schedule a showing. You were just dialing the number when they arrived. Sit up. You'll draw more attention by looking suspicious. We have every right to be here."

"So who are we investigating?" Mac asked.

I looked over at her. "Your dad."

Her eyes got big. "Oh Mom, no. I'm not ready, and look at what I'm wearing! Look at what you're wearing!"

I frown down at what I thought had been a stylish choice. "What's wrong with what I'm wearing?"

"You look like you spent the night with your artist boyfriend and threw on his shirt to cover your pit stains."

I looked up at the ceiling. "This is why we shouldn't teach children to talk."

"Mom, focus. I don't want to meet him."

"We're not going to meet him. We're going to tail him."

Mac's panic ratcheted back a little. "Why?"

"Well, to see what kind of guy he is. I want to know more about him before I bring him into your life."

"And?" My kid knew me too well, knew when I held things back.

"And so I can practice tailing a car. If he doesn't make me, it's been a success."

"And if he does make you?" Worry crept back into her voice.

"We'll jump off that bridge when we come to it," I said as Brett's front door swung open. "It's show time."

CHAPTER SEVENTEEN

"No one runs away without telling someone else first. The trick is finding his or her confidant."
From the *Working Man's Guide to Sleuthing for a Living* by Albert Taylor, PI

"That's him?" Mac starred at the figure emerging from Brett's house the way I stared at designer boots I couldn't afford—hungrily.

"Yes."

She watched as Brett trotted down the steps, flipping his keys around his finger and catching them in his palm. She pressed her own hand to Fillmore's dirty window. "What if he doesn't like me?"

Something pinged in my chest. Taking her out on surveillance had seemed like a good idea when I'd first come up with it, but seeing her lost expression made me rethink the scenario. "Babe, how can anyone not adore you?"

She didn't turn her head from the window. "You're biased."

"He will be too."

"Do you think he'll be mad, when you tell him?"

"I honestly don't know. He used to be a very easy-going guy, but people change. If he's mad at anyone, it'll be me, though, not you."

"Are you going to do it now?"

Coffee churned in my stomach. When I told him. Not if. It was one thing to know I had to come clean, another entirely to waltz over to my high school boyfriend who I hadn't seen for more than a decade and a half and ruin his life.

"Not now."

"Mom," Mac pleaded.

"I thought you weren't ready?" I asked.

"I'm not, but I want him to know about me. He should know about me." She lifted her chin to a stubborn angle and for one second was the spitting image of her grandmother. Java help me.

"Don't, hon, I can't right now. Let me call him and set up a meeting."

"Tomorrow. You need to do it tomorrow." She turned back to the window. "I don't want to keep wondering how he'll take the news. It's making me feel sick."

"That makes two of us. I promise, I will call him tomorrow." Brett's SUV pulled away from the curb. I waited until he'd turned the corner before pursuing.

"We lost him," Mac said, not even five minutes later. "You weren't kidding when you said you needed practice."

"Hey, I've got mad driving skills. I just didn't want to risk having him bust us." I cruised through again at the intersection where we'd been held up. No sign of the Escalade. "Damn it."

"It's probably better this way," Mac soothed. "We should get you some GPS tech to tag vehicles you need to follow. That way you don't have to worry about getting made."

"Technology isn't the end-all and be-all of life. There was a time we made due without it."

"Yeah, but why would you want to if you had another option?" Mac shuddered and her phone barked.

"Who's the dog?" I asked as I turned toward home.

"My lab partner," she grumbled, ignoring the bark. "Five minutes into our review he asked if I wanted to make out. When I told him no, he asked if I was a lesbian."

"Not short on confidence, is he?"

"I think the only thing he's short on is brains. He couldn't even handle the gene diagraming when I asked him to do that. It's, like, so simple."

"Awe, babe, sorry it didn't work out."

Mac snorted. "You're such a bad liar."

"Hey, I'll have you know I'm an excellent liar, but I only use my superpowers for good, not evil."

"Mom," she said.

"Okay fine. Sorry, not sorry. You happy now?"

"Might as well throw an I-told-you-so on for good measure."

What the kid didn't understand is that I hadn't wanted to be right. Pete the Pervert worshiped the ground Mac walked on, but my daughter looked at him like he was a brother. And meatheads like Todd would never see her worth until they were old and paunchy and the shine was completely off their jockstrap.

"Mom?" Mac asked as I pulled Fillmore into his customary place in the street in front of Uncle Al's. "What are you thinking about?"

"Shiny jock straps."

"Ew! Sorry I asked. Seriously though, what are we going to do about this dinner thing?" Now that the danger of running into her bio dad had passed, Mac had reverted back to her normal quippy self.

We both climbed from Fillmore, and I turned to face her. "Mac, relax, I have this. Just work on your project and text me if you need anything."

"Therapy," she said. "Massive doses of therapy."

"Noted." I headed over to Helga.

"Hey, no fair. You're taking the good car now?"

"It's a mom perk. To compensate for the stretch marks. Wanna see?"

She held up her hands quickly. "I'm good."

I watched her dart inside, smiling to myself. Just as she reached the door, Hunter stepped out and waved to me.

I flashed hot and then cold as he trotted down the steps, moving like a great big predator. "Where are you headed?"

"Um, errands?" Shoot, could that have sounded less convincing?

"Nona told me about your party tonight."

Shoot. "Um, it's not a party so much as a set-up for my parents and a social outing for my elderly strays."

The corners of his mouth turned up slightly. "I'm sure it'll prove eventful."

I shifted from one foot to the other. He still hadn't said whether he was coming or not. Or mentioned that bone-melting kiss from the night before. "So, where are you off to?"

"My sister's place. My family takes turns hosting Sunday dinner."

I glanced at my phone. It was barely afternoon. "It's a little early for dinner."

"I'm on duty tonight. So they're eating at two."

So I guessed that answered my question about him dropping by later. "Have fun."

"I was going to ask you to come with me," he said. "You and Mac."

My eyebrows went up so high I swore I felt them hit my hairline. "You want to introduce us to your family?" One kiss, no matter how fantastic, didn't equate to meet-the-parents time.

Hunter didn't bat an eyelash. "Yes, Mary Alice leaves her kids here sometimes, and I thought it would be a good idea if I introduced everyone."

Oh, that made more sense, the stranger danger factor. "Well, we already have plans. Maybe another time?"

He nodded and headed toward the shed. I watched as he situated his helmet, started the thing up, and guided it backwards. My inner wild child wanted to leap onto the back of that thing, wrap my arms around his broad form, and ask him to drive me off into the sunset.

He lifted the visor. "Do me a favor. If you get into any trouble, call me."

"I don't have your number." I had to shout to be heard over the thunderous engine.

"Check your phone," he mouthed then flipped his visor down.

I did as he rode off. Sure enough, Hunter Black was programmed into my contacts list. He must have done that when he'd taken my phone the other night. The man thought of every eventuality.

It felt amazingly good to get behind Helga's wheel again, and I had to retrain my brain for her power. She really wasn't meant to be a city car. If I was a responsible adult, I'd sell her and buy something fuel efficient that was better suited to surveillance. Good thing I'd never mastered the adulting shtick.

And my current missions didn't require discretion.

The location of Right Touch Pharmaceuticals was common knowledge. After being stonewalled every time I'd tried to call the drug manufacturer, I'd decided to show up in person on a Sunday. Because while they were open, I was betting that the pit bull they had manning the phones would be off for the weekend.

The large, modern, steel-and-glass industrial building was located in Brighton, a few blocks from the New Balance headquarters. There was no sign, but I double-checked the address on the corporate website. It was the place.

On-street parking was practically nonexistent, but I managed to squeeze Helga in behind a snack cake truck.

I was sizing up the building when I spotted a black Escalade.

Oh, no. No way. What were the odds that I'd lost Brett back at his place only to stumble across him here?

As casually as I could, I strode over to his car, and rested a hand on the hood. The engine was cool, meaning that barring a coffee run, Brett had most likely been here awhile.

I cracked my knuckles, considering my options. Going into the office building meant risking running into him, something I wanted to avoid. And not just because of our personal drama. No, Brett knew I was a PI, knew I was investigating Paul Garner's murder—information I didn't want to share with any of the Right Touch people.

Wait a second.

I frowned at the Escalade. Why was Brett here? If he'd been investigating a workers' comp claim for Right Touch, he wouldn't still be meeting with them. I thought his story about checking up on Mrs. Fox sounded a little too altruistic for him.

People lie for all sorts of reasons. Hunter's warning from the night before haunted me.

Brett had lied to me. To my face. And I was going to find out why.

* * *

"Hello?" Mac said.

"I need your help," I told her as I slid into a booth in the coffee shop across the street from Brett's Escalade.

"Mom?" Mac asked. "What number are you calling from?"

"It's a burner phone." I smiled at the bored-looking waitress who offered me coffee and waited until she filled the heavy-duty ceramic cup then hissed, "I planted mine on someone I want to follow, and I want you to track it. You have that finding app on your phone, right?"

"Yeah." The sound of clicking keys came over the line. "Looks like he's standing still."

"Yup. I have eyes on it right now."

"Then why am I tracking it?" Mac sounded put out.

"Because, I want to know where he goes."

"He?" Mac inquired.

"The guy I'm following. Plus, I kinda want my phone back."

"Where is it?"

"His sunroof was cracked, so I tossed it in the back seat."

"What if he finds it first?" my little naysayer inquired.

"Come on, Mac. Just track the stupid thing for me."

"Okay, okay," Mac grumbled. "I'll call you if the signal moves."

"Awesome. Gotta go." I closed the phone and slipped it into my shirt pocket.

"Can I getcha anything else?" the waitress asked on a long-suffering sigh.

I wanted pie. Or maybe a burger and fries. Sadly, I'd blown what was left of my petty cash on the burner phone and had barely had enough to cover the much-needed java and a meager tip. "I'm good, thanks."

She skulked off to a corner, and I sipped the burnt-tasting coffee while keeping my gaze locked on the Escalade and trying to come up with a plan of action.

Mac tracking my phone was the plan of last resort. I'd also considered waiting for Brett and calling him out on his lie.

In some ways it was like we were back in high school again, when some random girl, out of sheer bitchiness, told me she'd seen my then boyfriend making out with someone else. I'd confronted him about it, and he'd told me that no, of course it wasn't true. And he'd done so ever so smoothly. The strip had turned pink on my pregnancy test before I'd discovered that he had been screwing around. In my more honest moments I admitted to myself that was part of what made me hold my tongue about the baby.

The sour-faced waitress refilled my coffee twice more before Brett emerged from the building, golden hair gleaming in the sunlight. I breathed a sigh of relief. The thought had occurred to me that it hadn't been his Escalade and I'd have to think quickly if I ever wanted to see my cell again.

After dropping the scant amount of money on the table, I waited until Brett was secured in his car before exiting the diner and heading to Helga. I was still ninety-nine point nine percent sure that Brett wasn't a sociopathic murderer. I reminded myself of this nonstop as I tailed him into the Jamaica Plain neighborhood. Just because he'd lied to me about what Right Touch had hired him for didn't mean my character assessment was totally off base.

Maybe it was because I had the tech backing me up, but I didn't have a problem keeping the Escalade in sight. I drove in a relaxed manner, listening to classic rock, just another urbanite out doing Sunday errands. I didn't run any lights and kept at least two vehicles between us the whole time.

Of course I wanted him to be a good guy, for Mac's sake if nothing else. But the personal connection had nothing to do with the job. If I found out he had anything to do with either Paul Granger's or Kimmy's murder, I'd turn his homicidal hide in so fast his head would spin.

He pulled to a stop on Child Street, across from several triple-decker houses, and parked. I kept going, taking the next side street turn, and zipped around the corners to come up behind him. My heart thundered in my chest. Had he recognized Helga? There was no way to tell, so I had to proceed under the assumption that I hadn't been made.

By the time I made the turn back onto Child, Brett was striding across the street to a dove-gray house. He didn't look in my direction, so I idled halfway down the street and waited to see who would open the door.

Of course, when the door did finally open, I couldn't see a damn thing. Brett stepped inside, and the door closed behind him.

So was this stop personal or work related? I needed more information. I drove around the block again, this time cutting up a side street and parking around the corner, before securing Helga and walking up to the house.

There were three buzzers beside the intercom labeled *A*, *B*, and *C*. No names, which didn't help. I scribbled down the address and dialed Mac's number. "Is there any way to check who lives at a particular address?"

She responded right away. "Tax records would show the owners."

I thought about our particular set up and took a step back to study the house. It wasn't uncommon for these kinds of houses to have multiple tenants. "What about renters in a building with multiple apartments?"

"Give me the address, and I'll see what I can do," my own personal girl wonder ordered.

I rattled it off and waited while she did her little tech thing.

"The owner is Rita Fuller, and she lives in apartment A. I could try to track down leases for the other two if you want."

I eyeballed the buzzer for the bottom floor apartment. "Does it say how long she's had the property?"

"Fifty-seven years. You gonna putt the squeeze on her, Fogey-Whisperer style?"

"Hey, one day we'll be lucky to make it to senior citizen status," I cautioned.

"Especially with the way we eat," Mac said and disconnected.

I depressed the buzzer, and almost instantly the intercom crackled. "Who's there?" a reedy and yes, elderly, voice called out.

"Rita Fuller?" I asked. "This is Mackenzie Taylor. I'm a private investigator. I was wondering if I could ask you a few questions about your tenants."

Telling her exactly who I was and what I wanted was a gamble. If she had something to hide, she might not admit me. I was banking on the boredom and loneliness that often plagued older people.

Sure enough, the door buzzed, and I slipped inside, praying I wouldn't run into Brett in the hallway.

Rita Fuller's door was open, and the woman herself sat there in an automatic wheelchair, a devilish gleam in her eyes. "You don't look like any PI I've ever seen." Her accent was soft but distinctly Chicago, not Boston.

"Seen a lot of PIs, have you?" I grinned.

A smile kicked up one side of her mouth. "Enough to know that you have to have a license. Let's see some ID"

I pulled my driver's license from my wallet and handed it over for her inspection. "I'm actually working for a lawyer right now, just learning the ropes, so I'm not licensed. But that's me."

She looked it up and down then studied me before handing it back over. "Okay then."

She maneuvered the chair backward and ushered me into her apartment. It was small but clean, with photographs of handsome men and smiling women, stylish art, and comfortable furniture strategically placed out of the way of her wheelchair. "Want some coffee?" she called over her shoulder as she headed into the kitchen.

"No, thanks." It wasn't natural for me to turn down coffee, but I already had to use the bathroom. There was a large bay window facing the street, so I took the chair opposite it to keep an eye on Brett's car. "You have a nice place. Are these all your kids?"

She moved around expertly in the kitchen. Obviously she had her system in place. "And grandkids. And great, great, well, you lose track of the greats after a while."

"Good-looking crew," I told her as I moved from photo to photo.

Rita returned, coffee cup in hand. "Now, tell me what you're investigating and what I can do to help you."

"A man came in here a little while ago. Did you see him?"

She nodded. "I've never seen him before. He went upstairs."

"Do you know which apartment?"

"It has to be the third floor. The girl on the second floor is a friend of my granddaughter's."

"And who lives on the third floor?"

"A couple. The man's a no-goodnik. The wife supports him. I forget the name, but it's on the rent check." She headed down the small hallway to what I assumed was a den before I could even ask.

She was back a moment later, check in hand. "It's a good thing I didn't cash this yet, or you'd be out of luck. The name's Brown, Ruth Brown."

I blinked in surprise. "Is Ruth about five-foot-five, a curvy African American woman with a no-nonsense attitude who looks like she eats tacks for breakfast?"

Rita nodded. "Oh, so you know her then?"

"Our paths have crossed," I said, just as the sound of glass breaking came from upstairs.

Rita shook her head. "Fight like cats and dogs, those two. They don't make men like they used to, that's for sure."

"I don't know about that," I said as footsteps thundered down the stairs. "I need to go, Rita, but it was real nice meeting you."

"Come back anytime," my hostess called.

I hit the hallway the same time as Brett barreled down the stairs to the second floor landing, a pissed off Ruth hot on his heels.

"Come back here, you, so I can squish you like the no-good cockroach you are!" Ruth thundered.

"I'm sorry," Brett said. "I didn't mean to upset you."

Neither of them had noticed me yet. I ducked back into the shadow of Rita's doorway to listen.

"Upset? Why would I be upset? What with you accusing my poor dead friend of dealing drugs. Nu-uh, nothing to be upset about there." Rita had, for whatever reason, a fistful of pennies, and she lobbed one at Brett's head every time she paused her tirade.

He put his hands up as though to ward her off. "Mrs. Brown, the company who hired me knows for a fact that someone was helping Paul Granger fake orders for Alphadra."

"Is that right?" I said stepping out so Brett could see me. "Funny, this is the first I've heard about it.

Brett's hands fell to his sides. "I'm so busted."

CHAPTER EIGHTEEN

Trade Secret—A formula, pattern, process, device, information, or compilation of information that gives the owner of that secret an advantage over competitors who do not know or use it. I'd tell you mine, but then I'd have to kill you.
From the *Working Man's Guide to Sleuthing for a Living* by Albert Taylor, PI

"You know this loser?" Ruth huffed from the stairs. She looked different in jeans and a purple hoodie, with her hair down, though her expression remained as menacing.

"Intimately."

"He's asking if Kimmy was helping the leg-humper forge orders for that stupid drug that didn't even work. I been telling him Kimmy wouldn't do such a thing. He's a damn liar."

"No argument here," I said.

Brett's face was flushed, his gaze split between the two pissed-off females who had him in their crosshairs. "Look, ladies, I didn't mean to disrespect your friend."

"And then when I told him Kimmy wouldn't do it, he said *I* was helping him." Ruth's nostrils flared—she was practically breathing fire.

"I'm sure he didn't mean it," I tried to soothe her.

"Mean it or not, the man owes me an apology." Ruth crossed her arms over her chest and tapped her toe.

"Brett, apologize."

"But—"

"Apologize!" I barked, not wanting to see Ruth commit murder, even if it was justifiable.

"I'm sorry." Brett lowered his gaze. "I never meant to impugn your honor."

"Hmmph," Ruth said. She whirled on her heel and stomped up to her apartment, slamming the door behind her.

"Impugn your honor?" I raised a brow.

Brett trotted down the steps and took me by the elbow. "Heard it on *Game of Thrones*. Come on, let's get out of here before she changes her mind and decides inflation demands nickels."

"Let go of me." How dare he try to perp walk me like I was the one in the wrong? Well I was, but not at the moment.

"Take it easy," he said when I yanked my arm back. "It's really not that big a deal."

"Oh, lying to me isn't categorized as a big deal, huh? Good to know." I saw the irony that I was the one accusing him of being a liar when I was the one with the big Mac Daddy whopper of a secret, but still, I was too pissed to care.

"What did you expect?" He rounded on me, a few feet away from his vehicle. "That I was just going to spill my whole case to you when you magically reappear in my life after sixteen years? Why should I tell you anything, because you woke up one day and thought 'Gee, today I'd like to be a private investigator, and I'm Mackenzie so I can just do whatever the hell I want'?"

"Bitter much?" I asked him.

"Now that I've thought about, yeah. I am bitter. But this isn't about us or how you abandoned me."

He made it sound like he was a puppy I'd left by the side of the road in a basket. "I didn't abandon you, you idiot. My parents made me move. And besides, I'm sure Tina Yates stepped right into my place."

"Who?" Brett looked genuinely confused.

"Oh don't bother lying. I saw you making out with her in that empty alcove by the cafeteria." My hands flew to my hips as I glared at him. "Or did you think I'd forgotten about that?"

He grimaced. "Mackenzie, *I've* forgotten about that. What can I say? I was a dumbass at sixteen. Now, get in the car before someone calls in a domestic disturbance."

I opened my mouth to argue with him on principle before recalling that I needed my phone back. "Fine. But, only because I want to know what *you know* about the Alphadra. No more talk of what a lying, cheating, no-goodnik you are."

"Glad we got that cleared up," Brett muttered and held the passenger door for me.

I waited until he shut it and turned away before leaning into the back to search for my phone. Unfortunately it was a big back seat, and he had a bunch of gadgets stowed there.

"What are you doing?"

"Looking for my contact. It popped out."

"All the way into the back seat?" His tone was incredulous.

There was the phone, half hidden beneath his seat. "Almost got it."

"Do you want help?"

I snagged the phone and slid it forward. Cool air brushed my stomach as my contortionist act revealed about six inches of well-fed belly. "Nope, I got it."

I sat up, making sure to blink one eye as if I'd just replaced my imaginary contact. "There."

"Where are you parked? That old lady is staring at us and looking like she wants to call the cops."

"Her name is Rita, and don't worry about her. We're friends." I waved and after a moment she waved back. "And my car's on a side street."

Brett turned the engine over. "That's why I didn't spot you. When did you pick me up?"

I lifted my chin and crossed my arms. "At the Right Touch office building."

"Wow." He looked suitably impressed.

"So tell me about the missing Alphadra. Every doctor I spoke to says it doesn't work."

"Oh it works, just not the way it's supposed to."

I made a rolling motion with my hand, the universal gesture to keep going.

"Mackenzie." He sounded pained.

"I'm not trying to horn in on your case, but I want to know how it involves two dead people."

"Fine. As an ED drug, Alphadra's a bust. But cooked up with a few over-the-counter medications, it becomes a powerful stimulant."

"Like meth?"

"Milder than that. It's mostly an energy booster and causes rapid weight loss, but it can be just as toxic. There were several deliveries that Paul made to various practices that have no record of stocking it. Right Touch hired me to find out who was helping him hide the trail and sell it on the street. Ruth and Kimmy were the prime suspects, mostly because they have the financial need."

"What about the doctors in the practice?" I asked.

"I've checked them all out. They aren't flush with cash, but most have their medical loans paid back and aren't facing any major malpractice suits. There's no motive."

I thought back to the day I'd fist gone into the clinic, how Hunter had just happened to be in the parking garage. "Do the cops know about this?"

"Yes. After Granger's death, Right Touch told the police about my investigation. So far they haven't gotten any further than I have." He parked behind my car and laid his head against the wheel. "When I heard about Kimmy's murder, I thought for sure she must have been the one. She sent money home to her parents in Cambodia on a regular basis. I underestimated Ruth's loyalty."

I drummed my fingers on the leg of my jeans. "You're sure someone from the office had to be helping him?"

"Yes. The orders were made through the office computer systems, so whoever made it had access."

"And it has to be someone with financial motive?"

He nodded again.

"Was Ruth's husband there?"

"Yeah, why?"

I looked at him, waiting for it to click.

He smacked himself on the forehead, saving me the trouble of doing it. "He has no job, plenty of time to deal, and could probably obtain access to the system through her. Why didn't I think of that?"

"You realize you'll have to go back up there." I warned him. "Ruth might put your head on a pike."

"No need. I have surveillance equipment in back. If I can catch him dealing, I can call the cops and have them bust him. Case closed."

"That easy, huh? You don't suppose he's a murderer too?"

"Nah, no motive. Why bite off the hand that feeds him?"

"So I'm still spitting into the wind."

"Chin up, Mackenzie. Someday you, too, will be a great mastermind detective like me. In the meantime…" He moved in to kiss me.

My back slammed against the side door. "Whoa there, Sparky. What are you doing?"

"Trying to kiss you. As a thank you."

"Ha, I'm not sixteen anymore. Say it with cash." I held out my palm.

He looked from it to my face and back. "What do you say I buy you dinner sometime?"

All the case cracking had shoved my original purpose in following him to the backburner. Dinner might be just the thing. "Give me your number, and we'll set something up."

Hope flashed in his eyes, and he rattled off his number. "Can I have yours?"

"You'll get it when I call you."

He shook his head. "You always wanted all the power in our relationship."

My hand was on the door handle, but I froze at his words.

Brett noticed my odd mood shift. "What? Did I say something wrong?"

"No, but you aren't the first person to tell me that this week. See ya." I slithered out onto the sidewalk on rubbery legs, leaving him behind.

* * *

"Mom," Mac met me at the door. "Where were you?"

"Cracking a case wide open."

"Does that mean you're getting paid?" My daughter looked hopeful.

"Unfortunately not. Shoot, is that the time?" I glanced at the Felix the Cat wall clock.

"Yes, and we still have no plan for this dinner that's supposed to be starting in less than an hour."

I set my shoulder bag down and shucked my coat then rubbed my hands together. "Bring me everything we have. Cabinets, fridge, freezer. Let's empty this mother out."

Mac looked at me like I'd lost my mind but did as instructed. Fifteen minutes later we had a passable feast, at least if we had a bunch of eight-year-olds. Peanut butter and jelly sandwiched between crackers, cheese cubes, cheese puffs, apple slices dipped in caramel, candy, cookies, and popcorn. And the pièce de résistance, root beer floats, though I wouldn't make those until the guests arrived.

"It's all in the arranging," I told Mac as I set a bowl of M&M's as a centerpiece. "Oh, and see if we have any candles."

"Because then it will look like we tried?" Mac shook her head.

"Always with the quips," I muttered. "Trust me—you don't want people coming to you for food. Once they do, they never stop."

The doorbell rang, and Snickers leapt from her favorite couch cushion to sound the alert.

"You don't think she'll bite anybody, do you?" I asked Mac.

"Only you." My daughter headed for the door and peeked through the peephole. "Mom? Did you invite Atticus Finch?"

I nudged her out of the way so I could see. "That would be Len, the kind soul who sees fit to employ me. Hold the dog."

Mac backed up so I could open the door and usher Len inside.

"Mackenzie." He nodded at me and handed over a lovely autumn bouquet and a bottle of Moscato. "Good to see you."

"Len, may I introduce my daughter, Mackenzie Elizabeth Taylor the Second, though we just call her Mac."

Mac extended the hand not holding a squirming puggle and, like the true southern gentleman, Len took it and raised it to his lips. "Just as beautiful as your mother, I see."

I watched as Mac's surprise faded into pleasure. The charming devil had ensnared her, too. I bet opposing counsel never saw Len coming.

He wore a seersucker suit and matching fedora, which he'd removed the second he crossed the threshold. He also carried a cane, but since this was the first I'd seen of it, I got the feeling it was an accessory more than anything else. Kindly older man comes a-calling. "Am I the first to arrive? I'm not too familiar with this area, so I left early."

"It's fine. We just set the table." I waved at what looked like a dentist's wet dream and asked, "Root beer float or wine?"

"Lord have mercy, what a choice." Len laughed. "It's been a dog's age since I had a root beer float. Set me up with one of those. This looks like a carnival!"

"Coming right up." I circled the counter to retrieve the vanilla ice cream out of the fridge. "Would you like a tour, Len?"

"I'd be much obliged." Sure enough, he set the cane aside.

Mac set Snickers down and offered him her arm. He grinned and took hold of it.

I made three root beer floats, adding a generous dollop of whip cream, and tried to make a plan of attack for when my parents both arrived. Unfortunately, having them in the same room at the same time caused me to break out in hives, so I'd never given much thought to their couple's dynamic. What I did know for a fact was that neither one liked surprises.

The plan had "harebrained scheme" splattered all over it.

I was still fretting when the doorbell rang again. I checked the time, ten minutes to seven. That had to be Mom or Nona dropping by early since The Captain was perpetually punctual. I wouldn't be surprised if he was sitting out in his car, watching the clock so he could arrive on my doorstep at seven thirty on the dot.

"Mackenzie, looking good as always, doll." Nona wore a long shapeless sack covered with giant tropical flowers and a wide-brimmed Sunday hat. Her press-on nails were tipped in what looked like gold dust, and she wore bright pink lipstick. "I brought latkes."

"Excellent," I said taking the dish from her. "Mac's never had them, so this will be a treat."

I set the plate on the table and opened the aluminum foil to let the fragrant steam wash over me. "These smell delicious."

"I'm out of sour cream, but there's apple sauce for dipping. I really should have gone to the store, but my knee was bothering me," Nona fretted.

I debated offering to go get the ketchup, but didn't. "Maybe I should run upstairs and see if Mom has any sour cream?"

Nona sagged in relief. "Oh, that would be great. I was gonna knock on her door but my hands were full."

"I'll do that then. Mac, you're in charge till I get back."

I shut the door behind me a second after hearing Nona whistle and say, "Well, hell-o, handsome." I smiled to myself. Somehow I had a feeling they'd hit it off.

I took the stairs and knocked on my mother's door.

"Go away, Mackenzie," she called.

"Is that any way to talk to your only child?" I called.

There was a pause and then the door opened a crack, the chain still in place.

"Seriously?" I asked, waving at the chain. "Do you really think I'm going to bust the door down?"

"I never know with you," my mother replied tartly. "You run hot and cold."

I bit my tongue. Hard enough to taste blood. Getting her downstairs to see dad was the goal, and me losing my temper wouldn't help. My root beer float would be well earned. "Didn't you get my note?"

"You think I'll come down only to go through the humiliation of having you kick me out again? This time in front of witnesses?"

"I won't. Look, for what it's worth, I'm sorry I made you leave last night. You have the right to your opinion."

She didn't say anything, and I sighed. "Mom, I wrote you an apology note. I'm here groveling right now. Judas Priest, what do I have to do, order a singing telegram?"

"Don't be ridiculous." She spoke without venom. "Well, I didn't make anything."

"That's okay." My mother's contribution would probably contain kale or some other superfood and ruin my theme. "If you have any sour cream though, could you bring that? Nona's plotzing because she made latkes and didn't have any."

"Let me check the fridge." The door shut, and a minute later the chain rattled, and she reopened it.

"I'm not really dressed for a dinner party." She fussed, plucking at her navy sweater and taupe slacks.

At least she was worrying about her own clothing instead of mine for a change. "Trust me—it's a very casual affair."

She went to her stainless steel fridge, opened the door, and pulled out a container of light sour cream. "Will this do?"

"Perfect." I could always put it in a bowl and try to forget that it was low fat.

"Do I need my purse?"

"Yes, because Mac's carding and charging a five spot at the door."

"Oh, you and that smart mouth." She swatted my arm then turned to lock her door.

We were headed down the steps when the front door to the building opened and The Captain strode in and marched toward my door.

"What's he doing here?" my mother hissed. Loudly. She'd never gotten the hang of volume control.

My father froze mid-step, then looked up, his expression blanking as he looked at the woman he'd been married to for thirty-five years.

"Dad wanted to see our new place." I looped my arm through my mother's so she wouldn't get away. "And meet my boss. Just like you."

"Agnes," my father said curtly. "Mackenzie. Good evening."

"This isn't a good idea." In spite of my grip, my mother tried to pull back, to retreat back up the stairs.

"I should go." The Captain was also backing toward the exit.

"Now hold on one minute," I snapped. "I've gone to a lot of trouble to get the two of you here. The least you can do is tell me what the hell is going on."

"Language," Agnes chastised, but it was a reflex more than anything else.

"You have bigger problems than my language," I said. "Can you two look me in the eye and tell me that after spending half your lives together you can't play nice for one dinner?"

My mother didn't move. Neither did my father.

I threw my hands up in the air. "Did one of you have an affair? Is there another man? Another woman? Both?"

"Don't be lewd," Reg Taylor barked.

I stared at him. Maybe it was my newly emerging PI skills or women's intuition, but I heard what he didn't say just as loudly as what he did. "You didn't answer the question. Is that it, Mom? Did he screw around on you?"

My father's face darkened to a blotchy red-purple. "How dare you? How dare you stand there and let her accuse me of throwing it all away when you're the one who's leaving."

"No one's accusing anyone—" I interjected, but he ignored me.

Coming closer one slow, menacing step at a time, he glared at his wife.

My mother had her arms wrapped protectively around herself. "You gave me no choice."

He laughed, totally without humor. "You disgust me anyway. I can't even look at you without thinking about his hands all over you."

My mouth fell open. My mother had cheated?

"Who would want you now anyway? You're nothing but a dried-up bag of used goods."

"Hey!" I came back to life and stepped between my advancing father and my silent mother. "Hold on here. I don't care what she did! You can't talk to her that way."

His attention snapped from her to me, and then he shook his head and headed for the door. He pushed it open so hard it slammed against outer wall with a defining bang.

Without a word my mother handed me the sour cream and disappeared up the stairs.

I let her, my head swimming as I replayed the scene from the last few minutes, shaken to my core.

My own door opened, and Mac's head popped out. "Everything okay out here? I thought I heard shouting."

My lips parted, but I didn't know what to say.

The front door opened and I blinked, dreading it would be The Captain all wound up for round two. Instead, Hunter stood there, filling the doorway, the western sun backlighting him like some romantic movie hero.

I rushed down the steps, eager to run into his arms, to let him hold me while I quietly put myself back together in the safety of his embrace. I was so focused on him that I didn't notice the swarm of uniformed police following hot on his heels.

"Hunter?" I asked.

"Mackenzie Taylor, you are under arrest."

"What did I do?" I barked, outraged, gaze locked on Hunter, demanding an explanation. Seething at the betrayal. If he was going to arrest me, he could have least sent me a heads up text.

"Not you," the uniform said and then broke my heart when he pointed at my wide-eyed daughter. "Her."

CHAPTER NINETEEN

Felony—A crime of a more serious nature than a misdemeanor; generally, a criminal offense punishable by death or imprisonment in excess of one year. Depending on the state, the judge and how much your lawyer charges by the hour.
From the *Working Man's Guide to Sleuthing for a Living* by Albert Taylor, PI

"What did you do?" I asked my daughter for the zillionth time. We were shut together in what I could only assume was an interrogation room—no windows, no mirror, just a video camera in the corner above the door. We were waiting for Len to get the 4-1-1 on why Mac had been arrested.

"Nothing." My daughter sounded offended that I'd even asked.

"You know the drill. You're not supposed to get incarcerated unless I'm sitting in the cell beside you." It was a lame joke, but admittedly I wasn't on my A-game.

"Len will find out what the deal is, and we'll get you out of here." As a parent, there's no worse feeling in the world than watching your only child being led away in handcuffs by the police. Except maybe being physically restrained by the sexy traitor you'd been running to for comfort only moments earlier while watching your only child be led away in handcuffs by the police.

My knee was bouncing spastically. I wanted to pace in the worst way but was afraid to telegraph my nervousness, lest it worry Mac more. She looked thoroughly freaked out. But the damn knee had a mind of its own and jiggled away.

"There has to be something. They wouldn't drag you down here in handcuffs for jaywalking."

Mac shook her head. "I really don't know. Hunter didn't say anything to you?"

"No," I snapped, the rage building to toxic levels. "He didn't."

"It's not his fault, Mom. He was just doing his job."

I didn't acknowledge her logic. My mind was preoccupied with one glaring fact: Hunter Black worked *murder* investigations. There was no way Mac could have anything to do with a homicide case.

The door opened, and Len shuffled in, followed by a glaringly handsome man in a rumpled suit.

I hopped out of my chair, ready to block my offspring bodily if necessary. "What's going on?"

The stranger was young, only a few years older than Mac. His hair was slicked back, revealing high cheekbones, a sharp blade of a nose, and piercing blue eyes. His body was lean and athletic. He looked more like a displaced surfer dressing up in his father's wardrobe than a cop. When he spoke I noticed the distinct lack of accent. "Ms. Taylor, Ms. Taylor, I'm Detective Carson with the Cyberterrorism Unit."

"Cyberterrorism?" Mac and I said in unison. We exchanged a look, and I swallowed hard before adding, "There must be some mistake."

"Hear him out, girls," Len advised.

"I'm here to offer Miss Mackenzie the Second a deal."

"We still don't know—" I began.

"I hacked into the police database," Mac confessed as though someone were holding her feet to the fire. "It was me. Well, Pete helped."

Carson nodded. "You did a damn good job of it, too. Left virtually no tracks. If it had only been the once, I might not have caught on."

Mac blushed and looked away as though he'd told her she was the most beautiful girl he'd ever seen.

I'd known she'd accessed Hunter's files, but I hadn't realized she'd hacked into the police database to do it. And she'd done it more than once? A sinking feeling took up residence in my stomach. For me—she'd broken the law for me. I must be the worst mother on the face of the planet.

"How bad is this?" I turned toward Len, but it was Detective Carson who answered.

"It's not good. The Commonwealth could ask for the maximum. A three thousand dollar fine and up to two and a half years in prison."

Prison was on the table? I swallowed hard. "But she's only sixteen."

"Cybercrimes are different." Len patted my hand. "They could try her as an adult."

My heart was pounding, and I had the urge to confess, to tell them it wasn't Mac, that I had done it. It was unlikely anyone would believe me. My chest tightened, and I couldn't seem to get enough air.

Just when I was sure the terror would drown me, Detective Carson tossed me a life preserver. "That's if we pursue criminal charges. We don't want to do that, however. What we want is for Mackenzie to work for us."

"Work for?" Mac asked.

"Technically volunteer for. We can't afford to pay you. Or Pete, we want him too. I'll be speaking with him in a few."

"But how can she? She's only in tenth grade," I reminded them.

"Mo-om." Mac's tone was incredulous.

I gave her a palms-up gesture. "Well you are. He can't expect you to quit school for this." I looked over at the cop for verification.

He shook his head "The position is as a consultant only. Think of it as a part-time job—after school, weekends, holidays."

I looked to our attorney. "And they'll drop the charges, all the charges?"

Len nodded. "That's what he claims. If Mac agrees, they'll go ahead and draw up the paperwork, and I'll go over it with a fine-tooth comb before she signs it."

"Mac?" I asked. It didn't sound like we had much of a choice. Either agree to the deal, or roll the dice with a court case and risk her having to do jail time.

"I want to do it." She wasn't looking at me. All her attention was fixed on Carson.

"Excellent," he said and grinned, flashing even white teeth. "You'll start tomorrow. I'll email you with details of your first assignment."

"Will I need to come here?" she asked almost eagerly.

"Only on occasion. We have a closed circuit network that you can access with any top-secret information. I can show you the lab if you'd like, Mackenzie."

"I go by Mac." My daughter leapt up like an eager puppy, ready to follow wherever Carson went.

He opened the door.

"Carson," I called when Mac was out in the hall.

He looked back at me, his charming grin fading.

"Keep in mind that she's sixteen, and I have an awesome attorney. No funny business."

Carson blanched visibly but nodded. "Nothing like that, ma'am."

"I think you scared the poor boy." Len chuckled.

"Not nearly enough. Did you see the way she was looking at him? Computer geeks aren't supposed to look like that," I grumbled. "And he called me ma'am."

"He's also the reason your daughter isn't facing criminal charges," Len pointed out.

"You'll have to forgive me. I'm a little soured on cops at the moment."

He tucked an arm through one of mine. "I'll say this for you Miz Mackenzie. You throw the most entertaining dinner parties."

* * *

Later that night, I peeked in on Mac, sleeping soundly in my bed. When she was a baby, I used to sleep in the same room with her, lying awake, listening to her rhythmic breathing. After tonight's scare I might just renew the habit.

Restless, I prowled through the apartment, looking for something—anything—to take my mind off the awful events of the day. First finding out Brett was the same lying bastard he'd always been, then The Captain berating Agnes, Mac getting hauled out of our home in handcuffs, and Hunter's hands on me, keeping me from launching myself at the police.

Brett was who he was. The same went for my parents, and the Mac situation had resolved itself, at least temporarily. I paused and turned toward the door, my blood boiling with the urge to settle a score.

I locked the apartment and crept across the entryway until I was standing in front of Hunter's door, knocking before I'd even thought it through.

He must have been standing on the other side of it because the door swung open immediately. I waited for him to say something. He didn't.

"Can I come in?" I asked. "I really don't want to say what I came here to say out in the hall where anyone can hear."

He stood aside, and I marched in, trembling with rage.

"Before you say anything," Hunter said. "I found out about the charges at the last second and asked to come with the team."

If he thought that would somehow diffuse me he was dead wrong. "Why?"

"Because I didn't want you to go through that alone."

"You held me back," I accused, stepping closer to him, lifting my chin.

"Because I didn't want you to get arrested for obstruction of justice or assaulting a police officer," he responded.

The reasonableness of his answer pissed me right off. "You could have told me."

"How? Telephone? Text? I could have lost my shield."

Hot tears were stinging behind my eyes. I blinked them back, furiously. "You have an answer for everything don't you?"

"Red." He didn't move any closer. "There's nothing I could have done to stop it."

"That's what Mac said."

He tipped my chin up "But you don't believe it?"

I jerked my face away. "No, I don't. You don't just sit on the sidelines when people you care about are in trouble."

"She broke the law."

"Because of me!" I shouted. "Because she was trying to help me with a case."

Hunter was quiet.

"Don't do that," I snapped. "Don't just stand there and say nothing. It makes me want to hit you."

"Go ahead." His tone was flat, his stance stoic.

"What?"

"I said go ahead and hit me."

I stared at him, searching for the trap. "So you can arrest me for assaulting a police officer?"

"I'm off duty. If you need a punching bag, I'm volunteering. It wouldn't be the first time." A faint tinge of bitterness crept into his tone.

"You mean on the job."

He didn't answer, but something shifted in his dark eyes. The mood between us altered, the air ceased crackling with heat, and instead chilled me to my core. I recognized a deep pain, something that stretched out over years that took root in childhood and that, even as a fully functioning adult, you never managed to completely shake off. I saw that same nebulous something in my own eyes at times.

My rage dissipated, and when I stepped closer it wasn't to strike but to soothe. "Tell me."

He looked away first. "I don't talk about it. Ever."

I chose a line Mac sometimes used to bait me. "You wouldn't have brought it up if you didn't want to talk."

He glanced back at me, then, "What did you see when you were in here last time? You never said."

I hadn't. He knew I'd snooped, had probably invited me in for that very purpose. "I saw your screensaver, if that's what you're asking."

Hunter nodded once. "You saw my family then, probably noticed the lack of resemblance between me and anyone else. To answer your unspoken question, yes, they adopted me."

I reached out, took his hand in mine and squeezed once. "How old were you?"

He squeezed back and didn't let go. "Eight. They found me on the side of the road in New Mexico, covered in blood. Put something of a damper on their family vacation."

The lack of comfy furniture in the small space bothered me. This wasn't the sort of story a man should stand through while reliving. For lack of anything else, I pulled out one of his massive dining table chairs and guided him into it, before settling in across from him.

"My dad, Mr. Black, I mean, was a police officer. I think that's the only reason he stopped. A cop can't ignore a child covered in blood, even if the rest of the world could. And his wife was a nurse so out of all the people who could have picked me up, they were the best. It was the best and worst day of my life."

"How badly were you hurt?" I had images of an eight-year-old boy flung from a moving vehicle and left to die alone and scared.

"I wasn't hurt. It wasn't my blood."

I blinked but didn't say anything. I could pull the story out of him, one back and forth question at a time, but he needed to open up on his own timeline.

"My father, my biological father, I mean, he was a drunk. A mean drunk. Alcoholism is very common on Native American reservations, especially impoverished ones."

"I've heard that."

His gaze slid to mine. "We didn't have to live in squalor. My father was a big man, like me. When he wasn't lost in a bottle he was a hard worker. There were some good times. But that was almost worse. You can get used to any kind of ugly situation, but when you believe it to be over and think yourself safe—" he broke off, shaking his head.

"Did your mother know? That he hit you?"

His hand had been resting palm down on the glass-topped table but at my question, he clenched it into a fist. "She knew. Usually she patched me up after he passed out, if she wasn't too badly hurt herself. Before you ask, she stayed because she had nowhere else to go, no family, no friends who would take us in. The situation escalated, but she was trapped. We both were at his mercy. And he had very little of that to spare."

I was afraid to twitch, to draw a deep breath or do anything that would prevent him from talking. My heart went out to him as I imagined the terrifying unpredictability of his childhood.

"Things got better for me when I went to school." Hunter's gaze was unfocused. "We were bused off the reservation, and I was away from home for hours and hours. But I was always worried about what was going on back there, what he was doing to her while I was safe, and what I'd come home to. I think it was the guilt that made me pick fights with him. If he wore himself out beating on me then he wouldn't hurt her too badly."

"But you were just a little boy," I whispered, my heart breaking.

He looked at me then, his intensity scorching me where I sat. "I never had the luxury. My mother begged me to stop goading him, told me I should keep my head down and not rile him the way she did. I didn't listen because, well, her approach wasn't keeping her any safer. And there was some satisfaction in taking potshots at the old man. Some little revenges to show him he couldn't break me."

"Oh, I know that feeling," I mumbled. "It's heady."

"And in my situation, dangerous. The day of the blood he'd been drinking since he rolled out of bed, and my mother had taken me into town for new sneakers. I was growing like crazy then. Most clothing items lasted three months, tops. We had donations, but people rarely think to donate shoes. So it was an ongoing expense. That's what started it, the cost of a twenty-dollar pair of sneakers.

"She didn't even have her coat off when he landed the first blow. She went down hard, and I immediately put myself between the two of them. He snarled at me to get out of the way, that this was between them. I told him they were my feet and my sneakers so I wasn't going anywhere. He picked me up by my shirt and tossed me into the kitchen wall. I hit so hard it cracked the plaster."

"Hunter," I begged, not wanting to hear anymore.

He blinked, shook himself. "Well, it went on like that for a while, me refusing to stay down no matter how sore or dizzy because I knew he'd keep going after her if I gave in. He kept ranting and railing until finally my mother got up. She told him she was leaving him, that she'd had enough, and we were going. Her hands were trembling her voice shook, but she stood there and refused to give in. I'd never been so proud of her.

"She went down the hall to their room, and he followed. She called to me, told me to take any clothes that fit and put them in the shopping bag we'd gotten with my new shoes. I did, loading up the bag as full as it would get. I remember feeling, light, hopeful. My father was shouting, swearing, telling her he'd kill her before he'd let her leave. Then I heard the crash from the other side of the wall."

A chill crept through me, and I knew this story wasn't going to end on a high note.

"I dropped the bag and ran to see what had happened. My father stood there in the room, still shaking, and my mother—" He broke off had to clear his throat. "He'd shoved her through the window. She was lying outside the house, cuts all over her body. A jagged piece of glass was sticking out of the side of her neck, the blood spurting out, like a fountain. I ran outside, stripped off my shirt, trying to stop the bleeding but it was too late. She was gone.

He came out then, started howling like he hadn't just killed her. He killed my mother and wept over her body like he had any right to mourn. I remember looking down at the new sneakers that had started the whole thing. They were stained with her blood. I took them off and started walking and made it about two miles before they found me."

My throat had gone dry, but I managed to choke out, "I'm so sorry."

His gaze refocused, and he reached for my hand. "I've never told anyone that story. At least not with so much detail."

"But your parents, the people who adopted you, I mean."

"Oh, they found out what had happened through police reports. My father had disappeared by the time they arrived. They caught up to him a few weeks later though, passed out in a new place with a new woman like nothing had changed. He's serving a thirty-five year sentence for manslaughter and aggravated assault."

His story explained so much about him. Why he became a cop. Why he insisted on playing by the rules. Why he didn't smile much. Why the idea of me putting myself in danger upset him so much. He'd already seen one young mother's death and was doing everything in his power to prevent another.

"I'm so sorry about your mom," I whispered and reached for his hand.

"So am I." He tangled our fingers together. "Sorry, I didn't mean to burden you with all that."

"Burdens are meant to be shared. It makes them less…burdensome."

That provoked the half smile. "Burdensome?"

I rubbed my tired eyes with my free hand. "It's late. I should be getting back home." Though the likelihood of me sleeping after hearing such a story was nil.

"Stay. And not because you feel sorry for me or because you think I need comforting. Stay because you want to and because I want you to more than I've wanted anything in a long time."

"Hunter," I protested.

Without warning he pulled me off my chair and onto his lap. His free arm went around my waist like a steel band. "Say yes," he whispered and then kissed me in that all-consuming way of his.

Again I melted into him, and again he was the one to pull away first.

His hand traveled up to spear into my hair as he nipped my bottom lip. "I want you, Red. Say yes."

"Is that an order? Because I don't take orders well."

No answer.

I ran my fingers through his silky dark hair, studied his every earnest feature. He was so tempting, and I wasn't the kind of girl to say no to temptation for long. "Yes."

A slow grin spread over his face, stealing my breath. His smile intoxicated me faster than my mother's horrible cocktails and made my head swim. "Come on, I want to show you my bedroom."

I rose, and he took my hand, leading me toward our destination.

He didn't turn on the light, just shut the door closing us into the moonlit space.

I didn't look away from him as I said, "Nice room."

Then he kissed me until I lost all sense of time and place.

CHAPTER TWENTY

Private investigators who lack professional skill cause more problems than they solve. If this lack results in injury or loss to another party, the PI can be held liable for malpractice.
From the *Working Man's Guide to Sleuthing for a Living* by Albert Taylor, PI

I crept back to my apartment before first light and headed right into the shower. The hot water helped clear away some of the cobwebs but didn't touch the sense of icky confusion that clung to me like a second skin.

I changed into a faded pair of jeans with fraying cuffs and a black racer-back tank that proclaimed the java's honest truth in big block letters: *I can't adult today*.

Mac was at the coffeepot looking daisy fresh. "You got in late. I didn't even hear you. More work?"

"No." I couldn't even wrap my head around the investigation, just one more thing I was screwing up.

My daughter studied me closely as she poured her coffee. "You're not looking too hot. You coming down with something?"

"Nothing like that. Hey listen, you think maybe you could play hooky today? I'll write you a note. Tell them you have a fever." I said the last part in my best Christopher Walken inflection.

Mac groaned and stuffed a bagel in the toaster. "Mom, it's too early for SNL skits."

I couldn't resist and fell right back into it. "They don't need to know that the only prescription is *moar* cowbell."

Mac rolled her eyes at my Walkenesque pronunciation just as her bagel popped out of the toaster "I can't. I have a Spanish test, and I need to get some work done on the genetics project during my free period."

I poured my own coffee and took a fortifying sip. "Hey listen. I didn't get a chance to tell you yesterday that I ran into Brett again."

Mac froze with the bagel halfway to her mouth. "What happened?"

"It was all case related, mostly his case. But I remembered some stuff. About him and his issues with the truth. And then the whole debacle with the police happened and between school and your new internship…and I was just thinking that maybe we should wait on the grand reveal."

Mac was quiet. Like Hunter type quiet.

It made me nervous. "Yes? No? Maybe?"

"Were you with him last night?"

"What?" I blinked. "No, of course not."

"Where were you then?"

I blew out a breath. "I was with Hunter. I know I told you I wouldn't, and I didn't intend to, but it just happened. It was a mistake."

She turned and dropped her bagel in the trash, scooped up her backpack, and headed toward the door.

"Hey wait a second!" I scurried after her, snagging the strap of her backpack before she could escape. "Not only did you just waste perfectly good food, but we were in the middle of a conversation. You can't just leave."

"I have school, and my appetite disappeared." I could practically hear her molars grinding. "Let go."

"Not until we talk about this."

She rounded on me. "What's to talk about? You never do what you promise me you'll do. Do I have to sneak past his door now, avoid all eye contact? Should I remind you he was there when I was arrested and *didn't do anything to stop it*?"

"You told me it wasn't his fault," I argued back. "Yesterday, you were the one defending him!"

"Because I didn't want you coming down on him like a ton of bricks. But I didn't know the alternative would be you hopping into bed with him!"

I blew out a breath, tired of defending my actions to her. "Listen, I'm sorry if you're so upset, and I won't do it again, but I'm not sorry it happened. I really like him, Mac."

"Did you sneak out of his bed this morning?"

"That's not—"

She bowled right over the top of me. "Does he still live next door? Are you two on the same *it was a one-time thing* page or will my life get even more complicated? And then there's Brett."

I put my hands on my hips in classic showdown fashion. "Is that really what this is about then?"

"You promised me you'd tell him." She mimicked my pose.

"I will, but Mac, think it through. You already have a full plate."

"Stop pretending this is about me," she snapped.

"Hey," I snapped back, the leash on my temper frayed to the breaking point. "I know I may not act like it all the time, but I am your mother, and when I say now isn't the right time to invite your father into your life, I expect you to accept it as the truth even if you don't like it."

"Whatever." Mac wrenched her backpack free and yanked the door open. "You'll do what you want. You always do, no matter the collateral damage."

I gaped at her, open-mouthed as she stormed through the entryway and slammed out the front door. I wanted to call her back but figured the walk to the bus stop would cool her temper and maybe a little normal teenager type of distraction would help her get over her ire.

"Everything all right down there, doll?" Nona called from the top of the stairs.

I cleared my throat. "Yeah, just teenager versus mama drama. I'm not liking my odds."

"Come on up. I got a nice coffee cake," Nona insisted.

"Just let me put the dog out."

I let Snickers out in the back yard and then, remembering Nona's mini-cups, grabbed my coffee mug, and filled it to the brim.

Nona's door was open, and she was slicing into the coffee cake.

"You seem verklempt," she observed.

"I passed verklempt a few days ago." I lowered myself into the chair. "Right now I'm at the regretting-I've-been-born phase."

She patted my hand. "Tell Nona all about it."

I blew out a sigh. "The long and short of it is that Mac's angry because I won't tell her father about her existence."

"He doesn't know he has a daughter?"

"No. When I first saw him he was all cool and collected, and I felt bad, but then I caught him in a lie, and all the reasons I thought he was too immature to handle parenthood came back." I fiddled with my napkin. "And I don't want to share her."

"Ah." Nona nodded. "I see."

"She's my best friend as well as my daughter. Even when she's being the quintessential difficult teenager, I'm lost without her. If Brett knew about her, he might want to spend time with her, and between school and her new obligation with the police…"

"The police?" Nona's eyebrows went up.

"It's a long story. And she's also mad at me about Hunter. We… that is Hunter and I…" I looked her in the eye, lowering my chin as I waited for her to catch my drift.

"Schtupped?" Nona waggled her eyebrows. "I knew you two would go together like pastrami and rye. How was it?"

I blushed.

"That good, huh?" Nona fanned herself with her napkin. "Honey, give yourself a break. It's okay to enjoy life to the fullest. And as for Mac's father, you did what you believed was right for you and for her then, and you'll do what's right for both of you now."

"But what if what's right for her is not what's right for me? She'll be heading off to college in a few years, and I'll hardly see her. I want to savor the time we have together before she's gone."

"The tighter you hold on, doll, the sooner she'll leave."

She was right. I knew she was. "Thanks, Nona. Now, if I could only solve my murder case, I'd be set."

"Can't help you with that, I'm afraid. Give my regards to that handsome lawyer when you see him."

I pushed back my chair. "Will do, Nona. Will do."

After letting Snickers back in and changing into more suitable work attire, I was all set to head out the door when someone knocked. "Open up Red. I know you're in there."

Judas Priest, I wasn't ready to deal with Hunter yet. For one thing, I'd snuck out of his bed in the wee small hours like a coward. And for another, I was hoping Mac would come around to our relationship. Sure, it had all the potential for a romantic disaster, but with great risk came great reward. And, for maybe the first time I was almost ready to take the risk. Which scared me to death. But still, I had promised Mac it was a one-time thing, and I didn't want to renege on yet another front. Me and my big, fat mouth.

"Mackenzie." He knocked louder and Snickers barked. "Let's talk about this."

No, no, no. Warning, warning, danger, danger, Will Robinson! I backed slowly away from the door, heading back to the bedroom and out the sliding glass door. After climbing the low fence, I crept through the bushes and over to where Fillmore was parked. Though I had no clear destination in mind, Fillmore was the better bet for surveillance.

I called Brett and let out a relieved sigh when his voicemail picked up. "Hey, this is Mackenzie. Can we meet up? You can reach me at this number."

My phone rang just as I hit the end of the street. "Hello?"

"Mackenzie? Hey, it's Brett. I have some information about your case."

"You do?" I asked eagerly. "That's good because I need to talk to you about something. Where can we meet up?"

"How about your lawyer's office. I'm not far from there now." His voice sounded a little strained.

"Sounds good. Is everything okay?"

"Yeah, sure."

"How did it go with your case?" I probed. "Did you catch Ruth's man dealing your drug?"

"I don't want to get into it over the phone." He definitely sounded distracted.

"Okay, it'll take me about twenty minutes. See you then." I disconnected and drummed my fingers against the steering wheel. Had I mentioned Len to Brett? Well he was a PI after all, and he'd been at it longer than I had. Traffic was backed up, and I distracted myself thinking about Paul Granger, aka the leg-humper.

The man had the morals of an alley cat, and considering what I'd learned about him, I was surprised he'd had the intelligence to repurpose the Alphadra. The fact that Right Touch had hired Brett showed that Paul wasn't at all careful about hiding what he'd been up to. Even his wife had known the company had been paying him.

His wife. The doctor. Who presumably had the knowledge of drugs and how they interacted with the human body. Who was going through a messy divorce and maybe needed the money.

Could Jessica Granger have hired someone to kill her husband the way Hunter thought? She had certainly put off the type of vibe I would have associated with a murderer. But I kept coming back to Kimmy. How would the two women have met, except through Paul? And if Kimmy had been helping distribute the drug, why would Dr. Granger have killed her?

The number for the men's health clinic where Kimmy had worked was in my notebook. I pulled Fillmore over, plucked up my cell phone, and dialed.

Ruth picked up on the first ring.

"It's Mackenzie Taylor." I said. "I was just wondering, did a Dr. Jessica Granger ever stop by the office?"

"Not that I'm aware of," Ruth said. "And I'm getting a little fed up with all your questions."

"Kimmy was your friend, Ruth. Help me find out who killed her."

"Make it snappy," Ruth said. "I don't have all day."

I got down to business. "Do you know of anyone who would want to hurt Kimmy? An ex-boyfriend or maybe a relative who was abusive?" I asked, thinking of Hunter's story.

"If she did have anyone like that lurking around, she never told me about it," Ruth responded.

"We think Paul Granger was killed because he was messing with the drugs he was supposed to be selling, faking orders, and selling them on the street. Is there any way Kimmy maybe caught on to whoever was helping him?" I said. "Any secrets that were maybe eating her up?"

"Now that you mention it, she was acting a little weird since your visit. She'd been quiet and jumpy. I thought that was maybe because one of the doctors barked at her, but it could have easily been something else. Now if you'll excuse me, I need to keep this line open." Ruth hung up before I could thank her.

Some thanks it would be, too, if her significant other was arrested for dealing the Alphadra. Damn, I really needed to find out what Brett knew if I were going to have any chance of piecing the answers together.

I parked across the street from Len's office. There was the Escalade, a few spots down. Good, Brett was there already.

My phone rang, and the sleeping profile candid I'd snapped of Hunter that morning popped up. So, he knew I was no longer in the building.

"I'm just heading into a meeting. I'll talk to you soon." I cradled the phone between my shoulder and head so I had a hand free to open the door.

"No, wait, Mackenzie," he began, but I fumbled the phone and accidently disconnected.

The front door was unlocked, and I pushed my way inside calling out, "Len! It's me. I hope you have coffee because—"

The words died in my throat as I saw Len and Brett tied to chairs and an unconscious woman lying face-down on the floor. And over by the desk sat my wide-eyed daughter and a familiar man holding a handgun to her head.

CHAPTER TWENTY-ONE

There are times when you do everything right and the situation still goes sideways. A good private investigator needs to think on his feet.
From the *Working Man's Guide to Sleuthing for a Living* by Albert Taylor, PI

"You?" I blinked in confusion at Dr. Bernard Dole as he held a gun on my daughter. My daughter, who was supposed to be in school, not in mortal peril at my place of employment. "You were the one stealing the Alphadra?"

"It wasn't stealing." The not-so-good doctor's tone was even, as if he didn't have five people held hostage. "Right Touch was paid for those drugs, and paid far more than they were worth. Lock the door."

I did. "But why?" I asked, partly because I really wanted to know, but mostly because I needed to draw his attention away from Mac. As long as the barrel of that handgun was trained on my daughter, I couldn't do a thing.

Brett spoke up. "That's what you get for going into business with a loser like Paul Granger. Someone smarter would have covered his tracks better. How about you let the girl go. She's got nothing to do with this."

I could have kissed him for trying to secure her release and crossed my fingers that it would work.

Dr. Dole didn't turn so much as a hair as he studied Mac. "I'm afraid that's unacceptable. You've seen my face. It's unfortunate that you chose this very morning to show up here. I'm assuming this is why you came here, to see your mother?"

All the blood had drained from my daughter's face. Her lips were clamped firmly together, and she didn't answer him. Good girl.

Brett frowned. "Mother?"

The doctor made a derisive sound. "Well, she looks exactly like Ms. Taylor, doesn't she? Genetics don't lie."

Brett's gaze swung to me, and then back to Mac. I could see the wheels spinning. "You have a kid?"

Dole studied Mac more closely. "No, genetics don't lie. And if I'm not mistaken, she has your eyes, Mr. Archer. In fact, I'd wager you spent some quality time with Ms. Taylor sixteen or seventeen years ago." He chuckled at Brett's obvious astonishment and Mac's hands clenching into fists, her whole body braced for impact.

I didn't stop to worry about the personal atomic bomb that had just gone off. We could deal with the fallout later, if we survived. "So what's your plan then?" I took a step closer, intending to wedge myself bodily between Mac and Dole's weapon. "You're just going to murder an office full of people and expect to get away with it?"

"I have a convincing scapegoat." His free hand indicated the woman on the floor. "Dr. Garner's personal and professional slipups have her primed for a breakdown that ends in mass murder."

"But she has nothing to do with Alphadra." I risked another step, bringing me about five feet from Mac and the doctor. "And Brett knows Kimmy didn't either."

"Poor Kimmy. Wrong place, wrong time. I was sorry she had to die, but what else was I supposed to do when she discovered the phony orders? It was all because of that idiot, Paul Granger. Who did he think he was, demanding a bigger cut of the profits? I was the one who faked the orders under Kimmy's office ID code, paying for the drug out-of-pocket and cutting it down before handing it over to various contacts."

"But why?" I really didn't care, but a good investigator would want to know what motive she'd missed.

"Cancer research. My funding dried up, but I was so close, within a few months of coming up with a real treatment option without the horrific side effects. Now tell me, who deserved the lion's share of the profits?"

Another step. If I reached out my arm, I'd be able to touch Mac's chair. "So it's all about the money? You took a father away from his children, killed an innocent girl, and why? Because she figured out what you were doing?"

"Sacrifices must be made for the greater good. And that's far enough, Ms. Taylor."

I froze mid-step and swallowed hard. "It doesn't matter what your reasons are, you're a drug-dealing murderer."

He raised the gun but instead of shooting me, cracked it over my face. I went down hard, catching myself with my hands.

"Mom," Mac cried.

I held up a hand, trying to ignore the throbbing pain. "It's okay."

"Just for that, I'm going to shoot your daughter first, so you can watch her die." The click of the safety was audible.

I was about to scream when there was a loud knock behind the door.

Doctor Dole extracted a syringe from his jacket pocket. "Who is that?"

"A walk-in probably," Len spoke for the first time.

"Tell whoever it is to go away."

"We're closed," Len shouted.

"Mr. Copeland? It's Agnes Taylor, Mackenzie's mom."

Dr. Dole cursed. "Am I going to have to wipe out your entire sodding family tree?"

My mouth opened, and I was about to scream for her to run and get help when the barrel of the gun was pressed against my temple.

"Stand up. Let's greet her together. The rest of you, not a sound."

I nearly vomited as I pushed myself to my feet, and the room tilted like a really bad case of the drunk spins. Dole was right behind me, gun in one hand and syringe in the other. I tried to think of some way to warn my mother, some secret code that would let her know she needed to run and get help. But between the braining and my terror not one single thought came to mind.

We were all going to die because I wanted to play detective. Regret filled me. Hanging up on Hunter, fighting with Mac, not telling Brett the truth when I'd had the chance. And that was just one morning.

Would Uncle Al have found a way out of this mess? Uncle Al probably would have caught on to Dr. Dole immediately, would have stopped him before Kimmy was killed.

And then we were at the door. "Open it," Dole ordered.

"I'm sorry, Mom," I whispered and turned the deadbolt and reached for the handle.

The door exploded in, knocking me back into the doctor. A defining boom resounded as the gun went off and a familiar burn stole my sight, clogged my nose, and made me gag.

Mom had spritzed us both with pepper spray.

Even with the ringing in my ears, I heard Dole curse. I tried to roll away from him, but rendered temporarily deaf and blind, all I really managed to do was flail like a fish tossed on the bank. I coughed and choked and sputtered for untold amounts of time before someone dragged me to the side of the room, got me a handful of wet paper towels, and stroked my hair.

My vision cleared first, though it wasn't exactly twenty/twenty. Agnes sat next to me, soggy paper towels in hand. She moved to replace them, but I shook my head then pointed to my nose. She handed me a box of tissues, which I used liberally. Mac knelt next to me. I could see her lips moving, but the ringing was getting worse, not better. I pointed to my ears and did a palms-up.

Mac turned and waved someone over. Dark boots and jeans appeared, and Hunter Black knelt down in front of me, his dark gaze assessing the mess.

"Sorry I hung up on you." I must have spoken loudly because several heads turned our direction. "It was an accident, I swear."

He tucked some hair behind my ear and touched a spot so sore it made me flinch. His gaze darkened, and he turned to Mac. I watched Mac's lips move and Hunter said something back. I was feeling dizzy again, so I closed my eyes and leaned back against the wall.

Someone tapped my knee. I opened my eyes and saw a yellow legal pad with the word *hospita*l written on it.

I looked from the word to Hunter's face. "You aren't asking, are you?"

Slowly he shook his head.

I sighed. "Fine. Mac, stay close."

She took my hand and pulled me to my feet. I'd take that as a yes.

* * *

Six hours later I was seated comfortably on my couch, my hearing and sight mostly restored. The headache persisted though, even after a hot shower. The doctor had advised that we treat my head injury like a concussion, meaning I had to be wakened up every two to three hours and have a person or people ask irritatingly idiotic questions every time I woke up.

There were plenty of volunteers, but I knew who I had to talk with first.

"What in the name of java were you doing there?" I bellowed at my daughter when we were alone. "If you wanted to talk to me you could have called. Or texted."

"I wasn't there to see you. I went there to talk to him." Mac flushed.

"How did you even know he was at Len's office?"

"I tracked his cell phone."

I blew out a sigh. "Well, cat's out of the bag now. I'm sorry, hon. None of this would have happened if I'd just fessed up yesterday."

Mac picked at a thread on her shirt. "Nona told me why you didn't. You know nobody could ever replace you, right?"

I reached out and pulled her into a hug, the motion making my head pound. It was worth the added misery, as children always were. "I know, but buried underneath my outer exterior of goddess-like fabulousness, you're mom's an insecure neurotic mess."

That got me a snort. "Not too deep underneath."

"Wiseass. Now, go get Calamity Jane and make sure she isn't packing heat."

Mac left, and Snickers hopped up onto my lap. She turned three circles before plunking down into a tight little ball of fluff.

"Oh, are we gonna be friends now?" I stroked her fur in a slow, soothing caress.

She let out a contented sigh, and her eyes drifted shut.

"That's what happens. I grow on people."

"Like a fungus," Mac retorted as she reentered the apartment, my mother following in her wake. Agnes appeared apprehensive, almost nervous.

"I'm so sorry I sprayed you," she blurted.

"Considering it was either that, I get stuck with whatever the heck was in that needle, or shot at point blank range, I'll take the pepper spray."

"You saved our lives, Grams." Mac put an arm around her shoulder. "You were kind of incredible."

"Well, Detective Black is the one who kicked the door in," Agnes said.

"I'm not buying the false modesty for one second," I told her. "You might as well buff your nails on your shirt and claim it was nothing."

"Honestly, Mackenzie. Can't you just say thank you?"

I took a slow and steady breath. "Thank you, Mom. For everything."

She blinked then blushed. "Well, you're welcome. I have to look after my girls. Have you eaten? I have this fantastic soup recipe. It has kale in it."

I made gagging sounds.

"Just try it. You never know if you might like it."

Mac and I bit our lips in tandem and then glanced at one another, both filling in a mental *that's what he said.*

I broke first, a crack of laughter escaping. Snickers grunted but stayed put. Mac doubled over, wheezing with giddy delight.

Agnes looked back and forth between the two of us. "What am I missing?"

"Nothing, Grandma." Mac recovered enough to say. "It's an inside joke."

"Tasteless lowbrow humor," I added. "The best kind."

"I don't know," Agnes mumbled. "Maybe I should take my own advice and try it."

Mac and I exchanged another look, this time of the is-she-serious variety.

"We could break her in slowly," I said. "A little *Caddyshack*, maybe some *Blazing Saddles*."

"*Dumb and Dumber*, oh, and *The Duff*." Mac looked thrilled with the idea of indoctrinating new blood into our cult-classic film family.

"Soup first," Agnes said with authority. "Mac, you want to help? It'll do you good to learn to cook."

"But not because you need it to lure some man to love you," I countered.

My mother actually rolled her eyes. "No, because good nutrition is important and because your mother is a lost cause."

"Thank you," I said and watched the two of them head out the door.

Five minutes later, my next visitor knocked.

"Come in, Brett." I called.

The door opened. "How'd you know it was me?"

"I saw you lurking in the shrubbery." I gestured toward the adjacent chair. "Have a seat."

He lowered himself into the chair across from me and studied my face.

"Go ahead." I said. "Though I have to warn you, if you're contemplating hitting me, I have an attack puggle here, and I'm not afraid to use it."

As if on cue, Snickers let out a warning growl.

"I'd never hit you." Brett looked utterly appalled.

"Well, you lured me to that meeting with a homicidal doctor."

He scowled at that. "I didn't know he was homicidal when I made the call. He just said he had information that would wrap up both of our cases. It wasn't until Dr. Granger walked in that he drew on us."

I shivered, recalling just how close the call had been. "Well, I guess I'm officially out of the PI business."

"Why? You're good at it."

I blinked. "You think I'm a good PI?"

"Well, yeah. You solved my case."

"But I made so many mistakes."

"That doesn't mean you're not a good PI. It just means you need to practice and build your skill sets. If you don't want to work for the lawyer anymore, you can come work with me."

My mouth fell open. "Aren't you angry? That I didn't tell you I was pregnant?"

"Getting right into the heavy stuff are we?" He sighed and scrubbed a hand over his face. "Well, I'm not thrilled that you didn't tell me. Obviously. And I gotta say it blows my mind. I have a kid—not a kid, a teenager. But no, I'm not mad."

"You don't feel cheated? That I kept her from you?" I probed.

He shook his head. "It's still sinking in. But I guess what I most wanted to say is that I get it, why you didn't tell me."

I jolted as if hit with electric current. "You do?"

"Well, yeah. I mean I wish you had, but it took me a long time to grow up. Hell, some days I think I'm not there yet."

"You're not alone in that." I let out a sigh. "It wasn't just because I thought you were immature. My life had to change, but yours didn't. And I didn't want you to be tied down, obligated to us. I always wanted the best for you, and I knew if I told you that would have impacted every decision you made going forward. Eventually you would have resented both of us, and that wasn't fair to any of us."

He nodded. "So, she knows about me?"

"Only just. After I ran into you again, I knew I had to come clean with both of you."

"What's she like?" He sat forward, eyes alight with eagerness.

"Brilliant. She's quite the little whiz with computers. In fact, she just got an internship with the police." I went on for some time, describing various bits of Mac's personality while her father listened raptly.

"Does she…" Brett cleared his throat. "That is, do you think she will want to get to know me?"

"I think she wants that more than anything."

Brett smiled, that natural-born charmer grin that lit up the room. "Really?"

"Would I lie? She's upstairs with the battle-ax. Maybe you two could talk a little bit."

He rose to go, but hesitated. "Seriously Mackenzie. I think you're going to be one of the best PIs in the business someday. Stick with it."

I glanced away, embarrassed.

Another knock sounded on the door, just three hard raps.

"Did you see anyone lurking in the bushes that time?" Brett asked.

"No, but that's Hunter. Let him in."

Sure enough, Detective Black stood on the other side, and he wasn't alone. Len was with him, the older man holding a large bouquet of autumn flowers.

"I didn't realize you were entertaining," Len said.

"I'm always entertaining." I waved them in. "Brett was just on his way up to see Mac, so I guess I'm ready for a new babysitter."

Len shuffled forward as the two younger men studied each other warily. If they'd been dogs there would have been a lot of circling and butt sniffing as each took the other's measure.

"Mackenzie," Brett called from the door. "I'll see you around."

I rolled my eyes. He had to get in one last shot. "Later, Brett."

As the lawyer approached I saw the bouquet was in fact two different arrangements. He handed me one, and I looked up at him, surprised. "What are these for?"

"To celebrate your first successful case. Detective Black assures me that all the charges against Dr. Granger have been dropped."

I craned my neck up to meet Hunter's gaze. "Is that so?"

He nodded mutely. His gaze was once again dark and inscrutable.

"Have a seat." I waved to the chair and the empty couch cushion beside me.

"I'm not staying. I just wanted to drop off the flowers and this." Len reached into his pocket and extracted a check, which he handed to me.

"But I haven't compiled my hours yet," I protested.

"I know. You can do that when you're feeling better."

My hand shook as I took it from him. It wasn't a ton of money, but it would help. But it was more than the money. I'd solved my first case as a private investigator. With a ton of help and a heaping helping of luck, but still…

"So get some rest." Len twinkled at me. "I'll see you in the office as soon as you're fit to be back on the job."

"Who are those for?" I gestured toward the other bouquet, wondering if the arrangement was a thank you to my mother.

"Nona. Poor dear felt left out so I thought I'd bring these by to cheer her up. Have a good night." Len tipped an imaginary hat and then headed out the door.

I shifted and leaned back against the couch. "Please sit down. My head is throbbing, and tipping it back to look up at you isn't doing me any good."

"You assume I'm staying?" Hunter said quietly.

I flinched. "You probably have a ton of case things to tidy up."

"I do," he said, not moving.

"On a scale of one to ten, with one being not at all and ten being ballistic, just how mad are you?"

Hunter thought about it. "One hundred and ten."

"Yowch. I really screwed up, didn't I?"

He heaved out a breath and then sat on the couch next to me. "Why did you leave like that?"

I almost played the injury card, but decided against it. "I broke a bunch of promises last night to my daughter and to myself. Mac was mad and even worse, hurt. I'm not saying I regret what happened, but I'm not in a place where I can go forward either."

Hunter nodded. "So where does that leave us?"

"As neighbors. And friends, I hope." I reached for his hand and laced my fingers through his.

"And Brett?" Was that a slight trace of bitterness in his voice?

"Brett is Mac's dad, and I guess he'll be around."

He searched my face. "Nothing else?"

"No. Same rules apply. I have my daughter, and she's my number one priority."

As if summoned, Mac appeared, a sunny smile on her face. It dimmed a little when she saw Hunter seated beside me on the couch. "Oh, uh, hi."

"Did you talk to him?" I asked, releasing Hunter's hand.

"I should go." He stood up.

"Oh, no. That is, you don't have to. I was just coming to ask Mom if it was okay if we ordered pizza. That soup smells vile."

"Try it, meh meh meh," I mimicked Agnes.

"You need to be nicer to your mother," Hunter said, surprising us both. "She's one of the bravest women I've ever seen. She spotted what was going on through the office window, and I tried to get her to stay outside, but she knocked on the door and had the pepper spray ready before I could do anything about it."

I remembered the story he'd told me about his mother and how she died and felt ashamed. "You're right."

"Let me know if you need anything." His gaze devoured me for an endless moment, and then he was gone.

"Is it hot in here?" I asked Mac.

She plopped down on the other side of the couch. "No, it's just you two."

"I meant what I said, you know. I called a halt to things with him. So there won't be awkwardness."

"Good," Mac said distractedly. "That's good"

"Where's your dad?"

"He had to go. Do we really need to eat the soup?"

I plucked the check from my pajama pocket and handed it to her. "Order a pizza and we'll dip it in the soup."

Mac laughed and took out her phone. "Done. Oh and Mom?"

"What?"

"I'm proud of you."

Tears stung my eyes. "Ditto, kid. Now, what do you say to a John Hughes movie marathon until I can see straight?"

"I have school tomorrow," Mac pointed out.

"I'll write you a note." I hit the Walken accent express again.

"Mom."

"You've got a fever, and the only prescription is more cowbell."

Mac shook her head. "It's a good thing I love you."

I closed my eyes and sighed, content. "It's a dirty job, but somebody's got to do it."

ABOUT THE AUTHOR

Former navy wife turned author Jennifer L. Hart loves a good mystery as well as a good laugh and a happily ever after is a must. When she's not playing with her imaginary friends or losing countless hours on social media, she spends her free time experimenting with both food and drink recipes and wishing someone else would clean up. Since she lives with three guys and a beagle, that's usually not the case. Her works include *The Misadventures of the Laundry Hag* series, the *Southern Pasta Shop Mysteries*, and the *Mackenzie & Mackenzie Mysteries* from Gemma Halliday Publishing.

To learn more about Jennifer, visit her online at www.jenniferlhart.com

Enjoyed this book? Check out these other fun reads available in print now from Gemma Halliday Publishing:

Printed in Great Britain
by Amazon